THE GOVIL

And The Hidden Symbol

2nd Edition
ISBN-13: 978-1-7343981-1-3

The characters in this book are entirely fictional. Any resemblance to actual persons living or dead is entirely coincidental.

Edited by Dana E. Kaufman.
Front cover image by Jennifer B. Litherland.

This book is dedicated to my children, Noah and Avery.

CONTENTS

Chapter 1: Jack

Jack Newton lived in a small cottage located at 14 Pumpernickel Drive, centered in a field of tall grasses just outside the village of Stonevue. There was no hustle or bustle in this small, quaint town. The streets rarely ever saw anything other than feet and wagon wheels; yet news had its way of traveling quickly in a town where everyone knew each other.

In a place where it always snowed in the mountains and the forest was ancient, this town was nestled somewhere in the rolling hills of Sylvermyst, the name so given to the region. A large span of unchecked land, Sylvermyst had a dark secret within its shadow.

There were no more than a few hundred people living within Stonevue's boundaries. Most lived peaceful lives. And, although the landscape around the town was vast and unscathed, many of the buildings were sporadically placed at best. Few buildings were more than two stories high. The main road, or what resembled one, was a blend of old cobblestone, broken bricks, short grasses, and vibrant mosses. The houses lay on the outskirts with dirt roads that meandered between small hills, large trees, and the occasional rocky outcropping. As far as the eye could see, there was not much more to the land than rolling hills and forests, with the exception of a very distant mountain range to the north.

Most houses were neatly tucked between the hills, with their amber rooftops lying nearly even with the grassy hilltops. Some were built with stone and others were built of wood, but the poorest built their homes from the dirt itself. Only a few houses had their own wells, while the others shared the main well in the town's center. A few fence lines drew clear property lines with their brick and stone pillars and black iron bars. Many homes, though, had no such luxury of knowing whose land was whose exactly. Vegetable gardens crossed into neighbors' lands and many pathways were shared by neighbors before reaching the road.

The town hall stood three stories high on the southern side of the town center. It was the most magnificent building in town with stone pillars from the ground to the eaves, on all sides. The main doors were comprised of heavy oak from around the area and had big bronze straps across the bottoms and tops. The handles were built solid and grand from darkened steel by the town's blacksmith. The building stood strong and proud in Stonevue, a symbol of the greatness such a small town could accomplish.

Across the plaza, on the corner of the northern road, stood a much smaller building with similar architectural features as the town hall. It was the same in most ways except for the size and the door, which was old and plain. That building was the constable's office. A thick wooden sign hung out from above the door by chains with a burned-in image of something that probably once had meaning but was mostly too hard to make out any longer. Only two constables worked in town.

The most respected man in Stonevue was Chief Marion Hiksum. The townspeople were more apt to listen to him than the mayor. The chief, however, would never allow such a thing. He was a quiet fellow, old and wise, but rather quick witted. Most of the time, Chief Hiksum walked the streets of town, keeping the peace, but mostly conversing with the people. He liked knowing what was going on in his town.

The other officer was a bit rowdier, as he was much younger than the Chief. Sully Kroug was his name. Although he had no real title other than Officer, he liked people to call him Doc. Maybe it was a joke to him, or maybe he really thought of himself as doctor of sorts. Nobody really cared and many only called him Doc for their own amusement. Sully was dedicated to his desk. He only left if it were called for. Otherwise, he played cards by himself. The three jail cells in the office were rarely ever occupied, and two of them were used for the town's record storage.

In what was considered the center of town, stood a bronze statue atop the town's water well. It was of a man on a horse, sword drawn and pointed north as if he was ready to attack. Among his saddle gear were less triumphant articles - explorer's gear like a spyglass, compass, rolled maps, and the sort. The man depicted was definitely not a warrior, fierce, or anything else, but looked willing to stand his ground against an unseen enemy. He was not wearing a suit of armor; rather, his apparel was more like a light leather patchwork.

The center of town, referred to as "The Center" by the townsfolk, was dissected by three roads. One road came from the north, where most of the houses could be reached. The other two roads came from the west and from the east. Those two roads were considered the main stretch. The eastern road was named Glacier Drive and the western road was Palms Row. The northern drive was Ironstone Way and was narrower than the other two.

Up and down the main stretch were small shops with very aged fronts, some of which could use some work. The town was nearly two hundred years old, and the shops looked just as old. There was a lot of color on the streets and the smell of fresh baked bread always filled the morning air. Flower baskets and thatches of grass here and there livened the scenery. Although old and faded, many shop fronts had chipped, colorful trim work that drew attention to them.

The occasional horse wagon was parked in front of a shop with supplies. Shop owners and shop workers all worked hard as they went about their daily tasks. Massive oaks grew between some of the shops up and down the stretch, casting shade over the roads and buildings. Large lampposts lined the streets in every direction with glass tops that towered above the roads and into tree canopies. At night, these posts burned brightly and cast shards of flickering light about the streets.

Many of the shops' top floors were the homes of their owners. Clothes were pinned to lines between some of the buildings' top floors and rugs lay draped over window balcony railings. Some of the alleys were so shaded from trees and rooftops they never saw the light of day. Those alleys were always cold and wet and very few shop fronts could be found in them. As the roads got further away from the Center, the shops became fewer and fewer. They were replaced by small farms and a flour mill until all that was left was a thin, dirt road leading far out of town. Despite being rather quaint, the town had several different roads leading to it from faraway places that could not be seen.

This tale begins like all others in all of time; it begins at the end of another. It all started on a moonless summer night. The breeze whispered through the trees. Waves rolled in the tall grasses. Exotic flowers scented the air and the smell of expired fires drifted out of their tired ovens. Darkness had completely swallowed up the stars. Moonless was nothing special, but something happened that dark and wondrous night that was significant. It was so many years ago, but a vivid memory to those who knew its secret. A secret that was larger than its keepers could ever have imagined; larger than anyone could have imagined.

Hastily a horse made its way down the drive. Its passenger carried in his arms a blanket as dark as the night. There was a small baby boy wrapped in it quietly sleeping despite the thunderous noise of the neighing horse and hooves stampeding the ground. At the front door of Pumpernickel Drive awaited a small group of robed men and women. They all seemed anxious. As the horse drew closer, the group murmured amongst themselves. One, dressed in a dingy and pale robe, calmly walked out to the restless horse and grabbed its reigns. The passenger jumped off and made his way straight to the door.

The shortest of the group, by nearly half, shouted out to the horse rider. "Is this the boy?" He held a book up and followed after the man, "I must know, Tristan, is that the boy?"

Tristan, the rider, slender, pale, and disheveled, looked to the others. He held the boy close to his chest and replied, "They think he is the one, yes."

A gasp quickly followed from the group and they began to murmur amongst themselves.

The short man spoke to the rider again, "Then you must make sure he gets this." He thrust the book at Tristan.

"Now hold on just a second, Hearny," another man grabbed the book. "We don't know if this really is the boy and we don't know what the book is all about!"

One of the ladies shouted out from the back, "It can't be him."

Some of the others shook their heads. "Where's the guard? Where's the one who is supposed to protect him? Is there not a Protector, did something go wrong?"

The others began talking again. "Surely they have it wrong, Tristan." Another man spoke in a deep voice, his heavy chest and arms hardly fitting in his robes. "The Protector is supposed to follow him. That was the way it was told."

The rider, tired and weak, replied to them, "I do not know where the Protector is. I do not know who the Protector is. I do, however, know that there was a fierce and relentless battle. I did not have much more than a few moments to get out of there. I did not notice if the Protector appeared. I do not know if I have lost him or if he is on his way."

He made his way to a small cot in the corner and gently placed the baby boy in it. Then, slowly, he walked to the table near the kitchen and sat in a chair close to the fireplace. He looked heavy hearted and life looked gone from his face.

"I do not think Sam made it." His eyes were glossing over as the others expressed disbelief. "There was so much happening, and right as I turned to leave there was an explosion. They had found out."

He looked up into their eyes, frightened, "They knew. They were there to stop her. I think they had the whole Reign seeking her out. I just don't know what happened. They were furious and frantic." His hair slowly turned white from its light brown as he spoke. "All I can say is I hope with all my heart that he is the one they fear. There isn't going to be another chance. Sam risked everything believing it. It'll only be a matter of time before they break through."

His hands now began losing their fullness and weakness took over his arms. His face became thinner and his legs became still. "You have to trust me. They will find a way. They are in an unbreakable rage. The Reign cannot be allowed to continue."

The muscular man knelt beside Tristan and held him from falling out of his chair.

"For my faults, I am done." Tristan whispered as his eyes grew heavy. "Through my love, I am again."

"What are you saying?" Hearny asked.

The rider gave one last look up and, with his last breath, forced out his last words. "In time, my boy, unlock what you have in store."

As his last words faded from his tongue, the rider slumped in his chair. The man by his side gently rested Tristan's head upon the table. Some of the members wept silently. Others stared at his lifeless body in fear.

The member in white stepped forward, looked over to the boy in the corner. He quietly knelt beside the baby and whispered something under his breath with his hand holding the boy's. For a moment, he looked fondly at him while he slept so peacefully in the makeshift bed.

Then he addressed the others, "The dawn of darkness has knocked upon our door. If you intended on turning back, you have missed your cue."

He walked to the open window and watched the yard. Marion had wandered this town for many years, and nothing he had ever encountered had made him feel so uneasy. Before his eyes, he could see the faraway lampposts of Stonevue dimly breaking the shadow of night. Silence awaited his remarks as his calm voice called upon the members in the house.

He made his way to the door and then he turned and faced them. "In haste we will find nothing but despair. We must take action upon the evil that will befall our village and our way of life. The evil that seeks eternal power over the goodness of mankind will meet with our will first. We cannot fail, for no other power in the world can challenge what has begun. This is what we have prepared for. You all know your parts and mustn't forget what we will be fighting for. For now, be at your ready. The time for our sworn duty is coming, until then, we are adjourned."

With not so much as a goodnight or a goodbye, he opened the front door and began shuffling the robed individuals out. There were murmurs of protest, but no one questioned his resolve. Within minutes the last of them had exited the small cottage and made their way down the street.

Chapter 2: The Symbol

The day was getting late and the sun lit up the treetops. Bright oranges and reds slowly swayed in the breeze as the branches whispered their songs. A disarray of dancing colors made its way through the air and up the drive, meandering without purpose, as the trees rained down their leaves. The biggest oak trees lined an old street with their oversized canopies shadowing even older cottages. The fall had always been the best time of year as the old oak trees blanketed the lawns with loud bursts of color. The shades of all the trees showered the usually sheltered street with light and warmth; as they stood tall and mighty and their trunks revealed their age. The street looked unwilling to accept the approaching months of harshness, as winters brought ice and snow and weeks of gray skies. The grass stubbornly held its green against the cool days. The roads refused to fade under the mounting fall of leaves. The wind reminisced the summer in its breath as it filled the land.

There were not many houses on this drive, as all the homes around were scattered about the region. One in particular had a pathway that reached passersby with a dark cobblestone lay and thickets of grass pressing through the cracks. The tired remnants of a rotted wooden fence lined the ragged edge of an overgrown front lawn. A weeping willow stole the sun from most of the driveway and the rooftop.

This house was the home of the police chief. It was also the home to Jack, a young boy who had no parents. Jack was unaware of the specifics surrounding his birth and the death of his parents. It was going to be up to the chief, the man who adopted Jack, to one day explain to him. But even the chief was not fully sure what had happened on that night fourteen years ago.

As Jack sat at his window with his head cradled in his arms, he stared down the road. The scent of the brisk fall air was just outside the window and he smelled it permeating the room through the cracks in the doors and the worn corners of the sills. No matter how cold it got outside, something about home made him feel warm. The other cottages were old and reminded him of the architectural drawings on the wall in town hall. The chief's house had been passed to him from previous generations and was one of the oldest around.

Although he knew otherwise, Jack had always looked up to the chief as his real father. Chief Hiksum was commonly gone, walking the streets of Stonevue. And when he was home, he mostly spent much of his time reading in a small study at the rear of the house. Jack had been taught many things by the chief and was considered learned. That was more than most of the kids his age. Many children in Stonevue did not receive any kind of formal education unless their parents could afford it. The chief, however, went through great lengths to educate Jack in the ways of the world as best as he could. About as many things as he had experienced himself, the chief passed that knowledge on to Jack.

He never realized how well educated Chief Hiksum was. Some children in the village had similar educations as Jack, but most parents were only educated as apprentices in their crafts. Chief Hiksum had traveled many years to places many villagers had never heard of. His journeys gained him knowledge and deeper understanding of the world around him. And those acquired skills are what he intended to pass to Jack.

One set of skills Jack learned from an early age was how to manage a small farm. There were times he had to help Chief Hiksum tend to the land, which included a large pumpkin patch immediately behind the cottage. The patch did not bring in a lot of money, but it helped them get through the winter months. It was deep in the season of fall and harvest was going full force. Jack would spend hours every day with or without Chief Hicksum's help and prepare a cart to bring to market. There, he would unload them at the local grocer where the owner would simply point to where Jack should put them for the day. He never collected anything for the trade, which was all taken care of by the Chief.

The pumpkin patch also provided food in many forms. Jack never tired of the smells of pumpkin baking or stewing, and he loved the breads and pies they made for many months following the harvest. By the end of winter, though, he looked forward to a change in diet as he could only love pumpkin concoctions for so long.

Jack liked to read. So much so, he was probably the most frequent visitor of the town library. He would spend many hours a day there when he could. After bringing in a batch of pumpkins, he would make it a point to stop into the library to read another book. He was a fast reader, something he developed over time. Sometimes he could even start and finish a book in one sitting. This was to his detriment, though, as the library only had a few thousand books to read. Most of the books were penned by hand, some with intricately drawn maps and creatures of the world, and others with fantastic stories that enlivened the mind.

Sylvermyst had a small, faded yellow star painted next to its name on a large, raised map in the library. It was indeed the capital of the land it resided on, but that did not mean much in a vastly unknown region. To the north of the capital's star was a dark green, wooded representation of the Shadow Lake Forest that gradually became whiter to the upper north. To the west stood a mountain range standing unusually high, representing the White Ridge Mountains. The snow never stopped blowing on the mountaintops in White Ridge and the range cast a shadow for miles across the plains beneath them. The shadowed lands were unusually named The Glow and even more unusual was the fact that no roads led there. The East was mostly a smudge of browns, greens and blues, representing the endless fields, swamps, and lakes of Everess. The southern edge of the map showed a massive lake that filled most of the bottom of the map. Painted in large, blue, cracked letters across small cresting waves was the name, Black Loch. Each area of the map was unique in its own way, but few places had ever been fully explored. Engraved in the front side of the map's table was the name Avnoli.

Several books Jack had read in the past had referenced the library's map. It was something amazing to look at. In fact, Jack had spent some time admiring its beauty. It was more than just a table with a map on it. The map itself was raised and carved out of solid wood. The sides of the table were adorned with wooden etchings and carvings, some of gargoyles and others of things one could see every day, like depictions of animals and people. Jack liked to think of the map as a piece of art.

One day, Jack was gazing over the map. He ran his fingers over the rough edges of the small waves and imagined himself exploring the unexplored. He wondered what it would be like to go on an adventure or to just leave Stonevue for a little while. It was not that he disliked Stonevue, but he felt like there must be more to do and see beyond the borders of town.

"What are you doing?" a voice called from behind him.

Jack stood up straight as his thoughts were so abruptly broken. He turned around and saw a girl his age with long golden blond hair. She was holding several books in her hands and looked concerned about him touching the map. He immediately noticed her as the daughter of the librarian. He saw her in the library from time to time helping out.

"I was just admiring this beautiful piece of art and history," he said. He thought that was going to be it, but she continued to press him.

"Why were you touching it? You really shouldn't do that."

Slightly annoyed, Jack responded back, "I just like the work is all." He motioned to the books she was carrying and asked, "Are you reading those or putting them away?"

She looked down as if she had forgotten about them, "Oh these? I was just putting them away for my mom. I was kinda bored. There's not much to do in the cold."

"Well, if you get a chance, that one's a good one." Jack pointed to a small green bound book that read: Sylvermyst – A Short History.

She looked down again and agreed, "Yeah, I've read it. It was definitely short. He could have put more in it."

Jack gave a little laugh and introduced himself, "I'm Jack, by the way."

"Anna. I'm Anna. My mom is the caretaker of the library. I help out when I'm bored." She looked like this was definitely one of those times. "I've seen you here lots of times before. I can tell you like to read."

"I bet you have." Jack laughed and agreed. "I love reading. You wouldn't have any recommendations, would you?"

Without hesitation, Anna suggested, "If you think the map is interesting, you might like the book about it. It's got loads of schematics and drawings and some history about its planning."

Jack was half expecting that she would suggest something he had already read, but this particular book he had not come across before.

"Sure. Where is it?" Jack asked.

Anna led Jack to the back of one of the bookshelves and pulled a small, leather bound book with the words "The Avnoli Map" burned into the front cover.

"You can't check this one out, so you'll have to read it here." Anna said as she handed him the book. "Anyway, I'm gonna get back to it. Have fun."

Jack had some time to spare, so he found a comfortable chair near the map itself and began to read. The book was like most of the books in the library in that it was handwritten, and its binding was hand crafted. Jack did notice, though, that the book was unusual because it appeared to be written by multiple writers. It was not common for him to see several different handwriting styles in one book. It seemed more like a small collection of short stories and accompanying drawings of the map's intricacies. At first glance, the book was just the blueprints of the map. But Jack was already comfortable and did not feel like looking for another book. He figured he would read a little and call it a day.

The book was full of symbols and drawings of mythical creatures. Each of the different carvings on the side of the map table seemed to have its own dedicated page that explained the significance of it. The first such page depicted a large tree with an intricate root system. The writing was partially faded and hard to make out. Jack could make out the words "Arbolio" and "dying." He wondered why the roots were so emphasized.

Jack read through a few more of these pages before he got curious about the gargoyle and what it represented. Jack flipped through the pages until he found the drawing of it. On the page was the drawing of the gargoyle-like creature with some kind of depiction in the upper right-hand corner. It was a symbol of sorts, but Jack did not recognize it from the map. He continued to read the passage under it, which read:

Strong and fierce, these gargoyle-like creatures can carry hundreds of times their weight. They are very handy in dire situations. Although friendly, these creatures repel human interference. However, they have been widely accepted as participants in the Govi...

That was it. The words were too difficult to read after that. Jack was confused about what he just read. Everything he had ever known about gargoyles was that they were entirely mythical. This book, though, talked about them as though they existed. Jack thought that seemed like a frivolous thing to put in what would otherwise appear to be factual book. He chalked it up to superstitions that people used to have and the influence those superstitions had on people in the past.

Jack read several more pages before it was about time for him to head home for the day. He had to do a little more work in the pumpkin patch before it got too dark outside. On his way out, he decided to look at the map once again. It was intriguing to him that there was so much thought and backstory to each component of the map and its adornments. He looked closely at the carving of the tree and appreciated the intricacies of the roots carved into the wood. Then, he looked over the gargoyle. It was depicted as a small creature in flight while carrying a large boulder. Carved into the boulder was a small circle that Jack had not noticed before. It was the circle with the symbol that was on the page of the gargoyle. He ran his finger over the carving in awe.

"Again?" Anna called from behind him. "You're gonna break something."

Jack snapped back to a standing position. Her voice broke a deep silence and startled him.

"I, er, I was just looking at … never mind." Jack did not feel like explaining what he did not understand.

"My mom wants me to get a pumpkin from you if that's okay?" Anna seemed slightly annoyed that she was now in charge of a chore.

"Um, sure." Jack looked confused, "I brought some to the store earlier. You might try there first."

"She said they're out already." Anna was obviously annoyed now as she began to realize that her mother was just trying to keep her busy. "She said she doesn't want to wait until morning. She wants to bake a pie tonight."

Jack smiled, "Well, I'd be more than happy to pick something out for you. It's a bit of a walk, though."

"Great," she said sarcastically.

The two set off for the cottage outside of town. He had to push his empty cart while she walked beside him. Anna was bundled from head to foot while Jack wore a light leather jacket. He did not think it was cold enough outside to dress like she was. For a while they walked in silence. Eventually, though, the silence was unbearable, and Jack tried to make conversation.

"I wonder how old these trees are," Jack pondered aloud as he looked at the mighty oaks that lined the road.

"They were planted by the founders of Stonevue," Anna stated matter-of-factly, "So, they're somewhere around two hundred years old."

Jack looked surprised that she knew that off the top of her head. Then, he recalled that he had read that in the Sylvermyst history book before. Now he felt foolish for asking, especially since she knew he had read that same book.

"Oh right," Jack replied.

The trip was slower than normal because Jack had to push the cart. The walk to the cottage was normally a half hour, but they walked for nearly forty-five minutes before they finally arrived at the pathway that led to 14 Pumpernickel Drive. It had a large wrought iron lamppost at the roadside, which served to welcome visitors. The front lawn was unkempt with large swaths of tall grasses and weeds. They walked up the pathway to the front of the house.

The cottage was nestled between two hills and slightly buried underground. There was a large tree growing out of the top of the roof with roots tangled all around the outside. There were a few windows located on each side of the front door. The cottage, overall, looked dilapidated but functional.

Jack opened the front door. "Well, here we are."

He motioned for her to enter and she followed. They entered into a cozy cottage crowded by decades of belongings. The main room had a fireplace that looked like it had been used recently. There were three nonmatching, soft and tired chairs located in various spots. They walked through to the kitchen in the back. There was a massive wooden table surrounded by four heavy wooden chairs. The kitchen was tidy, but it was in desperate need of cleaning. All throughout the cottage, belongings had a layer of dust.

Jack opened the back door to the pumpkin patch, "Right this way and we'll get you back on your way."

Anna was busy looking around the cottage. She slid her finger across the mantle above the oversized fireplace and looked at the dust in disbelief.

"Why is it so dusty in here?" she asked.

Jack stepped back in the house. "Well, we don't spend much time inside the house."

Anna instantly changed her train of thought as she noticed a sketch of the parcel of land they were on hung haphazardly on the wall. Jack noticed her gazing at it.

"That's been here since before I was born, I think. It's a drawing of everything my dad owns." Jack was relieved they were not going to be talking about dust.

"It's really detailed," Anna said as she looked it over, "Someone must have spent a lot of time drawing it. How much do you think it cost?"

Jack never considered that it might have cost something, but it made sense. "I dunno. I never really thought about that."

Even though he had looked it over in the past, Jack decided to look over the map with Anna. He watched as she straightened it on the wall. It had the usual North pointing arrow located in the upper left-hand corner and a small scale drawn on the bottom right hand corner that indicated distance. The cottage took up a very small portion of the land indicated in the drawing. A fair portion was dedicated to the pumpkin patch, but the remainder was unused land. The entirety of the plot was nearly a mile long and a half mile wide.

After a few moments of mutual gazing, Jack finally said, "Why don't we get that pumpkin for you? It'll be dark soon and you'll wanna be on your way before it gets too cold outside."

Anna nodded and began walking toward the back door. Jack took one last glance at the map and just about walked away, too. But something he had not noticed before caught his eye. On a large boulder located about midway through the pumpkin patch was a small drawing. He leaned in and squinted his eyes as he fixated on the detail. Any other time he would have probably thought nothing of it, but this time was different. The small drawing on the rock was the same symbol he had just seen earlier at the library, in the book and on the map.

"Are you coming or not?" Anna called back to Jack.

He looked at the symbol for a moment more. Then he shook his head, thinking it must be a signature or trademark of the map's creator. He figured the map must have been drawn by the same person who drew in the book at the library. Perhaps the artist had some major part in the creation of the map at the library, he thought.

"Sorry, thought I saw something." Jack said as they made their way out the back door.

The air in the cottage was thicker and warmer than the air outside. Although they were only inside for a few minutes, the air outside already felt colder than when they arrived. Their breath filled the air in small clouds in front of their faces. The crunching of grass, leaves, and twigs underfoot broke through the air in a fit of crispness. They walked about fifty feet before they arrived at a small wooden shed next to a cobblestone fireplace. The ground was matted hard around the area, indicating constant use. Indeed, Jack and his dad, Chief Hiksum, spent more time out back than inside on many occasions.

Jack opened the shed door slightly and reached in. His hand knew where to go and he grabbed a small tool to cut a pumpkin off the vine. They headed into the field. He knew where to find the ripest pumpkins and headed about halfway up the field to get one. Anna followed closely. After about a minute or two of looking around, Jack located the perfect size pumpkin to make a pie with. He grabbed it and showed it to Anna.

"How's this?" He asked.

Anna shrugged, "Sure." She really did not care much about the pumpkin. It was just another chore her mother was making her do.

He quickly cut the vine and wiped off the dirt. He then handed her the pumpkin. Not far from them was the boulder that the map had shown the symbol. Jack wondered if, like the gargoyle on the map's table at the library, the boulder also had a mark on it. He thought it was a foolish thought, but decided to check it out, nonetheless. After handing the pumpkin to Anna he began walking towards the boulder.

"Since we're out here, I wanna check something out really quick." He said to her as he walked away.

"What could you possibly need to check out in your own field?" she asked annoyed.

Not wanting to simply stand in the middle of the field by herself, she followed him.

"I saw something on the map inside that was drawn on this boulder over here." Jack replied. "It had a symbol on it that was the same symbol from the map book I was reading at the library. It's probably nothing, but I'm curious is all."

He walked around the boulder a couple of times, looking up and down. He did not see anything out of the ordinary with it. For all intents and purposes, it was just a big rock sitting idly in the middle of the field. He was about to give up when he noticed something low on the north side of the boulder. He furrowed his brow and looked harder, thinking maybe it was just an imperfection in the rock. He moved the grass out of the way and there it was, the same symbol he had now seen in four different places that day.

"What d'ya see?" Anna asked plainly. She was half expecting nothing.

"It's the same symbol engraved in this rock" Jack said perplexed. "I wonder if this rock isn't from around here, ya know? Like, maybe someone was going to make a monument or statue out of it, and something happened that made them just leave it here."

"That sounds dumb." Anna mused aloud, "Why would someone carve that symbol in it if they were just gonna leave it here?"

Jack shrugged. He could not think of what or why this was the way it was. He figured he would just have to ask his dad to see if he knew anything.

"It's probably nothing," Jack responded, "but it's certainly perplexing."

He ran his fingers over the symbol, which was only about four inches across. It lit up in a purple glow and began to spin slowly. Anna dropped her pumpkin and her eyes were wide in disbelief. Jack nearly fell backwards before he caught himself. Then, right before their eyes the boulder cracked from bottom to top with the same purple glow. The air suddenly filled with warmth. The sky above them grew dark and the wind picked up from behind them. It was only a moment before the two of them found themselves trying to brace against the ever-growing wind rushing past them and into the middle of the open boulder. Before the minute was up, they were swept into the bright purple light and then darkness.

Chapter 3: The Oasis Garden

Collecting himself and his thoughts from the violent burst of energy, Jack stumbled back to his feet. As his eyes cleared, he could not gather where he was or what had just happened, but his surroundings were incredibly different from only a moment before. There were large, wispy trees and tall, broad-leafed plants all around him. A small stream trickled not far from his feet and flowers of every color were in blossom everywhere. The rich smell of crisp, cool air filled with the perfume of flowers and grasses caught his nose as he became more puzzled over where he was. He stood there for a moment trying to figure out what was happening around him.

"I've never seen this place before. This is nowhere near Sylvermyst and I'm pretty sure it's not in Avnoli either." Anna was stunned by the beauty of their new surroundings. "It's beautiful; it's absolutely amazing! Where are we?"

A small group of multicolored birds flew just over their heads, lightly singing as they flew by.

Jack could not believe his eyes. "I'm not sure how this happened, but I think that symbol may have been some sort of key and we just passed through a door of some sort;" he rubbed his sore ribs from his rough landing.

"C'mon, that little engraving couldn't have done this," Anna said.

"I don't know what this is, but it isn't ordinary. I intend on writing the library a strongly worded complaint about this."

"You can't possibly think the library had anything to do with this." Anna was slightly annoyed at Jack's suggestion, "That symbol was obviously put there by the map's maker."

Jack looked for the door they came through as he walked around the area.

"We need to find where we came through and get out of here. I'm not too keen on the idea of being here ... wherever 'here' is."

Anna began looking around as well and almost instantly exclaimed, "Jack!"

He ran over to her and noticed she was standing on a small path with a small wooden sign only a few feet away with more of the strange symbols. It was pointing right at the clearing in which they had arrived.

"What does it mean?" Jack asked, knowing Anna probably had as little of an idea as he did.

They looked at the clearing the sign was pointing at and realized there was a large boulder almost suspiciously by itself near the stream. It was dimly glowing.

Jack started running towards the boulder, "This has to be it! The symbol is on here somewhere!"

He searched the boulder all over, feeling any crevice he could find and knocking on other areas. Yet, there did not seem to be any crack, symbol, or door of any kind.

"Jack?" Anna pressed.

"Anna, c'mon, help me find a door or lever or anything." Jack said hurriedly.

"Jack!" Anna yelled in a whisper as she ran behind the boulder.

Jack looked behind him and saw movement coming down the path.

"What are you afraid of?" asked Jack. "Maybe they'll know how to get us out of here."

Jack was beginning to approach the path when an arrow flew past his head and struck a tree trunk a few feet behind him. He immediately ducked and ran back to where Anna was hiding.

"Did you see that? I think someone just shot an arrow at me! We have to get out of here!"

He grabbed Anna's arm and they ran to the brush on the other side of the clearing where they hid behind a large trunk.

"Maybe it was an accident; maybe they thought you were a deer or something." Anna was breathing fast, "We should watch to see who it is. I'm going to report them."

They watched as a large figure jumped off a carriage pulled by horse-like creatures. The large figure stood in silence for a moment before retrieving his arrow.

The carriage was in grave disrepair. It looked like it would fall apart at any moment. The wood it was built from bowed from its own weight and creaked with every movement. Then, the half-broken door flew open and a small, old man with pointed ears and oversized eyes climbed to the ground. His long, white beard got stuck in the splinters of the door as he was about to touch the ground and threw his small frame off balance. He stumbled to the ground and used a cane to clamber back up.

"What is that?" Anna motioned toward the small man.

Jack pushed her back behind the tree.

"Be quiet," he whispered hurriedly, "I want to know why they shot at me and I don't think it was an accident."

He turned back to look around the tree and watched the clearing again. The large manly figure was closer now and appeared to be more like an ape than a man. He was sniffing the air and searching the ground for something. The old man was shouting out commands as he searched the still glowing boulder.

"Maybe he knows how to open the rock back up," Anna pointed at the old man, "he seems like he knows something about it."

"Yeah, but he doesn't seem too pleased either," Jack whispered.

Jack was watching the old man intently. He was trying to see if there was a way to open it. The old man kept walking around the boulder. As he walked around it, he ran his hand across it and it looked as if he was talking to it.

Jack felt a sudden pull at his shirt.

"We gotta get out of here!" Anna was whispering frantically.

The large ape creature had just found their scent and was coming their way.

"Go! Go! Go!" Jack pushed Anna through the tall grass as they ran as fast as they could.

They could hear the old man yelling at the creature and the sound of the brush being flattened as it followed their path. A large arrow whizzed by their heads and disappeared into the distance. Then another arrow, this time it sounded like it was shot from closer behind them. Then a bolt of light shot by and singed a path into the brush next to them.

Anna stopped, "What was that!" she was yelling in bemusement.

"I don't know but run!" Jack shoved her on.

Another bolt of light ran through the brush and hit a tree. The trunk of the tree exploded, and it crashed to the ground.

Jack grabbed Anna by the arm and pulled her further into the forest.

"This way," he said, "and try and get as many trees behind you as you can."

"Why are they trying to kill us?" Anna was panting. "And what are they shooting?"

Another arrow just missed Anna's head and landed itself into a tree in front of her. As Anna kept running, Jack stopped for a moment to see where the arrows were coming from. Another arrow whizzed by, but he could not tell where it came from. He began running again and caught up with Anna.

"We need to find somewhere to hide and quick." He was looking all around him as they ran. "They are catching up on us."

A bright flash of light shot by them again and struck another tree. It exploded as its canopy smashed into the forest's floor. Dust and smoke filled the air and their ears filled with a ring. Another flash of light came at them again, but this time from the front. Within a moment, more arrows and more flashes were coming at them from both directions.

"We're surrounded!" Anna yelled over the sound of the crashing trees.

Jack immediately changed direction and yelled back at Anna, "This way!"

From behind them, the flashes and arrows were still flying rampantly about, but none of them were coming in their direction.

Still running, Jack panted, "I think we lost them."

They hid behind a tree and caught their breaths. There was smoke and bright flashes still going in the distance and moving away from them.

"They're going to find out soon enough that we are not in their crossfire." Jack stated. "We have to keep going. We need to find somewhere we can rest. It's already getting dark."

"I'm going back to that rock," Anna said, "as soon as I get some rest. We have to find that rock and get out of here."

"Something tells me when we came through the boulder's purple light it alerted those things to come to it. I don't think we can go back there for a while. They'll be watching it."

Anna sniped, "Well, we have to try. We have no idea where we are, but we know where the stupid rock goes and no one on the other side was shooting at us."

"What if those things didn't know there was an opening there or how to make it work? What if we've just made it possible for them to go through? Or, what if they intend on following us through if we try reopening it? We need to have a plan and we need to lose them completely before we get that boulder back open." Jack responded.

He was speaking fast as he was becoming aware of the possible danger they may have put Sylvermyst in. The thought of his dad getting ambushed by a bunch of ape creatures made him instantly regret ever finding the symbol on the map.

"Jack, look at that." Anna pointed at the sky through the forest's canopy. "Is that the moon?"

Jack instantly saw what she was looking at. The moon was much bigger than usual and filled much of the sky above them.

"That can't be," Jack looked confused.

He walked over to a half-fallen tree that was hanging from the branches of the surrounding trees and began climbing up. Anna quickly followed him as he made his way up the dead trunk. As it became too small to walk up any longer, Jack leapt to the closest tree and continued climbing up to its upper most branches.

Anna stopped and watched as he made his way up the other tree. "Obviously, I have not been trained in the fancy art of 'Monkey', so I'll just wait here."

Jack looked up at the sky above him and saw a moon unlike any other he had seen before. And as he scanned the sky, he noticed something else that nearly made him lose his grip.

"What do you see?" Anna called to him.

He made his way back down the tree some and sat down on a large branch. Jack looked lost in his thoughts as he stared at the forest floor.

Anna called from the dead tree, "What's wrong, Jack? What was up there?"

"I think we're in a lot of trouble." He said slowly.

"It's just a big moon. How much trouble can that really be?" Anna asked sarcastically.

"It is a big moon; I'll give you that. That is definitely the biggest moon I have ever seen. But that is not what worries me."

"What is it then?" she asked impatiently.

"There are two suns setting on the horizon," he said gravely.

Chapter 4: Another World

Anna and Jack found a place in the treetops to tuck away for the night. As the suns slowly made their way down the sky, Jack began noticing all the color in their new world. The air was warm, but the trees and plants varied in color as if it were autumn. He had never seen some of the colors in nature like they appeared here. There were purples and indigos mixed throughout the canopy and the foliage. It all seemed so mystical to Jack, but he could not help fearing the potentially deadly actions he and Anna had taken today by opening the door to another world.

Jack wondered how they were going to get back and how to find the way they came through. He was usually good with his sense of direction, but he had no idea where they were and how far they had gotten from the boulder. On top of all his fear and worry, his stomach was grumbling. The last thing he had eaten was breakfast before going to the library in the morning. He did not know what was edible or what kind of wildlife to expect, and he definitely knew the locals were not going to help.

As the stars lit up the night sky, Jack noticed how the heavens looked more colorful than he was used to, and he could make out several distant planets. It was truly an amazing place to be, but Jack could not forget why he was sleeping in a tree and not comfortably in the meadow near the boulder. All the beauty in this world or his could not make him forget that someone, or something, was intent on killing him and Anna today. He remembered the arrows just barely missing his head and the strange, but deadly streaks of light he had never seen or heard of before. Tomorrow was going to be a long day and he had no clue what to do about any of their new problems.

The night passed by. As the first sun rose into the sky, the forest began to wake. The songs of the birds and the sounds of the forest creatures filled the air again. Anna awoke to a large bird landing next to her head.

She jumped in a startle, "Wh-what's th ... eeeyaah!" She flailed her arms at the bird.

Anna had forgotten she was in the tree and pushed back in fright. She quickly lost her hold on the branch and began falling back when Jack caught her from the branch above and pulled her up. He had been awake for an hour, waiting for the suns to come up.

"How long did we sleep?" she asked.

"I'm not sure, but I think the nights here are longer." Jack was already fully awake. "I've been up for a while and I don't feel tired at all. I think we slept far longer than normal."

Anna looked around at the forest in awe. She had fallen asleep much quicker than Jack did and had not really noticed all the color and beauty of the forest.

"Wow. Can you believe this? I mean, look at all the color. It's beautiful." She finished correcting her balance on the limb and looked at Jack, "By the way, thanks for catching me."

"I didn't want to have to carry you around all day if you got hurt," he said jokingly.

They stayed in the tree for some time, monitoring the forest for anything that looked like it might be hostile. After they decided it was okay to come back down, they started walking away from the direction of the attack.

"Before we try getting back to the boulder," Jack said as they walked through tall grasses and brush, "we need to find something to eat and get some water. I just don't know what we can eat."

Holding her stomach, Anna replied, "I know. After yesterday's running, I'm starving. What about some berries or something? Maybe an apple tree will come along our path."

"We'd only be so lucky," Jack smirked, "but I'd stay away from the berries and mushrooms. Everything is different here."

Then there was a sound in the distance. Jack and Anna ducked down instantly.

"Did you hear that?" Jack whispered.

"Yeah, it sounded like a cry or whimper of some sort." Anna looked ahead through the trees and pointed to a small cabin nestled between several trees.

They could smell food cooking and the clanking of metal coming from the cabin. It did not have any neighbors or clearings around it. Jack could make out a small trail of smoke coming from a chimney and a flickering red light coming from a window. The cabin was in a similar condition to the carriage they saw the day before. There were missing windowpanes and large cracks between the boards on the door. The stones were covered in moss and cracking, and the roof had a large hole next to the chimney.

"I think we should go around this place," Jack said as he observed the condition of the building. "What if this is the home of those things from yesterday? We barely escaped that, and we had a head start. I'd hate to think of how it would turn out if we walked right up to them so willingly."

"What if no one is home? We could go in and get something to eat and get out before anyone ever knew we were there." Anna was licking her lips as she watched the old cabin.

"Someone is home, we heard them yell." Jack said.

"Maybe we thought we heard something, or we heard them leaving," Anna was beginning to move forward slowly.

Jack protested, "We should just continue on. Or, at the very least, we should watch the place for a little bit to make sure no one is home."

Anna quickly replied, "Are you ki…"

From the cabin came another cry. But this time it was easy to tell that it was from someone, or something, that was in pain. Jack moved in a little closer to see if he could tell what was making the sound. The cry came again.

Anna pulled at Jack's shirt, "Okay, someone is definitely home. We should get out of here."

Jack paused as Anna turned to crawl away, "I saw something move in there."

"What?!" Anna froze in place. "Did it see you?"

"No," Jack was squinting his eyes and staring into the window directly ahead, "I don't think so."

"Well then, let's get out of here." She insisted.

"Wait!" Jack whispered as he ducked further down into the brush, "I think they are leaving."

Not a moment later, the front door swung open and slammed against the wall. The old man from the day before walked out, leaning on a cane and slowly making his way around the other corner of the cabin. Jack wondered if they had been seen and was beginning to think they were about to be ambushed. Just as he tried to see where the old man disappeared to, the same carriage from the day before sped away from the cottage on a worn down, overgrown path.

Jack felt a quick sense of relief as the carriage vanished into the forest and silence had once again taken over. He stood up and slowly walked up to the cabin window as Anna continued to kneel in the bushes with her eyes wide with fear. Jack carefully peered into the missing windowpane, all the while ready to run for his life.

As soon as his eyes peered in, he could see a warm, glowing fire in the fireplace with a black pot boiling something in it. There were shelves full of little glass bottles in different shapes and colors, filled with liquids and powders. The hole in the roof had a large, banged-up piece of metal tubing with a curved piece of glass at the top situated under it. Jack remembered seeing something similar to it at the library in the 'Astronomy' section. There was a table made of thick, heavy wood and covered in little vials and papers. The place was cluttered and hard to make out if anyone else might be in it.

Jack looked back at Anna who had a questioning look on her face, "I think it's clear," he whispered.

He cautiously moved to the front door.

Anna moved forward.

"Think it's clear," she mumbled sarcastically under her breath as she met up with Jack at the front door.

He slowly turned the doorknob and pulled open the door. As it moved, it creaked with an astonishingly loud cracking at the hinges. They both paused for a moment, expecting to hear some sort of reaction. Jack was sure someone heard that, even if not in the cabin.

After a moment of silence, Anna sniped, "Thanks for making that so subtle. I doubted you, but you shined through."

Jack looked back at her and rolled his eyes as he opened the door the rest of the way. They made their way in and could feel the warmth of the fire filling the small cabin against the cooler morning air. Jack began looking around for anything useful to use as a weapon in the forest. He did not see any knives or blades of any sort. He could not even find a table knife.

As he looked around on the table, one of the vials began rolling toward the edge and Jack reached out to catch it. In doing so, he had backed into something behind him. He turned and saw a few wooden cages stacked indiscriminately upon each other. The top one, however, had a creature inside of it. He could see it breathing, but it was lying on the floor of the cage and looked badly wounded. What was more interesting to Jack was that the creature was wearing clothes. They were simple clothes, but not something one would dress their pet in.

"Jack," Anna whispered over to him, "are you going to eat or what?"

Anna was sipping out of a large wooden ladle from the pot brewing over the fire.

"It's horrible, but it's food." She was making a disgusted face as she put more in her mouth. "C'mon. We need to get out of here before that guy gets back here."

From behind Jack came a small noise. They both looked back to see where it came from and noticed the creature in the cage had moved. Jack quietly walked back over to the cage and peered in at the creature. It had moved to the back corner but was again motionless as before.

"What is it, Jack?" Anna questioned with concern.

"I don't know. I haven't seen anything like it before," Jack studied the creature the best he could without touching it or the cage.

"Why would that guy dress it in clothes if he's just going to eat it?"

Anna took another sip from the ladle and motioned for Jack to do the same. Jack walked away from the cage and looked into the boiling pot over the fire.

"How do you know that isn't some sort of poison?" Jack was pointing at the steaming ladle in her hand.

Anna's shoulders drooped as she looked at the ladle in her hand and swished its contents around some.

"Well," she spoke slowly, "I don't know that, but I also don't know what we can eat from the forest either."

With some renewed confidence she perked up a little, "I mean, what's more likely, the guy brews five gallons of poison next to his dish plates and doesn't eat anything?"

She pointed at the dilapidated, bare shelving with only a few items strewn about them. Jack looked at the shelves in agreement. He noticed that not much looked like it could be food, but that the place did look like it was lived in. A small bed was tucked away in a smaller room to the back of the cabin, and, despite the mess of small cages and trinkets all over the room, the bed showed signs of being slept in recently.

Anna continued, "Or, he was hungry and made something to eat?"

Jack sighed and motioned for her to hand him the ladle. He sipped some and stood motionless for a moment. He tasted some more and swished it around in his mouth a little before swallowing it. He stood up straight and looked Anna in the eyes with a shocked look on his face.

"Well, don't do that then." She grabbed for the ladle, "The trick is to not think of it and just drink it quickly."

Jack pulled the ladle away from her reaching hand, but still had a surprised look on his face.

"Oh, get over it Jack, it's not that bad." Anna rolled her eyes.

Jack quickly drank the rest of the ladle and scooped up some more. He began blowing on the contents of the newly filled ladle and drank more of it.

"Actually, I was just saying that it wasn't that bad, but it isn't that good either." Anna was watching him in amazement as he started his third scoopful.

After he had a few more, Jack wiped his mouth on his cuff and handed her a full ladle.

"I can't believe how good that is!" Jack was excited, "Smell this."

He was leaning over the black pot attempting to waft the steam toward his face. He smelled as much as he could and stood back up with his eyes closed and held in his breath for a moment as he savored the smell of the most delicious meal he could ever remember.

Anna, still clutching the steaming ladle, watched Jack and rolled her eyes again.

"Jack, stop teasing, I was just saying we need to eat something."

She sipped on the ladle again and contorted her face in disgust as she fought to drink more.

"This is disgusting!" She said with a repulsive look.

She finished the rest of the ladle and quickly returned it to the pot. She looked at Jack, who was gazing into the fire. She attempted to wave a little steam in her direction and took the smallest smell that she could. As the scent hit her nose, she instantly backed away, coughing and gagging.

She said angrily, "I can't believe you let me do that! That's awful! How did you not get nauseous from that?"

Jack looked at her, "You're kidding right? This is probably the best food I've ever had!"

"What does your dad feed you, dung beetles? Well, I guess you can't be good at everything. He obviously can't cook."

Jack looked around the room for an empty container and saw one sitting at the edge of a shelf. He stood on an old chair and climbed on top to grab it.

"Jack! What are you doing?" Anna was getting anxious, "Don't move things around, we don't want him to know we were here."

Without looking at her, Jack headed straight for the pot, "I'm taking some of this with us."

"Are you nuts? That was disgusting; I'd rather have dung beetles. Besides, we don't know if it's poison, remember? "

Jack laughed, "I thought you were so sure a moment ago that it wasn't likely to be poisonous."

He blew out the dust from the container and wiped it out with the bottom of his shirt. The container was fairly small but held more than it looked like it would. Jack screwed on its lid and shoved it into a small, leather satchel he found on a shelf.

"Okay, we need to get out of here," Jack said quietly. "He's not going to be happy that half of his dinner is missing."

Anna looked into the pot, "Oh we're dead; so much for going

unnoticed."

They headed for the front door when they began to hear the sound of the carriage in the distance.

"I think he's coming back," Jack peered out the door and down the path. "We can't go out this door, he'll see us."

Jack could see the carriage in the distance and did not want to risk being seen. He closed the door and looked back into the cabin. He headed for the window in the small bedroom in the back and Anna followed anxiously.

"Did he see you?" Anna asked worriedly.

"No, but he will if we have to run across the front yard to get away." Jack spoke sternly.

Jack was stacking a couple old cages up under the window and stepping on them. He put his weight on one of the cages and it creaked and bent under his feet.

"I'm not using those, they're going to break," Anna was trying to pull the old chair into the bedroom, but it was hard to maneuver around the clutter on the floors.

Jack reached out his hand for her, "C'mon, if it can hold me, it will definitely hold you."

Anna gave up trying to move the heavy chair after it got caught in the doorway to the bedroom and ran to Jack. He moved off the cages and hoisted her up. She climbed through the window and fell noisily to the ground outside.

Jack was just about out the window when he heard a small whimper come from inside. He paused, half in and half out of the window.

"Let's go Jack!" Anna was trying to grab his hanging foot, "What are you doing?"

"Shhh," Jack motioned back to Anna, "I think I heard something."

"Me too," she whispered back, "it's the carriage. Remember?"

Then Jack heard the whimper again and pulled himself back into the cabin.

"Jack!" Anna was frantically trying to jump up to the window. "What's going on?"

Jack looked around the room and out toward the main room. Then came a small voice from the cage with the small creature; almost like a whisper. Jack's eyes shot over to the stacked cages and he could make out the dressed creature still huddled into a curled position in the corner of its cage. But he could hear something coming from it. He moved toward it and stumbled over a leg of the large chair. He caught himself from falling to the floor by grabbing one of the closest shelves, which gave way under his weight. It crashed down, along with all of its contents and vial after vial slid off the shelf under it, smashing on the hard wooden floor. After regaining his stance and watching in horror as the wall of shelves undid itself in front of him, Jack stood absolutely still.

The sound of the carriage was getting louder and Anna's voice was calling through the window, beckoning for Jack to return quickly. But the voice coming from the cage was no longer whimpering or whispering or making a peep. He walked over to the stack of cages, wondering what he was doing or what he was expecting to find. The idea of a talking, dressed creature was intriguing to him. He looked into the cage and watched the creature lay still for a moment. He knew he did not have much time, so Jack quickly grabbed something to poke through the small wooden slats. He gently pressed a small vial against the side of the creature, and it jumped up and grabbed the vial from Jack's hand. It bounced to the opposite corner and held a large splinter up like a sword, jabbing and swooshing it at the tip of Jack's fingers.

"You will not eat me!" the creature exclaimed loudly.

Jack jumped back and lost his balance against the side of the table. He fell back and cleared most of the table's items as well. Another series of loud crashes and bangs filled the air as Jack stared at the cage. He was entirely focused on the cage across from him, forgetting about the growing sound of the arriving carriage.

"What are you doing in there?" Anna yelled through the window. "Let's go!"

Stumbling over his words, Jack spoke to the creature, "Ex-excuse m-me? Did you say something?"

There was silence, so Jack slowly returned to the front of the cage, this time bringing a candle from atop the mantle. He watched the shadows dance across the cage and creature, as the dim light mixed details and emptiness together. Jack squinted as he tried to make out what he was looking at.

In a harsh, raspy voice, the creature, still clutching the long splinter like a sword, spoke with difficulty, "I am too important to your cause to be simply eaten! I am Geller the Great!"

The creature stood up straight and hit his hand against his chest as he spoke.

"I'm sorry?" Jack was stunned by what he was seeing, "You're who?"

"I am General Geller the Great, and if you wish to meet your maker," he jumped forward in the cage and wielded his weapon with a show of experience, "you will most definitely try your best, or your worst more likely, to bring any harm to me!"

Jack replied, "I'm not here to hurt you." He could not think of anything to say and he knew his time was very little.

"Ha!" The creature snapped back instantly, "I know what you want from me and you can't have it! I will die an honorable death and your death will be meaningless!"

"Look," Jack was still puzzled and amazed by what he was witnessing in front of him, "I don't want anything from you. In fact," Jack looked back at the door behind him. The sound of the carriage was loud, and he could feel the floor moving below his feet as it came closer. He looked back at the creature that called himself Geller the

Great and continued hurriedly, "In fact, you can stay there for all I care." He started running back to the bedroom, mumbling under his breath, "If you're so *great*, what are you doing in there?"

He was climbing up the stacked cages under the window when he heard Geller the Great call out.

"Wait! Wait! Come back here, at least give me something to eat, sir!" Geller was reaching through the bars with both arms as if trying to reach out to Jack. "I haven't eaten for years!"

Jack stopped and ran back to the cage. He hastily reached into his satchel and retrieved the canister he filled with the stew. He then hastily grabbed a small bowl from the floor and poured some into it. He handed it to Geller the Great, who sloppily tried his best to drink from it through the cage bars. Jack was out of time, so he stuffed the sealed canister back in the satchel and ran back for the bedroom. He quickly hurdled over the cages and through the window.

The carriage had come to a stop now and Anna and Jack were running as low and as quickly as they could away from the cabin. After the mess Jack had made of the place, he knew it would take no time for the man who lived there to know someone had let themselves in. They had no time and had no idea where they were going or how to get away. Then, he could hear the man yelling, but louder and more angrily than the day before.

Out of breath and still running, Anna yelled over to Jack, "What were you doing? That guy is going to kill us!"

Then, there was a loud bang with a ground shaking boom. Jack looked back and saw a bright flash of purple light pour out of every crack and window in the dilapidated cabin. Then the boards and the roof all came apart at once and blew into splinters and dust. Both Anna and Jack were knocked down by a burst of air that filled the forest.

Chapter 5: The Hunt

Jack came to with his body stuck between two tightly neighboring tree trunks. It took a few moments for him to wriggle himself free. It was already dark, and Jack could not find Anna anywhere. He searched all around the nearby trees and brush, looking for any sign of her. He could not even see where the cabin had been before or which direction they had been coming from. It did not take long for him to realize that he was in a lot of pain. He lifted his shirt up and saw that his left side was badly bruised. Jack was sure he had broken some ribs and feared Anna may have suffered much worse. Jack saw the blast coming and had a split second to attempt to duck down; Anna was still running when the blast hit.

"Anna," he called out in pain, "Anna." He stood still waiting to hear a response, but only heard his breath as it hit the cool air and formed small puffs of fog. There was quite a bit of light coming from the moons above the forest, but most of it came down as slivers and lit up small patches. There was also now a dense, cool fog that laid motionless and close to the ground.

"Anna," Jack called out in a loud whisper.

He was spooked by the eeriness of the forest. He stood waiting to hear something but found himself waiting to hear anything. There were no noises coming from the trees or from distant creatures of the night. He could not hear any birds or blowing leaves or a breeze to blow them in. He began wondering if his hearing was affected by the blast. When he shouted Anna's name, he heard himself, but he wondered if he could only hear things close to him. Jack bent over, picked up a stick and threw it up at the canopy as hard as he could. The stick made contact with a cluster of leaves and then a branch, all the while making loud cracking and rustling as it made its way through the trees and back down to the ground. The noise was loud against the still of the night and as quickly as it started, the forest became still and silent once more. Jack could feel chills overcoming him as he tried to make sense of his surroundings.

Then a resounding splash came from only a few hundred yards away. Jack turned around and looked in the direction of the splash. He could hear the light rippling of water against shallow shores as it was coming to rest again.

In a light whisper, Jack shivered and uttered, "Anna?" As quietly as he said it, he was not sure if he had even said anything.

He could hear the sound of something rustling through the vegetation and leaves on the floor of the forest, but he could not see where it was coming from. Then he saw movement in a lit area. The fog slightly rose and fell again as if something was moving under it. He could hear more rustling coming from several areas now and the sound of water becoming choppy against its shores. A purple glow began emitting from the distance where the sound of the splash came from. The forest instantly awoke as the treetops filled with the sounds of fluttering birds and the animals within the forest became excited. Jack began backing up quickly as the rustling sounds came closer to him. He could not see anything yet but was sure there had to be a hundred of them at least and the purple haze was lighting the tree trunks and underside of the thick canopy now.

Jack turned and ran, "Anna," he yelled for her.

He yelled her name several more times as he made his way through the trees and dense fog. He could hardly see his own feet as he ran, and he could feel the slapping of cold, small plants and leaves hitting his legs. Suddenly his foot caught something, and he flew down to the ground. The pain in his chest was throbbing now and his arms were searing with newfound pain from landing on large roots protruding from the ground. Jack winced in anguish as he tried sitting up. Then, he noticed the canister of stew from earlier. He quickly grabbed it as he pulled himself up, noticing that it was still hot, and shoved it back in the satchel he had taken earlier.

From the purple haze came a shot of light that headed straight through the treetops and lit up the sky. The light instantly lit up the veins of the trees and blades of grass through the fog and as the original shot of light faded, Jack could see that the canopy was also glowing an iridescent purple.

The scurrying on the forest floor was much closer now that Jack had lost some of his headway. He started to run again and could see much better through the fog due to the glow of all the plants. Then the fog began to move quickly toward the light, but Jack could not feel any wind other than the cool rush of air against his face as he ran. The forest floor was quickly becoming more visible as the fog disappeared like a flow of water running downhill. He looked behind him and could now see small figures running in and out of the shadows. All he could see were silhouettes blocking the lights of the forest, but he could not make out what they were.

The pain in Jack's side was becoming excruciating and the cold air filling his lungs with every pant he took felt like small knives filling his left lung. He could not think clearly and could not see anywhere to hide. He knew he would be seen in the treetops now because they were lit up and these creatures moved as if they knew the forest floor well. Hiding near a tree or behind a rock seemed fruitless.

The chase continued for some time and Jack could feel his body beginning to wear down. He was slowly becoming too tired to run anymore and the thought of rest was overcoming him. Nevertheless, Jack continued as best as he could, weaving in and out of large plants and trees, attempting to keep his dark figure behind other objects, hoping to make himself hard to see or track. His head was throbbing, and his hands were numb from the cold. His feet were damp and felt like wooden nubs banging against the ground. The sky was becoming lighter, but the forest was just as dark; Jack wished for warmth and rest. He fought to keep his eyes open as his legs began giving under him. He was stumbling against the trees and fighting to stay standing. His pain was ever growing and wearing at him.

All he could think about was how it was his fault Anna was here in the first place, and how he could not find her. She did not have the outdoors experience he had grown up with; she was sure to have been caught already. He tried imagining what these creatures wanted. It hit him; they were probably hunting him for food. He found a renewed sense of power in his steps as he thought about being something's meal.

Jack remembered the canister of stew in his bag and reached in and threw it over his head as a distraction. Maybe the animals would at least stop and look at it, he thought to himself. He just needed to get some distance between himself and them. If he could get just a little time to think, maybe he could find a hiding place or some way of getting away from these things. But Jack could hear the animals had already passed the spot where the canister landed, and they did not sound like they stopped or even slowed down any.

By now, the sky was lit enough to begin filling the dense forest with rays of light. The air was still cold, but the sight of light made Jack feel warmer and like there was hope. The purple lights were beginning to fade as the sunlight drowned them out. Then Jack came upon a small path. He instantly began running down it, hoping that something better was down it. The path gave him a much better advantage on getting some more distance from his hunters. And, as he gained, the animals began yelling out in high pitched squeals and whistles. The noise they made filled the air. Jack thought they even sounded frightened.

The air was becoming warmer and the light was breaking through the treetops more as the path continued. There were more grasses and fewer trees and Jack could see further down the path than before. The sound of the animals chasing him were a distant noise now, but still followed his footsteps. He stopped suddenly when he saw a large swath of burned grass and several burned trees. After looking around, he noticed this must be the same path that he and Anna had seen the day before. He began running again with a small sense of comfort. Maybe he could find the boulder he came through and set things right or at least get out of this forest. The severity of the burned land was becoming most of the landscape around him. Only a few plants and some tree limbs remained colored without char at this point.

A few moments later, Jack found the clearing where he and Anna had landed. He ran into it and straight to the large boulder. He called out for Anna again, hoping that she had found the same path. Other than the growing sound of the arriving animals that had chased him for the last hour, he could hear nothing else. He ran to the boulder and called out for Anna again. He looked around the rock for any signs of the symbol like he had discovered only a day ago, hoping to find anything he may have missed before. There was nothing.

He threw down his satchel and became more frantic as he tried climbing to the top of the smooth sided boulder. He could not get a good foothold anywhere and he was nearly out of time again. Frustration set in. The whole time he had been in this world he had been in some sort of danger. He was not used to such pressure and the constant fear of being killed.

"Anna!" Jack called out for her again.

The animals were close now, and he knew he needed to get out of the clearing. He grabbed his satchel and took off, but the bottom of the bag was so torn that several items fell out. An item caught his eye; a small looking trinket twinkled in the sunlight. If it was anything else, he might have just left it. However, this trinket looked peculiar and he felt it might be something important. He picked it up and shoved it back in the bag. He did not know what it was, but it had something to do with this place and he intended on finding out what it was … if he lived.

Then a few of the animals ran quickly down the path only a few yards away. They did not seem to notice him, so he threw his back against the boulder and crouched down. He had to get out of there, so he decided to crawl to the other side of the boulder and run in the direction he had the day before. As he shifted around the rock, the trinket fell back out of the bag and clinked against the base of the boulder. It began glowing and felt warm to the touch. There was a low humming coming from it.

From a very far off place came a loud and sudden sound of a battle horn. It blasted its note for nearly a minute, shaking loose leaves from the trees and rippling the shirt on Jack's chest. He stood up and tried to determine which direction it was coming from. Then silence. There were no noises coming from the animals or the forest, everything was once again in total silence; except for the sound of the remaining falling leaves rustling through the canopy as they made their way to the ground. The battle horn blasted again, just as loud and long as before. After the horn stopped, Jack could feel the earth beneath him begin to tremor rhythmically. There was a noise unlike he had ever heard before. The sounds of thousands of feet were heavily pounding against the ground as they marched their way through the forest. The battle horn blasted through the forest again and ended with a sudden blast that shook everything. Then, there was a blast of air, like the one that had knocked him unconscious the day before. It blew over the treetops. Millions of leaves and twigs and branches filled the air fifty feet above his head as they joined in the blast. The treetops swayed in unison for a few moments. Jack's ears hurt from the magnitude of the noise.

Only a moment later, the noise from the animals began again, but with much more ferocity and determination. And whatever was making the ground shake; whatever was marching his way, Jack knew he had no chance. He slouched against the rock. He was giving up. There was no way out of there, and everything was trying to kill him. He sat for a moment as the sounds of the quickly running creatures from the night were almost to the clearing. He thought about the library and about home. He yearned for a warm bath and a dry bed. He wished he had never read the book at the library.

With a renewed sense of urgency and adrenaline, Jack jumped to his feet. "Anna!" He called out.

He had to keep going at least until he was sure she was okay. He could not just leave her here to die. He started running the same way he had the day before. It only took a moment to pass the tree they had hidden behind while they watched the angry old man and his ape creature walking around the clearing. He could see their original path through the tall grasses because of the smashed down thickets; except they were much larger. He realized that was because the ape creature had been following them and must have been considerably larger and heavier than they were. He felt warmer now as the air was filling with sunlight, but the pain in his side was still constant. He knew he needed to find some help soon, and he desperately needed to find a place to rest for a while.

As he ran, he could see the damage done by the old man and the ape creature. Large tree bases stuck out of the ground only a few feet and were surrounded by large and small splinters and burned leaves. Huge holes were everywhere in the canopy as the trees that filled them were now gone. The light that was making its way to the forest's floor was already being soaked up by a variety of small flowers and plants. Jack saw random arrows that had missed his head by mere inches only a day before, and then he stopped as he passed one such arrow. He looked it over wide eyed as the sheer size of it made him realize how large the bow must have been. The arrow's shaft filled half of his hand and was much longer than his arm. It was the size of a small spear. Its tail shook at the sound of the slow stampede that followed him. He continued running, wondering how big something must be to shoot something that size.

He had experience with a bow and arrow from when he would go hunting, but the weight of many arrows and the size of the bow could slow down the hunter. It was important to keep this fact in mind when stalking a prey, and yet, the day before, something was easily on his tail shooting five-foot-long arrows left and right at his head and in rapid succession. And then he came upon the very creature he was so curious about.

It was lying face down on the ground; motionless. Jack ducked behind a tree and stood in silence while watching it. Then he noticed something gleam brightly against the sun. There was a small dagger sticking out of the creature's leg. Jack cautiously made his way over to the body and quickly grabbed the dagger out of the creature's leg. He jumped back into a defensive position as best as he could, hindered by his pain. He waited for a reaction from the creature; holding the dagger in the air. The creature did not move, and Jack could tell it was not breathing. He wrapped the dagger in some cloth, stowed it under his belt and crept back to the creature. Using his feet, Jack turned the creature's head onto its side and was disgusted by the brute look of the creature's face. It was stuck in a permanent snarl look, with wrinkles and tough, folded skin stretched across its face. Its body was covered in very course, thick hair and was massive in size. It looked like it could easily weigh three or four times more than Jack himself and probably stood twice as high.

There were several belongings on the ape-creature that Jack could see. One was a large leather belt that held several small bags. Another was a tattered chest piece of armor, which, as far as Jack could tell, looked like it was constructed from a sort of wood. A similar armor covered its shins and it wore nothing for shoes to cover its oversized, thick-skinned feet.

Lying only a couple feet from an outstretched hand was the bow it was shooting from. It was just as massive as Jack imagined, nearly the entire length of Jack's body. He looked around for a quiver or scattered arrows, but he only saw the bow. None were on the ape-creature either. The noise of the animals was not far behind Jack at this point.

Jack stood back up and grasped his left side as the pain of his ribs shot through his body. His feet began running and he took off once again. There were trees shattered everywhere and burnt plants scattered about. Jack was in awe at the amount of damage done by someone he had never met before in his life trying to kill him. He felt a sense of relief that that ape-creature was dead, and he felt even better that the old man may also have been killed in his fit of rage when he blew up his house. Nothing, though, could make him feel better about the chase he was in now. This time he could not see what was coming for him, but there was no doubt in his mind that it was something he could not outrun.

His thoughts filled with fear as his path became full of life again and there were no more marks of havoc from the day before. He feared that Anna was already dead and that no matter what he did, he would soon be found and killed as well. He did not know this forest, but his hunters were obviously familiar with it. He felt lost and hopeless.

All the running he had been doing had taken its toll on him as he finally collapsed. His heart was pounding harder than he had ever known, partly due to the sheer amount of fear he was in. His feet were covered in blisters and sores, the side of his chest was becoming blood red and was covered in black and purple, and his arms were scratched all over from the scraping of the brush. He was nearly gasping for his breaths now and the sound of the animals was only yards away. He pulled himself under a large leafed plant at the base of a tree nearby and clumsily attempted to cover himself with its leaves. Then, he situated one of the leaves of the plant to hang in front of him and remained motionless the best he could.

Only a moment later, one of the animals following him ran by. Jack tried to make out what it looked like, but it was scurrying close to the forest floor and was well hidden amongst the plants. He could hear a good number more pass in front of him and behind him, howling and calling to each other. Then one ran right in front of the plant he was hiding under. Jack got a good look at what it looked like before it disappeared out of sight again. These creatures were the same as the one that was in the cage from before; except, these were more energetic and covered in armor. They held small daggers in front of them as they ran. Jack remembered the dagger he found in the creature and took it out. It was the same kind the animals were wielding. The only wound he saw on the ape-creature was inflicted by the dagger in his hand. He noticed how amazingly light it was in his hand, and the metal was incredibly thin. If this could kill such a large adversary, Jack thought, it will definitely be able to take him down. And, it only took one of these to kill the ape-creature.

There was a quick rustle near the plant Jack was under. One of the creatures had backtracked. Jack's heart, still pounding from fear and exhaustion, began pounding out of his chest. He was in the middle of everything now. If he tried running, everything chasing him would surely see him and he would not have any chance of survival. Plus, he thought, there was still something larger coming that was shaking the ground as it steadily made its way through the forest. From what Jack could tell, there was no way out of this. The rustle near his large leafed plant stopped.

Something stood near him and he heard small footsteps slowly walk toward his way. He tucked further into the plant and silenced his breathing. Then, the leaf he was hiding behind fell to the ground as the tip of a small dagger sliced through it. Jack froze in fear as the creature looked right at him and called out loudly a high-pitched squeal that beckoned to the others. Jack could hear all the scurrying creatures coming his way and they began surrounding the tree he laid under.

The creature stopped squealing and took a step toward Jack. All Jack could think about was the awful amount of pain he was in and what was about to happen to him now. Jack dropped the dagger. He was growing weak. The creature then outstretched one hand, its dagger remaining at the ready in the other, and leaned in toward him. Jack let out a gasp as the breath he held exited rapidly from his lungs and he was overtaken by pain and fear. He collapsed to the ground and the visions in his eyes became small and narrow until finally going black.

Chapter 6: Geller the What?

Jack woke to a dark, large, warm cavern lit by candles. The air smelled damp and he was lying on a bed of soft, fuzzy leaves. There were roots coming out of the ceiling and all the way to the floor, while some stayed suspended in the air. The distant sound of music lightly filled the cavern and was interrupted only by the sound of dripping water. Jack tried sitting up, but his bed moved under his shifting weight. He regained control of his moving bed, looked down and saw it was made from wood tied together like a raft and floated on a body of water. He tried to see the bottom, but the water was black in the candlelight, which was scattered amongst the hanging roots. The flickering lights danced like small stars in their reflections. Jack could not tell how large the cavern was. It seemed, though, that the candles only lit up the area near him.

As Jack tried determining how deep the water was, he noticed small, white nodules on his arm. He quickly retracted his arm and positioned it into the light. It looked like large blisters covered his arm in certain areas. He raised his other arm and saw similar blisters. His feet were covered in the same blisters. He moved his toes some and did not feel pain like he expected. All the running he had done had left his feet in bad shape and in a lot of pain, but now he felt like they were new again – albeit covered in large blisters.

He wondered how he would ever get around with his feet and arms the way they were. None were in pain, but he did not want to try and step on them either. Then, Jack remembered what his chest had looked like before. He drew back the linen cloth that was blanketing him and noticed his shirt had been removed. Covering a large portion of his left side was a single, white blister that stuck far out of his side. His eyes grew wide in disgust and fear of what this infection was.

There was no pain coming from his chest or when he breathed. The blister rippled across the top a little and Jack flinched backwards, causing his bed to lurch some and rock from side to side. Small waves crested against the side of the bed and the roots and they swayed in the moving water. The swaying, flickering flames slowly came back to a rest as the water became calm once again. Jack watched the blister avidly, but it did not move again. He lightly touched it with his finger, scared of what might happen. He only felt warmth as he touched it. Pressing on it a second time, this time a little harder, it felt tough.

Jack laid on the bed for a while, resting and wondering. He wondered where he was and how he got there. He wondered how he was saved from the forest creatures that had chased him all night. He could not think of anything that could possibly have saved him. He stared at the roof of the cavern for several minutes as small rocks in the dirt reflected the candlelight, bringing it to life. He wondered where the music was coming from. It sounded pleasant and inviting. It was a beautiful tune he was unfamiliar with, but he enjoyed listening to it. Jack tried thinking of ways to get out of the cavern, but he did not know which way to go or how long he would have to swim. And worse, he was not sure if he would have the energy to leave. His body spent the whole night running and in pain, and he felt rested now, but he was sure that was because he was still lying down. The thought of running again was stressing him.

Jack was remembering the chase from the night and into the day. He was trying to remember as much of it as possible and he closed his eyes as he tried remembering when he woke up after the explosion at the cabin. He was trying to remember anything he could about what he saw. Anna was out there somewhere, and Jack hoped she was still alive. Maybe, he thought, she was still lying on the ground near the explosion, or maybe she climbed up into a tree. But the small creatures that had hunted him had passed through that same spot, too. They surely would have found her.

He was frustrated with himself for getting her into this. It was his foolishness that brought both him and her into a world he had never heard of. And, what was more frustrating, he did not know how exactly his actions got them there or how to get back home. All he wanted to do right then was wake up in his bed and have his normal life back. Normally, he dreaded weeding the garden and constantly fixing the small cottage he lived in. Now, though, he longed for such chores.

Anger and frustration were filling Jack's mind and he yelled out, "Ahhhhh! What's going on around here? Helllooo?"

He sat up and decided he was going to try and get out of there. He swung his legs forward and threw the linen off of his body. He steadied the floating bed and looked in every direction as he tried determining where to go. He could tell there was a dirt wall not far from him as it reflected the light like the ceiling. His immediate thought was there had to be a door or opening along that wall. He began paddling his bed in the direction of the wall when a sudden wind blew through the cavern. All the candles went dark and Jack's bed soon ran into several roots and slowly spun in the water.

"Great!" Jack stopped paddling. He was not sure which way he was facing anymore, and he could not see the wall any longer. Then he noticed the blisters on him slightly glowed the same purple the trees were the night before. He looked around and saw the roots had small veins of purple running through them as well. The water reflected this and made him feel like he was floating in air, surrounded by bars of purple lights.

He looked back at the blister on his chest, "What's going on here?" he whispered to himself.

"I may be able to answer that for you," a very close voice said from the dark.

Jack jumped up and the bed flew out from beneath him. He fell into the water and floundered about as he tried swimming back to the bed. It had floated away from him and all Jack could do was tread water and look around.

"Who said that?" he yelled, "Who's there?"

A single candle relit on a nearby root, "Why, it's I, Geller!" The creature picked up the candle and held it near him. "You may remember me as Geller the Great." Geller took a small bow as he stood on one of the roots, "How do you do?"

Although the light was dim, Jack could make out that this was the same small and frail, man-looking creature from before. His ears were slightly pointed, his hair long and somewhat disheveled, and his fingers long for the size of his hands. He stood only about two and a half feet tall and Jack could see lots of hair on the parts of Geller's legs that stuck out from his pant bottoms.

"Geller? I mean, Geller the Great? I-I thought you died in the explosion." Jack was trying to remember the cabin as best as he could.

"Oh, yes, the cabin," Geller smiled, and he hopped down to a root that was positioned just above the water a yard away from Jack. "That old man kept me captive for years. You gave me the power to do something about that."

"What did I do?" Jack asked cautiously.

"You gave me food, of which I hadn't had any for years." Geller looked down and threw the candle into the water. Just then all the candle flames relit in their reflections but remained unlit in the roots.

"How is that even possible?" Jack struggled to find a root to grab a hold of. "I thought you were just lying to me when you said you hadn't eaten for years. That's not possible. Surely you were eating something to stay alive."

"Good sir, I am many things, but I am not a liar!" Geller's eyes glowed brightly in a show of anger at the remark.

"What are you?" Jack whispered.

"You don't believe me about my name either do you?" Geller clapped his hands together and all the candles relit with ferocity and their flames were much larger than they were in the reflection on the lake. "I saved your life out there! They were going to kill you, but I saved your life!" He was visibly agitated.

"Whoa, okay," Jack responded, "I'm sorry. I didn't mean to offend. I just had never heard of it being possible to go such a time without eating, that's all. I'm not from ..." Jack stopped himself. He did not want to give away that he was from another world for fear they may try to find the boulder with the symbol. It felt too soon to divulge that kind of information. He said softly, remembering all the people who could get hurt if he said otherwise, "around here. I'm not familiar with this forest or its …" again, Jack stopped himself from saying the word 'animals'. He did not want Geller to feel like Jack only thought of him as one.

Geller, curious, pushed Jack's remarks further, "Its what?"

"Its, um, its," Jack had to think quickly, so not to offend Geller. "Its inhabitants. I'm not familiar with the inhabitants of the forest, that's all." He attempted to grab another root.

"You should really get out of that water," Geller said while smiling back to Jack, "there are some unfriendly things in there."

Jack spun around in the water. "Unfriendly? Like what?"

"Vrooks. They have taken some of our best without warning." He pointed to a ripple in the water thirty feet away which was slowly approaching Jack's position. He continued as Jack cautiously watched the rippling water, "They rely on your movement, see. If you stay absolutely still, they can't detect you, they have no eyes." He moved closer to the water and pulled out a dagger from his boot as he watched the moving water.

"Help me get out of…"

"Shhh! Here he comes. Stay quiet and don't move. You may have a chance if you stay still, he may forget you are here." Geller crouched down and was getting ready to pounce on something. He motioned to Jack, "Just stay absolutely still."

The ripples on the water were following something close to the surface. The movement swayed back and forth as it got closer to Jack. Then the water stopped.

"Oh, that's not good!" Geller whispered to Jack.

Jack tried not to move as his eyes were questioning Geller, who noticed the looks of concern he was getting.

"When the vrooks stop, that means they've found their prey." Geller got close to the water, as if he was trying to determine the position of the vrook, "I think it's gone." Geller stood up quickly and wiped his brow, "Whew, almost thought you were about to lose a limb or two!" Geller was smiling.

Irritated at the lack of concern, Jack snapped back to him, "Why are you smiling? I don't know how it happens here, but if I lose a limb, it doesn't grow back!"

"Oh, really?" Geller jumped through the roots and over to one in front of Jack, "You don't say? How curious?" He patted Jack's shoulder with the side of his dagger, "These things don't come back? Why, everything on Lunia can grow its limbs anew." He studied Jack as he treaded softly in the water.

A sudden splash of water came from right behind Jack.

Geller jumped up, "Vrook!" He held his dagger up in a throwing position.

Jack panicked. "Where? Where?" he spun around in the water trying to see where it was. The water churned heavily from only a few feet away. "Get me up!" Jack struggled against the slippery roots as he tried climbing them. "Geller! Help me!"

Geller was sitting nearby laughing and pointing at Jack.

Still panicked, Jack looked over to him, "Please, Geller! They don't grow back!" He was still struggling to climb up the hanging roots.

The water stopped churning and splashing. Jack stopped climbing, aware that something was behind him. He slowly turned around, expecting to see something vicious and hungry. He had held his eyes shut tightly as he turned, slowly opening them to see what was coming.

"Hi!" a small, squeaky voice said to him from a tiny boat not much bigger than the width of Jack's chest.

He fell back in a startled reaction and righted himself. "Wha..."

"I'm Selini!" A small hand came forth as if expecting Jack to shake it, "I'm Geller's younger sister."

Immediately, Jack shot a glance at Geller, who was still laughing.

"I got you! You thought a vrook was going to get you!" He was wiping a tear from his eye, "You really aren't from around here. Vrooks are small and friendly!"

"I thought you weren't a liar," Jack said as he turned back to Selini. He reached out and shook her hand, saying in hesitation, "Pleased to meet you, Selini."

She shook his hand with amazing firmness and strength for such a small creature-like person, "Pleased to meet you, Jack!" She wore a smile on her face and was visibly excited, "The vrook thing was his idea." Her smile stayed wide and she continued shaking Jack's hand.

"You made all that noise?" he asked as he attempted to pull back his hand. Her small boat pulled toward him as she kept shaking his hand.

"Yep," she stood up straight, "that was all me!"

"Oh, pshh," Geller was next to Jack again, "it could have been better."

She dropped Jack's hand and pointed at Geller, "I was trying not to be too loud. I didn't want him to faint again."

Jack's face turned red in embarrassment, "A –actually," he held up a finger in affirmation, "I was in a lot of pain, really. And..." he stumbled to find an excuse, "...and, and I was really exhausted, I'll have you know."

Geller grabbed Selini's boat and pulled it in to him, "Tired, were you?" He let Selini get out of the boat and pushed it away from the three of them but held a small string that was in it.

"Yes, tired. More like exhausted, I might say."

"You were exhausted, eh?" Geller looked at his sister and was smiling, "and from what were you exhausted? Didn't get any sleep?"

"Oh, leave him alone," Selini jumped into the water, "he had a rough time."

"Oh, no doubt he had a rough time," Geller's smile could not have gotten any bigger, "but why?"

Jack answered for her, "Well, I was being chased by an army of your friends and they were trying to kill me. And, I had broken some of my ribs. And then there was an even bigger army behind your friends, just in case they didn't kill me, the bigger army would just have to run me over. I was running all night and day from some sort of killer army, hell bent on hunting me down."

Geller let out a laugh, "That's the best thing I've heard in years!"

Jack was confused, he was not sure why that was so good to hear, but he was sure Geller had misunderstood him. "I'm not sure you heard me right," Jack began.

"Don't give him the pleasure of thinking it was worse than it really was," Selini was about to go under the water.

"It would please you more if I told you it was worse?" Jack questioned in surprise.

Geller clapped a little and jumped in excitement, "Oh, please, oh please, would you? Was it worse?"

"This is getting weirder than it already is," Jack mumbled. Then he remembered something, "I guess the fact that your friends may have killed my friend might bring you some pleasure." Jack's face became heavy as he thought about what could have happened to her.

"Your friend, huh?" Geller was pulling the string back.

"Do you mean, Anna?" Selini said.

Jack's face lit up, "Yes, her name is Anna! Have you seen her?"

Selini rolled her eyes, "Yes, I've seen her."

"Really?" Jack felt reassured.

"From what I hear, she's quite the handful," Geller joked to Selini.

"Wait, she's here?" Jack was beginning to feel a sense of relief that Anna may be alright. "Can I see her? Where is she?"

"Oh, she's here alright. And if it weren't for the fact that she is a friend of yours," Selini sighed heavily, "we would have happily sent her to Earth by now! She's a real pain; constantly demanding and questioning." She took in a deep breath and disappeared into the water.

Jack was in shock, "You guys can send us to Earth?"

He instantly thought Anna must have told them they were not from this place. The fact that they were willingly discussing it was welcoming to him.

Geller kept pulling on the string, "We can. I don't see why anyone on Lunia would ever want to go to Earth. It's a horrible place; dirty, filthy people always ruining the land."

"Some people call Earth their home," Jack snapped back.

Out of the darkness appeared the boat at the end of the string, but it was now large enough to carry the three of them. And, without warning, Jack's feet were pushed up along with the rest of his body and he flew into the boat with a hard landing.

The boat hardly flinched under his weight and Selini jumped up out of the water and into the boat. Geller jumped in with a bound that defied his size.

"You speak of Earth like you know of it," Geller was looking Jack over, "but, if you've ever been, you'd know there's nothing to like about it."

"That's where most of the humans on Lunia live," Selini chimed in, "Rarely do we see a human this far south, and it's been a long time since any of them helped one of us." She looked at Geller and smiled,

"We thought we lost Geller a long time ago, but, thanks to you," she patted Jack's leg, "we have him back."

"How do humans live on Earth and on Lunia?" Jack asked, confused.

Geller responded, "Humans here live *in* Earth and everyone here lives *on* Lunia. I could tell immediately when I met you, you weren't from Earth. You didn't act like one of them."

"For such a young city, they've rapidly increased in numbers, but show little respect to the world outside their gates," Selini said while lighting a lamp at the front of the boat.

"Earth is a city?" Jack felt more confused now.

Geller looked at him, "See? I knew you weren't from there. But who hasn't at least heard of Earth; especially since you're human?" He looked over to his sister and laughed out, "Sheesh, where'd you come from, under a rock?"

Jack wanted to keep talking about the humans on Lunia, but he was sure his secret about being from another world was close to being discovered if they kept talking about it. He quickly changed the subject, "So, what did I do that helped Geller get out of that man's cabin?"

The boat began moving slowly through the water and the roots parted out of the way as it moved through them. The light from the lamp shined brightly forward and as far as Jack's eyes could see, there were roots everywhere.

"First off," Selini sat down at the head of the boat, "that wasn't any old man."

"No sir, he sure wasn't." Geller was pulling something out of a small pouch as he spoke, "He was one of Ghowla's wizards; he had direct contact with Ghowla."

Selini continued for him, "His name was Frinkul. He was almost 3,000 years old; been around for a while and had a good deal of power."

"It's not easy to beat a wizard that old," Geller took a bite of some bread he had pulled out. "Both sides have their fair share of wizards, but Frinkul was very powerful, very powerful indeed. That's why he was stationed in Wellwood Forest." Geller took another bite from his bread.

"That forest, above all else, holds an ancient power that the Reign of Karakaziem hasn't learned to control. And they are serious about learning its secrets."

Geller stood up and shifted around for a moment before lying down on the deck, "No one can learn this ancient power the Reign seeks. No one can wield its power. It remains outside the reach of them and that has made them frightful of its potential."

"I'm really lost," Jack admitted. He did not know anything about what they were talking about.

Selini responded, "That forest was grown one night by us, the Valindi, to conceal the secret hidden on the lands there. The Reign realized this, but they found it hard to fight us. There is a war going on between the Reign and those who are opposed to them. As long as we keep fighting, we have a chance to protect this ancient power."

"Why fight to protect a power you yourselves can't even use?" Jack was curious, but still unsure of what she was talking about.

"There's something about it that the elders feel we must protect. We don't question their motives because they have been around a very long time. Some even think the elders know something about this ancient power but won't tell us about it."

"Do you think they know something about it?" Jack asked, curious once again. He thought maybe the power they were talking about had something to do with the boulder Anna and he had been sucked through.

She watched Geller settle himself into a little ball, like the one Jack had originally seen him in at the old cabin. "The oldest elder is our father, Gubuyis. He is very well respected by the other elders. I have felt in the past that he knows more than he is letting on. I see him sometimes sitting by himself reading through old texts and looking at a small pendant that hangs from his neck."

"What makes that so suspicious?" Jack asked, but he still felt confused by the conversation as a whole.

"He used to always hate jewelry, but many years ago he began wearing this necklace like it was something to be treasured. He never lets others see it, and I have a feeling it has something to do with the powers that rest in Wellwood Forest. It was shortly after the night the Valindi elders seeded the very forest we are under now that he began wearing it."

Jack had many questions; many about where he was and what was going on. His head swirled with question after question and he did not know where to begin. Selini was nice, but Jack did not know if he should mention that he was not from this world. He did not know what reaction that would get or if that would automatically make them enemies. He was not sure if the Valindi were the ones he should be becoming friends with, or if it was the Reign who were the good guys. It was hard to tell, and he knew so little about everything. He could not help wondering if the ancient powers that she spoke of had anything to do with his arrival either. He decided to keep as much of his personal experience or whereabouts a secret as long as he could, at least until he knew who he could trust.

Jack leaned back against the side of the boat and it swayed under his weight. He decided to try and keep the conversation off himself if he could help it. He was also learning things about this new world from Selini, and he wanted to keep that going as much as he could.

"So, what's so special about this necklace?" he asked coolly, trying to learn whatever he could about what was going on.

Selini leaned toward Jack and whispered, "I saw it once. It was sitting on the table in the mess of books my father was very intently searching through. I wasn't supposed to see it, I could tell. He has always been protective of it, keeping it out of view and always sure to skillfully change the subject if you try and ask about it. I saw it though, and I got a good view of it."

"What did it look like," Jack whispered back, but was not sure why they were whispering.

"It was almost identical to a pencine, except it was shinier and gold; at least I think it was gold. Anyway, it was similar, but there was an inscription along its edges that was written in a language I am not familiar with. There was also a symbol in the center, but I couldn't make it out."

Jack instantly thought of the symbol from the library. He could not help but to think that Gubuyis might have information that could help him get home. Curiosity rolled through his head as he thought of what it might mean if the symbol was the same as he had seen before. Maybe, he thought, Gubuyis knew how to get him and Anna back home.

"You seem pretty curious about it." Selini continued. "You wouldn't happen to know anything about it, would you?"

He turned his face toward Geller and responded, "I don't recall ever seeing something like that before, no." Pointing to Geller, Jack then asked, "Is he asleep?" He intended on changing this subject as well.

"Oh, him," Selini stomped her foot on the boat's bottom, "he falls asleep pretty quickly." Geller did not move to the loud thumping from Selini's hardened shoe, "that probably came in handy while he was caged up for so long."

"How long was he locked up like that for?" Jack asked.

"He hasn't really talked much about it yet, but we thought we lost him three years ago." Her face was somber, "He was out to war he was. Father told him he should stay here to help him oversee the colony, but Geller insisted. Every year around this time, the Reign leads massive campaigns against us. They destroy anything in their way, fewer and fewer ever make it out of battle, and we are always on the losing side."

"Why don't the Valindi just move and stop fighting if you're losing so much?" Jack felt like this was a stupid question but could not take it back.

She was staring ahead as she continued, "I say we are on the losing side, but, by our efforts, we have managed to help hold the Reign within a boundary. They have gained much ground, but the further out they expand, the harder it is for them to continue on. You see, the winters here are treacherous. They last for many months and the snow becomes like a barren white stretch of mountains that expand as far as the eyes can see. We can't live above the surface during the winter. Very few creatures can live in that kind of weather, and the Reign doesn't have that ability. Thank Valinia, they haven't found a way to expand during the winter, or we'd all be doomed." She turned the boat some and continued on, "Now, don't get me wrong, I did say some things can live up there during the winter, and the Reign has some of them under their control. The Frost Birds, they can live up there, but they swear allegiance to no one. That works out for us because the Reign can't use them, but it would sure be nice to be their friends at times."

"Does the Reign live underground also?" Jack inquired.

"No. They live above ground in a grand structure in the middle of Gibblesville. They took over that town during one of their early campaigns and just stopped moving after that. They protect the town from the winter by the power of Vane Weather, which protects and shields them from the cold and keeps the town warm and sunny, like summer."

"There have been rumors that they found something there, something mysterious and strong that they could use to their advantage in destroying all of their enemies. But we haven't seen anything to confirm that suspicion. If we ever want to rid our world of the Reign that is where the final battle must take place; that is where the strongest of the six mages lives. His name is Karakaziem. He can't die while the other five live, it is impossible. As long as any of the others are alive, he is invincible. And even then, we don't know how to defeat him once that happens. No one has seen him close enough to know what his powers are, or what his weaknesses are. And after what happened eight and a half years ago, no one has seen him since."

Curious, Jack asked, "What happened eight and a half years ago?"

"Dear sir," Selini seemed surprised, "where have you been? These wars and this power struggle affect everyone everywhere. You must have heard of something; especially since one of them was human."

"I must have missed the news." Jack said cautiously.

Selini looked Jack over intently. "Where'd you say you were from?"

Geller made a few grunts and stood up. "We should just about be there." He looked out in front of the boat, "You don't need me to drive this contraption now do ya?"

"I've got it." Selini snapped at him, "I had to go slower with this thing being bulkier than normal. There are more roots down here than before, thank you."

"Okay," Geller threw his hands up, "no need to get testy. We are expected, though." He looked at Jack, "So you two are getting to know each other?"

"Oh, um, sure," Jack said, relieved that Geller had woken at the right time. "We were talking about your dad."

"Well, he's going to find you absolutely fascinating," Geller pulled more bread from his pockets, "he just loves seeing humans."

"That's only because he thinks one of them will be just like the one from before," Selini said exasperated at the thought of how delighted her father would be when he saw Jack. "He always thinks the humans have some sort of unknown power."

Geller poked Jack jokingly, "We all know you guys can't do much but eat and sleep and make a mess of things. Nothing too special there, we can all do that."

Selini added, "Hard to make your place in this world without power, and you guys haven't shown any."

"Maybe it's a secret," Geller laughed. "Maybe you guys are hiding it from us." Geller started moving his hands as if acting out his words, "Maybe the humans can snap their fingers and blow this world to smithereens and we are all secretly at their whim, but they are being kind to us and letting us all live here."

Jack snapped his fingers as Geller enacted a world blowing up.

"Or, maybe not," Selini said. "We're here."

Chapter 7: A Fire Storm

The boat came to an abrupt stop against a glowing shore that twinkled as far in both directions Jack could see. The cavern seemed much more open now and the ceiling could no longer be seen. There were many roots hanging, but none of them came down to the shore and they swayed slowly in the air. Although the shore was lightly glowing, along with the iridescent glow of the roots, it was still dark.

Geller and Selini hopped out of the boat and began walking toward the cavern wall. Jack decided to follow and stepped on to the shore. The moment his bare foot hit the warm, soft sand, a balmy breeze rushed by the group and small lights appeared high in the roots. Jack looked up and saw that it looked like he was now under a sky with freely suspending roots. The lights looked like fluttering stars floating in water as they drifted about high above him.

"I've never seen th…" Selini was interrupted by Geller.

He whispered a hush to her as he nudged her arm. Geller looked nervous and bewildered in amazement at the same time. "C'mon," he said nonchalantly as he moved forward, "we are on a schedule here."

There was no doubt to Jack that the appearance of a sky above them was not normal, even in this strange world.

Geller reached for a closed, stone doorway in front of him. As his hand fell upon the lever sticking out from its side, the entire wall in every direction disappeared as if it was a mirage of smoke. A storm began cracking loud thunder and lightning far in the distance behind them over the water. The three of them turned in startle and stared for a moment. The water on the shore was becoming restless as small crests began to form.

"What is this?" Geller was standing defensively, as if he expected to be attacked at any moment.

"What did you do?" Selini was also becoming defensive and the both of them looked prepared to fight anything that came their way.

Jack watched as the storm became more violent and the once peaceful water became crashing waves against the shore. The sand beneath his feet was still warm, but the air around him was becoming rapidly cooler and windy. The boat they came on had shrunk to its original size and was now being tossed like a leaf on the water.

"Let's get out of here," Jack yelled over the thunder and wind.

Geller called back to him, "Be at your ready! Quick!"

"My ready! My ready for what? What's going on?" Jack called back to Geller.

Selini grabbed his arm and then Geller's, "Something is coming!" She tensed up and a small shockwave ran through the sand from her feet.

Rain began pouring hard with small bits of hail. The wind was fierce now and the warmth was gone from the sand. Water was flying off the tops of the waves and making it hard to see. The stars in the sky were beginning to swirl from every direction over the middle of the lake and above the storm clouds. As the storm approached the shore, Jack lost sight of the stars. The waves intensified and the water became cold. Jack was shivering and he could not hear if Geller or Selini were saying anything.

Then he saw something. It was dark and hard to make out, but whatever it was, it was moving fast and with ferocity. It was the clouds themselves! He could see a cloud swirling fast and skipping across the water, picking up massive amounts of water and throwing it back out.

Jack had heard of this type of storm and knew it was bad news for them if they stayed. He tried to run toward where the wall was before, but Selini's grip was tight and she was much more powerful than her size gave her credit for. He was hardly able to budge from his spot. He pried at her clutch on his arm and was yelling for them to run, but he could hardly hear himself.

The storm was now at the shore. There was no more sight of the sky above them and everything was almost pitch black except for the light glow from the sparkling sand. Then he saw a glimpse of it, the twister was close. No matter what they did now, they were too late, it was too close. The ground was beginning to rumble, and the waves were high and fast as they smashed against the shore and water ran high up it. Jack could hardly feel his hands or his toes, everything was so cold.

Then something happened. A low growling sound came from the sky. He could not make it out, but he could hear it intermittently through the sounds of everything else. There was some light coming from the clouds that was growing and getting brighter. Jack could see it over the flashes of lightning and now he could see the swirling clouds and the sheer intensity of the storm before them. The twister was only about a hundred feet away. He could see more of them scattered about in the storm still far over the water. His heart sank; he knew there was no hope.

The brightly growing light kept his attention. The clouds below the light suddenly sucked upward and were rotating faster than the very twister in front of him. Jack could see the entire storm was being sucked up and beginning to shrink in size. The twister was still dashing back and forth above the shore, but its bottom was curving toward the light. Even the lightning was not making it to the water anymore. As it flashed, it bent in midair and flew to the swirling center.

The water was becoming quieter and Jack could hear Selini yelling something. There was still a lot of noise, but he heard enough of what she was saying to take action.

"RUN! ... IS COMING! ... RUN, JACK!"

She was still holding his hand and Geller was already ahead of them as they ran up shore as fast as they could. Suddenly a crash of water and a scowling roaring came from the lake. Jack looked back and could see a large snake-like dragon bursting through the water. It must have been a hundred feet in length and its body was thicker than several tree trunks tied together. The water around it was boiling and it was surrounded in steam, illuminated by the remaining flashes of lightning and the light from the clouds.

The dragon's head slammed into the water and its body followed. All Jack could see were a few parts protruding from the water and a massive tail fin high above the water. Within a moment, the head reappeared, but far up the shore. It was no longer fully in the water and it was moving quickly under the ground.

The three of them were still running. Jack felt like he had an abundance of energy and was able to make larger steps than Geller or Selini. He scooped up Selini and took off. As he approached Geller, Geller looked back and, without hesitation, jumped up and onto Jack's back. Jack took off as fast as he could, and he was moving much faster than he ever thought possible. The dragon, however, was making headway. It had almost caught up to them.

Jack could see tall grasses in the distance and hoped they might be able to find somewhere to hide while the dragon's head was underground. It moved through the ground like it was still in the water, and Jack knew they were doomed if it could get close to them.

"STOP!" Selini yelled into Jack's ear. The sounds of the thunderstorm were lessening, and the crashing waves couldn't be heard anymore, but she still yelled at the top of her lungs.

He stopped abruptly and looked at her.

"WHAT ARE WE DOING?!" Geller yelled angrily and nervously, "GO!"

Selini was pointing to the grass ahead of them. There were more of the dragon creatures slithering within them.

"It was a trap," Jack whispered in despair.

"WHAT DO WE DO NOW?" Selini asked her brother.

Geller was no longer on Jack's back. He stood silently on the sand and dirt, looking in every direction, studying their next moves.

The thunder and lightning ceased, and the winds died. The only sound they could hear now was that of the dragon's head thudding into the ground and the moving scales of the dragons ahead of them against the course grass.

Within a moment, the swirling light above the lake could be seen again as the last of the storm clouds evaporated into the air. The light slowly came to a stop and dissipated into the sky again. The dragon was still violently thrashing itself into the ground, back and forth, but only behind them. It had stopped moving forward. The dragons ahead of them were moving more restlessly and the ground beneath Jack's feet was rumbling and small cracks began appearing everywhere.

Selini grabbed the small bag from Geller's waist and tore it from him. She threw it at the head of the dragon behind them and it snapped it out of the air.

"What! Why?" Geller looked displeased as he watched his bag of bread fly through the air.

"Figured I'd try something," she shrugged off her effort as valiance.

Jack was trying to stay standing as the ground shook more intensely, "I think he wants a lot more food than that!"

"That was a lot of food, even for him!" Geller said angrily. "You do realize I didn't eat for *years,* right?" He looked like he would cry.

"Get off it, we're about to die!" Selini was annoyed, "Were you thinking about picnicking after defeating a horde of dragon monsters with rocks?!" She bent down and picked up a small pebble from the mix of sand and dirt and threw it at the dragon, who didn't take notice.

"Guys! Come on!" Jack was irritated at their arguing, "How about we figure out what to do about the shaking ground first!"

"That's us," Selini said to him. "Geller and I are doing this and it seems to be keeping him at bay for now."

"Hard to move through the dirt this way," Geller was still upset about his missing bag.

"It doesn't breathe fire, does it?" Jack watched the dragon move from side to side as it watched its prey.

"If it's anything like the ones the Reign use … then, yes. It can breathe fire." Selini said coolly.

"What?" Jack fell back as he tried backing up, even though the dragon was still a good distance from them.

"Relax," Geller chimed in, "it won't do that."

"Yeah, dragons don't spit fire at the Valindi. They'd quickly burn and die."

"But, how? Why?"

Geller snapped his fingers and a small flame ball formed above his hand. He then motioned his arms as if to throw the flame at Selini. The fireball flew at her quickly and bounced off her and back to Geller. It continued to bounce back and forth for a moment before Selini waved her hand at the approaching ball. It disintegrated in its approach and turned into a small puff of smoke.

"The Valindi are immune to dragon fire," Geller said. "If it spits fire at us, it would bounce back at the dragon."

"And he isn't fireproof!" She yelled at the dragon.

Jack stumbled back up and said excitedly, "Well, throw fire at it then!" He felt a small ray of hope as he said it.

"Sorry, Jack," Selini said back to him, "he isn't immune to dragon fire. Our fire wouldn't hurt him."

His brow drooped, "There's a difference?" he asked himself out loudly.

Their speaking was interrupted by the sound of the lake once again. This time it was the sound of the boiling lake that was gaining their attention. A dense fog was rolling off it and filling the air. It quickly surpassed their group and the dragons began breathing fire.

"What are they doing?" Jack asked nervously. "You said they wouldn't attack us, right?"

"I don't know what they are doing. But I never said they wouldn't attack us." Geller could be heard saying from the fog near Jack, but he couldn't see him anymore.

Jack looked around and could no longer see Selini or Geller. All he could see now were burst of orange and red lighting up the fog in various places. He could still see the sky and its hanging roots.

"Are they doing this?" Jack asked.

"I don't know," Selini was whispering now, "No one has come back from a fight with the dragons. So, we have little knowledge of what happens."

Jack couldn't believe what he was hearing. No one has won a fight with the dragons before? How could they be so calm about that little fact?

The air was dense and getting hot when Geller suggested they begin digging and bury themselves under the sand. "They might be trying to cook us without directly using fire on us. If we get below the surface, we might be able to survive longer."

Jack could hear them digging intently with their hands. Within moments he could tell they were almost buried.

He heard Selini's voice call up to him, "Jack, start digging."

Then, a large burst of flames flew right by his head. Jack ducked to the ground and began digging as fast as he could. Another flame ball slammed into the ground next to him and he felt the searing pain of intense heat against his back.

Jack yelled in pain as another flame grazed him and another and another. The dragons were not hitting him directly, but he was still getting burned by indirect flames and offshoots. He laid down all the way and continued to try and dig with one hand. He could not see how he was going to be able to dig a big enough hole before the dragons successfully hit him. He felt hopeless.

Jack heard the thudding of several dragons' heads hit the ground as they moved closer. The dragons were now beneath the surface and moving toward them. Jack called for Geller and Selini, but they did not answer. He pounded on the dirt around him, hoping to hit one of them, but nothing happened. Fire was still coming at him from every direction and landing near him. He yelled again, trying to warn them of the impending danger of the underground dragons. Still, there was no response.

He stood up and began running toward the closest glow of flames he could find. Instantly, fire was being thrown at him almost directly. He wished he had had a weapon on him, when he remembered the dagger he had found on the ape-creature in the forest before. He reached to his waist where he had last stowed it and felt that it was still wrapped in cloth and hanging from his belt. He continued to run as he unwrapped the dagger.

The dragon in front of him spit another flame and Jack raised his dagger. He felt sudden, excruciating pain as the flash of fire hit him. He collapsed to the ground and coughed for cool air. The dagger was still cool in his hand, but everything else burned, even the ground he crawled on.

Jack struggled to get up as he could feel a surge of energy filling him. He began stumbling toward the dragon again and lunged forward with the small dagger. He did not know how to kill a dragon, or what he was going to do about all the others even if he killed this one, but he wanted to distract them away from Geller and Selini the best he could. His dagger quickly sank into something at the end of his lunge. There was a loud squawking and squealing of pain as the air filled with stuttering flames.

Jack realized he had not hit the dragon's head, but only a part of its body. The dagger was too small to cut through the dragon and Jack was quickly becoming tired. He fell to the ground, his dagger still lodged in the dragon's hardened scale body and rested.

He had accomplished what he set out to do; the other dragons were now surrounding him and the injured one. The air was thinning, and he could see the figures of the dragons. There must have been hundreds of them, as far as he could see. And they looked very angry. Jack backed up into the flailing dragon's body, thinking the others might not spit fire for fear of killing the dragon behind him. For the moment, it seemed this was true, as the other dragons only occasionally snapped at Jack, but none shot fire at him.

For the first time, Jack looked back at the dragon he had struck and got a good look at his head. It was obviously in pain as it shrieked and thrashed its head back and forth. It had four very large eyes which gave it sight from all directions and a mane of hair-like scales around its neck. Horns protruded from atop its head, and they were moving back and forth. Jack stood back up, remaining pressed against the dragon as much as he could.

Jack wondered how such a small dagger could cause this much pain. He looked back to where his dagger was sticking out of a large scale the size of a shield and saw a large crack bleeding black ooze. Jack grabbed the dagger as he watched the other dragons become more agitated. Some took more swipes at him and others blew fire into the air. He twisted the dagger and the dragon flipped around more. The surrounding dragons were becoming loud, shrieking in panic. The dragons were showing fear! Jack grabbed at the dagger's handle again and looked at the dragons; they backed up some.

"Back!" He yelled, "Get back or I'll kill him!" He had no clue how to kill the dragon, but he counted on the fact that the others did not know that. "I said, BACK!" he slowly twisted the dagger some and the dragon shrieked and bled more intensely.

The dragons became more subdued and stopped shrieking as they backed up.

"So you can understand me, huh? Good! You will let me and my friends out of here!" Nothing happened. "NOW!"

Within seconds, a dragon threw Selini and Geller from its mouth to the ground in front of Jack. They looked to be in bad shape, but still able to move.

Selini got up and ran to Geller. They both backed up with Jack and they all stood there for a moment as the dragons reluctantly slithered further back, giving the three of them plenty of walking space.

"How do we get out of here?" Selini said panting for air.

"I don't know," Jack said, "I didn't think this would work."

"These are dragons, they don't lose," Geller said. "They simply kill. Unless you intend on dragging this three-hundred-foot-long monstrosity behind you as collateral, we are doomed the second we step away from him."

"I'm sorry guys, I was just trying to make it so you could get out of here alive by creating a distraction."

"Why? You don't even know us," Selini asked. "Why not save yourself?"

"I guess … I guess it's just not in my nature." Jack said as he remembered a time when his dad, a constable, had been talking to him about the importance of others' lives.

"Where?" Geller was looking Jack over, "Where are you burned?"

Jack looked at his arms and hands and couldn't see any burns. "I was burned! I was being hit with fire. Look at my back, is it still burned?"

Selini looked and responded, "It looks fine."

Now that Jack had a little time to think, he could tell he did not feel burning pain anymore. He still clutched the dagger, but the dragon was lying nearly motionless now, with the occasional shriek of pain.

"Brother, it must be the swampees, right? That would be the only way he would heal that fast." Selini hypothesized.

Geller looked at the blister on Jack's chest and responded, "I've never heard of a recovery from such wounds with that kind of speed before."

Jack looked down at his chest and pointed at the blister, "This isn't some kind of blister or infection?"

"Oh, no, no, no. Those are rare swampees. They aid in healing your body." Selini said back to him, "they just don't do it that fast."

Far on a hill a shot of flames was thrown high into the air. They all watched as dragons moved out of the way and a dragon much larger than any of the others was rapidly approaching the three of them. The other dragons became more excited and skittish as it approached.

"Hello." Geller stood in front of the group, "it looks like we have an upset mommy."

It disappeared underground and reappeared almost right in front of them. Jack quickly grabbed the dagger again and twisted it. The injured dragon began writhing again and flailing its head. The large dragon stopped and watched as Jack threatened to twist it some more.

"I don't think it intends to let us pass," Selini whispered.

Jack yelled out, "Maybe you didn't hear me earlier! I will kill this dragon if you don't let us go!" The dragon watched them intently as Jack shouted, "I said, I WILL *KILL* HIM!"

The large dragon slithered some toward the front of the injured dragon and they looked into each other's eyes.

"Prepare for the worst, because this looks real bad," Geller backed into the other two.

Without so much as a warning, the large dragon lifted its head and breathed fire at the head of the other. Within a couple of seconds, the dragon that Jack had so successfully disabled had burned into utter ash and the dagger was now stuck in Jack's hand; floating in air.

Geller instantly said, "I knew it!"

All the dragons began surrounding the three of them now and the occasional shot of fire was sent their way. Geller and Selini were moving about, deflecting the approaching flames and sending them back to their throwers.

"This can't be!" Geller was confused, "Why would they shoot fire at us?"

The flames were bouncing back into the crowds of dragons and shrieks of pain came in numbers. Then a small light fell from the sky like a heavy snowflake; then another and another. Within moments, the stars from the sky were endlessly dropping like a snowfall. They were landing on the dragons all over. Fire was still coming at the three of them, but now dragons were shooting fire into the sky, vainly attempting to hit the flecks of light that were falling.

As a fleck of light hit a dragon, it seared straight through its heavily fortified scales and out its other side. Dragons were dropping to the ground everywhere and bursting into fire and ash as they died under the fall of light upon them. Neither Jack, nor his companions, were being hit at all. Jack looked at Geller and Selini searching for any sign that one of them had anything to do with this, but they looked in awe as well. They all watched in amazement as the last of the dragons, even the largest ones, died violently fiery deaths.

Only a brief moment after the last dragon disappeared into ash, the wall reappeared with the door and the lever. They were back on the warm sparkling shore of the cavern's lake, under a starry sky with swaying roots. Jack had never felt so good to be in such a strange place, even if it *was* on a different world. The boat was lying in pieces on the shore and in the water, but everything else was just as peaceful as it had been before the storm had started.

Both Geller and Selini looked at each other and Geller said to Jack, "I don't know what it is yet, but something about you is different. Isn't it?"

"Um," Jack was sure he could share where he was from now, "I'm not from here ..."

The door to the cavern opened and out came another Valindi, followed by several others. They looked astonished at the sight of the three of them standing on the shore, clothes burned, and boat smashed. One motioned for them to come through the door, eyes still affixed to Jack.

Jack followed the others through the door and up a long, spiral staircase they climbed for a good deal of time before stepping into daylight. He was in a courtyard and the door closed behind him. It was part of a stone statue on the side of a large fountain. The air was warm and fresh and there were flowering vines of different colors covering stone structures and small grasses squeezing through cracks on the cobblestone covered ground. In front of them stood a large building made for people five times Jack's height, but he watched only Valindi going in and coming out.

Chapter 8: Gubuyis

From the stairs of the great building, walked an aged Valindi with long, scraggily white hair and a short, polished, wooden cane. He wore a light brown robe and a chain around his neck that disappeared under his robe. He looked very happy and was nearly jumping with delight in his step.

"Father!" Selini ran to greet him.

Geller kept walking, with a small limp, "I have a feeling he's going to like you."

"Oh yeah, why's that?" Jack asked, watching the frail old Valindi walking toward him.

"You just saved both of his kids' lives," Geller looked at Jack and smiled. "I don't know how you did that, but I thank you."

Before Jack could interject, the old Valindi was now in front of them.

"Father," Geller stated, "this is Jack. He has saved me twice now."

Geller and Selini proceeded to explain to his father the events of the cavern.

"I ask that you approve him for introduction to the Council." Geller seemed serious at this remark.

He looked over his son's savior with a stern face. Then, he simply smiled and stated, "Well of course I will!" He threw his arms up and motioned for Jack to bow down to his level for a hug.

Geller continued, "Jack, this is my father, Gubuyis. He is the elder of the elders."

Still caught in an awkward hug, Jack responded, "Very pleased to meet you sir." Jack was not sure how to explain that he also did not know what caused the stars to snow down like they did.

"The Council will be very pleased to hear from you. And, we are very concerned with what happened after you got off the boat. I believe we have some news for you, but we shall see. We have some other visitors with the Council in the city as well." Gubuyis stood up straight, "Walk with me."

Jack, Geller, and Selini followed Gubuyis back toward the main building. Gubuyis continued speaking as they walked, "You are welcome here in our great town of Gargantulua for as long as you need and whenever you need a place to rest. I am eternally grateful you have saved my children from peril, the kind we will need to discuss later. For now, though, I want to welcome you. These are trying times. The next war is about to start, and we are no better prepared than any other time. But, Ghowla has amassed his forces in greater strength this time. He grows stronger and with recent events," he paused and looked at Jack, "certainly with recent events, he will attack hard this year. We are concerned with our ability to protect this forest and the powers it holds. However, we will fight to the end, regardless of our decreasing number of allies. We must remain true to this cause or we will all suffer a fate much worse than death." Gubuyis stopped and watched the sky for a moment before speaking again."

"You are not our only visitor, Jack. Like I said before, we have a group of 'representatives' here set out to discuss a unique task. I fear you may not like the subject, but I would like you to join our discussion this evening when all parties are together." Gubuyis turned and looked at Jack.

Jack shrugged his shoulders, "Sure, I guess." Jack was reluctant, as he could not figure out what a fourteen-year-old could possibly contribute.

"JACK!" A voice from across the plaza called to him.

"Oh yes," Geller said, "your friend you were concerned about."

Jack's face lit up with relief and happiness when he saw Anna running to him. "ANNA!"

Gubuyis laughed as the two hugged, "Geller, I trust you can take care of these two until tonight? And, until then, I am needed back in the Council for other reasons. I bid you two a good afternoon." With that, Gubuyis turned and walked back up the steps of the main building.

"Follow me," Geller began walking away.

Jack and Anna followed along with Selini, who was happily trotting next to Jack as if she just made a new best friend.

"Where have you been?" Anna asked, "This place is marvelous! You wouldn't believe me if I told you where we are! And what are those?" She pointed in disgust atand, the multitude of blisters on his arms and his chest.

"Wait, you know where we are?" Jack asked in disbelief. He was still trying to figure out how she was alive and well.

"No, I don't know *where* we are, but I know we are somewhere you wouldn't believe."

"Try me," Jack was disappointed, he had actually thought for a moment that Anna had some idea as to their whereabouts.

"Here we go," Geller stepped up to a small wooden door front and slammed his small knuckles against it.

After a moment of silence, noise could be heard from behind the door as someone clumsily made their way to it. It opened with a couple jitters and creaks and in its place stood a little Valindi the size of Selini. She was a mess. Her hair was unkempt and so was her home.

"Come in," she stated matter-of-factly, as if they were expected. "Up the stairs and to the right," she pointed at a small, wooden staircase.

Selini and Geller went up the stairs and disappeared from sight. Jack and Anna took more caution. Although the place was large enough for them to stand in, they were not sure if the stairs would support them.

"C'mon, c'mon," the little old lady rushed them along from behind. She slammed the door shut and several things hanging from the wall clanked together. "Up the stairs and to the left."

She moved ahead of them and also went up the stairs.

"What should we do?" Anna asked, "I'm not sure what we're doing here."

"Let's just go along with it," Jack began up the stairs.

"Oh, fine, but remember, it could be dangerous." Anna spouted out.

"I'm sure I'm all 'dangered' out for the day," Jack said as he continued up the stairs.

The stairs wobbled some but held firmly under their weight. The stairs continued for a while before coming to a landing, which was the entrance to a long hall. They did not see anyone as they stood at the top of the stairs, but there were voices and noises coming from various rooms and closed doors.

"Which one did she say," Jack asked Anna. "She said to the right, right?"

"No, she said to the left." Anna said.

"But, which one?" Jack recalled the little old lady commanding both ways, too. There were dozens of doors, each with a unique symbol engraved in it.

"Just go in the first one," Anna walked over to the first door on her left and opened the door. "There's gotta be some sort of mistake here."

Jack walked over to the same door and looked in. It was a view of the forest they had originally started out in. There was a clearing several hundred feet ahead and Jack noticed it was the place where the cottage that had been destroyed.

"That's strange," Jack said in disbelief, "I don't recall seeing a door in the middle of the forest."

"You must not be a very good hunting partner, what with the lack of attention to details." Anna joked.

"It must be hidden as part of a tree trunk, that's the only way."

"Jack," Geller called from the end of the hall, "what are you two doing? Those doors will only get you into a bunch of trouble. This way."

"I'm positive she didn't say the only door at the end of the hallway," Anna sounded frustrated with the directions they had received.

They walked to the end of the hall and opened the door. In it was a large, warm room with more doors and a staircase of its own. Geller was sitting at a table next to a kitchen and drinking something hot. Selini was talking with the old lady quietly and was listening very closely. Once Jack stepped in the room, they stopped talking and Selini came over.

"Welcome to your new home for now," she introduced the room to them. "This place is set up according to how we have learned humans like to live."

Geller called over from the table, "I like the idea of a place to make food right here in the house!"

She continued, "By the way, Jack, this is Miss Junia. She is an expert with unique creatures, like the ones here." She pointed at Jack's blister.

"What!?" Anna backed away in disgust, "Those are living?"

Jack, also surprised, "This is a joke, right? There's no way these are creatures."

"Swampees, they prefer to be called," Miss Junia said as she walked over to him. "And, as you are visibly healed as well as you can be, I will be removing them now. They are some of my babies that I take care of here."

"What are swampees?" asked Anna, "And what do they do?"

Miss Junia walked over to a room and beckoned for them to follow, "They help heal your injuries faster. Of course, that is not what they live to do, but it works for you that it is an effect of what they do."

"What?" Jack looked confused.

"Yeah, I'm not sure I know what you mean by that," Anna also looked confused.

Miss Junia sat down next to a bed, "I need you to lie down here, please." She grabbed a stick from a small bag sitting next to the bed.

"Is this going to hurt?" Jack asked, concerned.

"Absolutely not," Miss Junia responded, "it may feel weird, though."

"Why do I have them on me? How badly was I hurt?"

"From the looks of it, when we found you," she rummaged through the bag while she talked, "you had some broken ribs and a punctured lung. Not to mention the many gashes in your skin on your hands and legs. You must have been in some serious pain."

Jack remembered the pain he was in as he ran for hours that night. He remembered how cold he was and how badly his feet hurt and how much it hurt to breath. It was flooding back to him now and it seemed so long ago; especially since what he had just been through earlier. Then he recalled the burns that had disappeared.

"Is that why all those burns from the dragons disappeared so quickly? Is that why I healed so fast?"

Anna lit up with concern, "Dragons …? Burns …? Broken ribs? What in the world did I miss?"

"It may be," Miss Junia replied quietly, "But the swampees don't work that fast. At least I've never heard of it before. Now I need for you to lie down and relax."

Jack slowly laid back and watched Geller drink his drink without concern. He looked at Selini, who was smiling anxiously as she watched Miss Junia's hand grab a small bowl from the bottom of the bag. And he looked over to Anna, whose concerned expression was as if she was about to watch him be killed, but she remained still.

"Found it." Miss Junia gave the bowl to Anna, "That's for you."

Anna looked the bowl over and glanced at Jack. She shrugged and set it down on the counter near her.

Miss Junia continued, "Now, like I said this won't hurt. However, you'll feel a little jolt as its tentacles come out of you."

Anna's and Jack's eyes widened. "The what?" they asked in unison.

Miss Junia did not answer, but instead took the stick and moved it next to the large swampee on his chest. The stick shot out a small bolt of lightning and the swampee fluttered on his chest.

Anna's eyes were still wide, and she was breathing heavily.

Miss Junia then grabbed the swampee by its sides and began pulling it away from Jack's chest. As it lifted away, Jack could feel something inside of him pulling out. The tentacles of the swampee were mostly small, like long hairs, and a few were the size of thin worms. They moved in clusters as they became dislodged from Jack's insides. He could feel the tentacles in his bones and stomach, and it made a squishing sound as it came out of him.

Anna quickly grabbed the bowl next to her and threw up. Then she ran out of the room. Jack felt like throwing up, too. It did not hurt, but the feeling was very weird and watching it was worse. Miss Junia finally got it off of him and set it into a large tank of water on the counter. It drifted to the bottom, its tentacles slowly swaying in the water and its color turned paler. Jack looked at his chest and saw hundreds of small holes that went deep inside of him. There was no blood though and he still did not feel any pain. Miss Junia grabbed a small cup of water from the tank and poured it over his chest. The holes began closing and she continued the same process with the rest of the swampees.

Chapter 9: The Govilian Council

J ack spent the rest of the afternoon resting in a soft, warm bed in a large cozy room with a small fire burning in an oversized fireplace. He woke to a sudden and loud banging on his door. Geller had yelled through his door for him to get up. Jack got up and felt amazingly rested and full of energy. He no longer felt pain in his side or on his legs, and there was no sign of scarring from the swampees. When he came out of the room, Geller, Selini, and Anna were all sitting at the table drinking and eating. The table was nearly covered in mounding plates of strange and exotic fruits and foods, and it smelled great. Jack took a large breath of air and savored it for a moment. Without hesitation, he made his way to the table and began eating.

Anna pointed to one of the dishes, "Jack, this stuff is amazing! You definitely want to try some of it."

"Who made all this?" Jack asked.

"I haven't the foggiest idea," Anna said without much concern, "but it's some of the best food I've ever eaten."

Selini broke in, "My father has assigned your living quarters a watcher. His name is Gryan, and he'll keep an eye on this place and do whatever you need him to do."

Jack looked around but did not notice anyone else in the room.

Noticing this, Geller chimed in as well, "He's always here. Whenever you need him, just call and he'll show himself. You two needn't worry about cleaning or cooking. Gryan will also act as a protector while you are here."

"Why would we need a protector here in the city?" Anna showed concern.

Jack let out a little chuckle and replied before the others could,

"Well, I could have used him earlier today."

"That's exactly why my father has done this," Selini responded. "He is concerned for your well-being and is very grateful for what you did. Jack," her eyes became watery, "you saved our lives and put your own in grave danger. We are forever in your debt."

There was a knock at the main door. Geller got up and opened the front door. He greeted the individual at the door like a friend and chatted with him for a bit before returning to the dinner table.

"We must go now, Jack." He motioned for Jack to get up. "We have an appointment with the Council, and we do not want to be late."

As Jack stood up, Anna grabbed his sleeve and whispered to him, "What did you do earlier?" She still had not heard what had happened in the caverns earlier in the day.

"It's a long story," Jack smiled to her, "I'll have to tell you later."

Selini smiled and lit up with excitement, "I can tell her while you're out!"

"That's his story, Selini. He should have the honor of speaking it." Geller was annoyed with Selini for offering so quickly.

"Oh, no, no. That's fine, really. I don't mind." Jack could see the tension between the two and could tell Selini would be honored to tell the story to Anna. He continued, "Anyway, I'm not all that good at telling stories. I always forget details."

"It's settled then," Selini stood up from the table and sat in a large, overstuffed chair in the main room. She picked up a small log and tossed it into the fireplace and flames suddenly appeared as if they had been burning softly for hours.

"I am doing him a favor, Geller." She said matter-of-factly, "A story this great has no business being butchered by a poor memory. Now come over here, Anna. I will show you what happened today." She snapped her fingers and waved her hand in front of her. Out of thin air, like a wisp of fog, appeared a large image of the cavern from earlier in the day.

Anna quickly got up and grabbed a muffin from the table. She sat in a chair next to Selini and eagerly listened as Selini began telling the story.

Mumbling under his breath, Jack concluded, "And I definitely couldn't have done that."

"C'mon now," Geller walked out the front door and into the hall.

Jack followed as they made their way out of the cottage and through the streets, which were crowded with Valindi walking about, conducting their everyday business. There were exotic plants and animals. Some animals were obviously pets and used for work, but others were scavengers and crept around alleyways. They made their way back to the city's center where Jack had met Gubuyis earlier. The large stone structure stood so massively and high, Jack found it hard to believe it was built for such small people. Geller did not say much on their walk, except for the occasional greeting to some of the merchants and others he knew in the streets. But, as they came upon the stairs to the large building, Geller turned and stopped.

"This is the Panthyun." He motioned to the building now behind him. "It was constructed more than a thousand years ago as our society became one of the most respected for diplomacy amongst nations. It houses our Council members and their gatherings. It is where our society remains civil through laws and courts." He turned back to face the building, "But, more importantly, the Panthyun has found itself as the single most important gathering spot for many struggling and warring nations to find common ground in their plights to freedom and peacefulness."

Jack watched as Geller stood proudly, speaking with confidence and admiration.

"We are going to a Council meeting tonight?" Jack felt nervous.

Geller began walking up the stairs as he responded to Jack, "Tonight is very unique. Much is to be solved and the state of our allies and the strength of our enemies are cause for concern as the fragility of diplomacy is yet again against a powerful foe."

"Who?" Jack was not sure why he asked, because he fully expected to hear a response about some war he knew nothing about.

"Not who, Jack, instead, what. What is this foe?" Geller stated.

"Okay, what then?" Jack questioned.

At that point, the stone monuments and carvings all around the Panthyun began glowing a shade of purple that Jack was now quite familiar with.

Geller started walking up the stairs more quickly, "Hurry, Jack. They have started."

Geller nearly jogged up the remaining steps, but Jack, with his larger stride, merely had to take larger steps. When they reached the top, they headed through a large opening into the Panthyun and walked through huge wooden doors that were propped open. They were met with the occasional greeting from members of the community who had finished conducting business and were on their way out.

Jack was amazed at the size of it all. Nothing was small, even though everyone living in the city was. Even the plaques labeling the different rooms and corridors were incredibly large. Jack noticed the letters on the signs scramble as his eyes would glance at them. That is when he realized that they were written in another language but were translating themselves as his eyes tried reading them. Geller was nearly running now as they made a turn down another large corridor. Jack looked at the sign on the wall and watched the letters fight to arrange themselves. Once they were finished, it read:

Govilian Council Room →

They came upon a set of large doors and Geller stopped. He turned to Jack, "Whatever you hear tonight may not be what you want to hear. You must remain quiet and listen. It is absolutely important that you not speak, as you could inadvertently begin a war upon an unsuspecting nation of people."

Jack thought Geller was being overly dramatic but promised to keep quiet all the same.

"Again, you must remain quiet. This is important. Even if someone speaks to you, do not respond."

Jack nodded and wondered what he was even there for.

Geller faced the door and placed his hand on the head of a gargoyle statue sticking out of the wall next to the door. Its eyes glanced at Geller and then to Jack. As it looked at Jack it squinted, as if to focus, and held its gaze on him. It then moved out of its perched position and turned into the wall. Jack watched as the stone gargoyle passed right through the solid wall and left only an empty space where it had been sitting a moment before. Then, several clanks came from behind the door and it slowly creaked open as the gargoyle pulled and pushed on the heavy wooden door. Once open, the gargoyle stood up straight and motioned for them to pass.

The room was large, like an arena. It had a grand dome ceiling with pillars all around the edges that were made up of detailed stone carvings of historical events. The walls lined with large spheres of floating fires that lit the whole place. The seating was arranged all around the room in concentric circles with a small center stage, which was at the lowest point in the room. On the stage stood Gubuyis, who was looking up at both of them as they entered. Jack could see him rather clearly, even though he was a good distance away. They were standing in the main aisle headed straight to the middle of the room. Jack could feel a number of eyes looking at him, but he dared not to look at anyone else other than Gubuyis.

After a moment, Gubuyis continued, "As I was saying, there is a fundamental difference in working for peace and making things go our way."

Geller leaned in toward Jack and whispered, "Over here, we'll take a couple seats back here. And remember, keep absolutely quiet."

They walked over to an empty row of padded benches and sat down. It was at that point the gargoyle pushed the heavy door shut. It rattled and scraped on its hinges several times, filling the room with its loudness. Jack's eyes widened. He knew there were eyes watching him in annoyance.

"So much for being quiet!" Geller whispered loudly back at the stone gargoyle, who was jumping up to a small landing. It then walked backed through the wall to its position outside the door.

Jack's spot on his bench quietly separated from the rest of the bench and he jumped up at the movement. Geller threw his face into his hands in embarrassment as Jack collected himself. He noticed no one was speaking any longer and looked at Geller. Geller watched him through his fingers and then motioned for him to sit down.

"What are you doing?" Geller was upset with the constant disruption they were causing.

Jack whispered back to him, "I felt my seat move."

"Jack," Gubuyis called from the floor, "is there something we can help you with up there?"

Jack's face turned red as he responded, "No sir, I'm okay."

"Please, then, take a seat." Gubuyis was smiling to his audience, "I admire your willingness to join in, so I will call on you later for your comments."

Jack slowly returned to his seat.

"That's just great!" Geller seemed more annoyed.

Jack felt his seat moving again and shuffled a little. Geller grabbed Jack's arm before he could jump up again and simply pointed at the chair. He looked back at what was once a bench and realized it was forming into a seat that fit Jack's size. He looked around the room and noticed that the others were also sitting in chairs matching their size, and Geller's seat was the same now as well.

Jack was not sure what Gubuyis was talking about, but he was being careful about what he said to the others in the room. There were only a handful of seats filled in the first couple rows and Jack could see some of them were rather large people compared to the Valindi. It now made sense to him why everything was so big in this building. It was built for all kinds of people of different nations and races.

He looked at the ceiling in awe, as he watched a slow-moving sky of stars and terrestrial bodies make their way across the dome. He studied several of the pillars and tried to understand the stories being depicted. One pillar caught his attention because it had a carving that looked just like a large dragon from earlier. It breathed fire at a human man holding a sword out. It looked like the sword was absorbing the fire much like a tornado might. The man stood mighty and covered in armor and there were many Valindi standing behind him for protection. Jack wondered how long ago that happened. The series of pictures went on to portray the human as slaying the dragon and taking its head as a trophy back to a city of Valindi. The city looked like this one, but the picture also showed the dragon's head positioned in this very room, covered in stone and atop the pillar with the story. Jack looked at the top of the pillar and then at the others in the room, but none of them looked like they ever had a dragon's head at its crown.

Suddenly there was a slam. One of the individuals in the front row stood up in anger and shouted, "I've heard enough of this! We cannot sit idly by and watch as they tear the life from our lands!"

There was some murmuring, and it sounded mostly of agreeance. Gubuyis calmly responded back, "It is imperative that we find a solution. Declaring a nation as an enemy and waging war upon them is not to be taken lightly. If I am to understand, your own messengers reported failure in attempts to communicate with them. Is there not the possibility that they don't realize there is a problem?"

The large figure held a staff in his hand that was as thick as Jack's arm. Without much hesitation, the man replied, "How could they not know?" He turned as he addressed the audience, "They have ruined the land by ripping out her trees and replacing them with oversized buildings and homes. They hunt recklessly in our forests; taking all that they can. They drink spirits all night and day and fight amongst themselves. They are dirty. They multiply faster than the land can take, and now we are to move our borders back to make way for them?"

He slammed his staff against the ground and a small shockwave burst from its top. "I am not so willing to give as you are Gubuyis." He pointed at Gubuyis, who remained standing in the center and listening quietly as the man spoke, "Or is that because you have nothing to lose by the shrinking of my people's borders. Would not your merchants benefit from the increase in sales as a result of our heightened demands, stemming from the very fact that we would have less land to support our own nation?"

Without a word, Gubuyis gave a small nod as he listened to the man continue.

"The nation of Monarkia claimed its borders thousands of years ago and has been forgiving of these trespassers for hundreds of years. We did not bring them here," he was walking around the bottom floor in front of the lowest row of benches as he spoke. "They were discarded by the Vampiria nation as a failed experiment. I say it is time for my nation to do the same. You all have the right to be skeptical, I agree. We are nations of peace, but your nations have not had to take on such a burden of disgusting creatures."

He spoke with slowness and more subtlety now, "They have brought new diseases to my lands. Their young die so easily of those very diseases and they bury their dead in my lands. They bury their disease in my lands. The water is tainted and so is the land. Am I to allow my nation's young to die the same? Is this what I should do in the name of peace?"

Again, he slammed his staff on the ground and another small shockwave burst from the top. Several papers blew off the tables of the people in front of him as he walked by. He raised his voice again, "Our nation, my nation, Monarkia, will not let ourselves die in such vain and call it peace!" He returned to his seat and sat down heavily.

"Thank you for your view," Gubuyis spoke, "and as always,

Cedric, good friend of ours, we could not agree with you more if what you say is in fact the truth."

The man responded loudly from his chair, "It is absolutely true!"

"Would you mind, old friend?" Gubuyis continued, "Please inform us, how many of your young have died thus far from such diseases you speak of?" He held a pencil and was ready to write as he listened for Cedric's response.

Cedric remained silent.

"Do you not know this staggering number you are so passionate about?" Gubuyis spoke gently to him from his post in the center.

Still, Cedric had no answer.

Gubuyis wrote something down and continued, "Very well, then, could you answer me a few more questions? I would like to make sure we have the facts right before waging war on an unsuspecting neighbor."

"Trespassers! They are trespassers, not neighbors." Cedric grumbled and shifted in his chair.

Gubuyis went on, "During your many celebrations throughout the year, does your nation not also hunt indiscriminately the animals of the forest? Does your nation not also take much more from her than is needed to adequately feed your people?"

"That is very different," again, Cedric shifted some more.

After writing some, Gubuyis continued, "Did our nations not replace trees with stone when we constructed this very building we are in now? Did your people not grow and multiply over the last several thousand years into large cities that required buildings and homes as well?"

"That's different, too!" Cedric was becoming more agitated as he could not defend his position well.

"Should we not also assume that these people are also trying to live? Do they not have the same rights as the rest of us to fight every day for life and freedom and to pursue an enriched life for their young?"

"I am here by the specific request of my nation to remove the humans from our lands. There is no request of this assembly that will sway the position of our nation," Cedric stood up and began walking up the aisle. Several other members that sat with him followed behind him.

Jack sat up alertly. Did he say humans? Was this man talking about killing all the humans in his country?

Still speaking calmly, Gubuyis called out to him, "Old friend. Before you leave, may I request your ears for only a moment longer?"

Cedric stopped in his step and turned, "I grow impatient, Gubuyis."

"I see you have made your decision. I know you are bound by the request of your people, so I will not continue the argument." He stepped down from his post and walked up the aisle some, "However, I would like you to meet someone."

Gubuyis pointed up to Jack and Geller nudged him to stand. Jack stood slowly and watched as the rest of the assembly turned toward him.

"Jack, dear boy, come, come," Gubuyis motioned for Jack to come down to the floor.

Chapter 10: Cedric

J ack shuffled down to the floor and kept his eyes on Gubuyis the whole time. As he passed Cedric, he could feel the air move from his heavy breathing. He stood much higher and was much broader than Jack, but it was only now that he really noticed his size. From the top of the rows, Cedric did not look as big, but now Jack felt like he was in the shadow of anger as he made his way around Cedric and his group.

After making it past them, Jack let out a sigh of relief. "Boy!" Cedric called to him.

Remembering Geller's instruction, Jack did not respond, but kept walking to Gubuyis, but a little quicker. He somehow felt like he would be safer in the presence of Gubuyis, although Cedric's size could no way be matched by Gubuyis's small frame.

"I said, boy!" Cedric yelled this time and the room fell silent.

Jack stopped in his steps and looked at Gubuyis. Jack's eyes were calling for help and looked for assistance from Gubuyis. He did not know what to do, but then he saw Gubuyis's hand make a small wave, telling him to turn around.

Jack turned and faced the group of tall men. They looked much like humans but had much more hair. Everything about them was bigger. Their hands must have easily been twice that of a normal human's. And, their build was very burly. Jack envisioned them as incredibly strong. Only Cedric held a staff at his side, and he wore different clothes from the others in his group. The others wore clothes of simple, but strong leathers and light furs. Cedric, however, wore more colorful, albeit dark in nature, apparel. He had large furs that lined all the edges of his clothes and his head stuck slightly higher above the others.

Jack did not know if he should respond as he shot a glance up to Geller, who looked worried. He was shaking his head as he could tell

Jack was thinking of responding.

"I'm very impatient young boy," Cedric began, "so if you have something to say, you'd better say it now. Otherwise, we have orders to arrest any human we cross paths with. Once I arrest you, you will no longer have my ears and your pleas will mean nothing more to us than a pitiful whining coming from a human condemned to death."

Jack's eyes widened. He did not know what to say, but he figured he should at least try and explain to this oversized man that he was not like the others.

Cedric motioned to a couple of the men at the front and they moved toward Jack. Without much time to think, Jack spouted out, "I am not like the other humans!"

The men stopped for a moment and Cedric spoke, "So you do have a voice. It is weak just like that of your brothers and sisters." Cedric looked at him and walked over to him; "You look just as weak as any other human; powerless and helpless. However, I do believe you are different," he laughed and looked at the others in his group, "He does dress a bit funnier looking and still has some teeth!"

They all laughed for a moment. Jack tried to think of what to say, but he had no idea what Cedric wanted to hear.

"That's enough, Cedric!" Geller called down to him as he walked down the aisle. "You would have no more right here to detain Mr. Jack than you would within your own borders."

"The humans are not in a treaty with us, nor are they with you or any other nation in this assembly." Jack could hear the sound of tightening leather from Cedric's gloves as his hand gripped the staff harder. "The nation of Monarkia has decided that the humans have no allies. They have no diplomats to reason with. And," he stopped and chuckled, "they have no power."

"All the more reason not to disturb them," Geller was now at Jack's side, "why hurt a people that wouldn't be able to defend itself against you?"

"Our decision has been made!" Cedric snapped back and turned to face Gubuyis, who was still standing at the bottom of the aisle, "And as per our treaty, we have the right to detain any enemy of our nation. You would be wise to remember this, Gubuyis."

"It is written as such in the treaty," Gubuyis nodded in agreement.

"It is settled then!" Cedric grabbed Jack's shoulder who nearly collapsed under the weight, "This boy is declared a captive of Monarkia, under the crime of being a human of the ...," he paused and looked at the other men with him, "uh ... well, for being a human of the humans, a crime punishable by indefinite prison until death by punishment or by life."

A small strand of sparkling dust and light left from the tip of Cedric's staff and began binding the hands and legs of Jack. His heart began to pound. He was just given up as a prisoner to someone who hated him for being human! He tried to run, but all that happened was a squirming motion. He was already partially bound. Then, a sudden flash of purple flew up from Gubuyis's hands and struck Cedric's staff, breaking the binds on Jack.

Cedric's face flared up in red as his staff flew from his hands, "YOU SAID!"

"Yes," Gubuyis replied quietly, "I agreed with you, and it is true that you have the right. However, you are punishing those who are human of the human nation are you not?"

"And you don't believe he is?" Cedric's staff was returned to him by one of the members of his group. "You think he's something else, do you?"

Gubuyis walked up the aisle, "Good friend, I know your rights in the treaty. Now know ours." Gubuyis looked Cedric deep in the eyes and continued, "We have the right to declare any person a citizen of our nation."

"You must know then," Cedric spoke harshly, "that does not protect him from being a criminal under our war against his people!"

"You are absolutely correct, my friend, correct indeed."

Cedric raised one eyebrow as if questioning Gubuyis's reasoning. He almost looked delighted to hear he won the argument so easily.

"However," Gubuyis continued, "you may not press criminal charges against a member of my army, unless you have undeniable proof the individual in question has done you or your nation purposeful harm. In this case, this individual has not."

"In your ARMY?! Wh..." Cedric was choking on his words as he became angrier. "In a thousand years, you haven't declared any other than a Valindi as a rightful member of your army!"

Jack was lost now more than ever. He did not know what to do, so he remained as still as possible, hoping no one would notice he was still there. This was his hope, but he found it hard not to be noticed when the whole debacle revolved around his presence.

"What's going on?" Geller seemed just as confused as Jack.

Gubuyis responded to Cedric just as calmly as before, "Oh, yes. This is not just Jack," he patted Jack's leg, "this is Captain Jack Newton."

Geller's jaw dropped open.

Cedric huffed loudly and clenched his fist around his staff. "How convenient for you, Captain," Cedric was glaring at Jack, "Hmmm, he's the quietest captain I've ever seen in any army. It seems like it'd be pretty hard to give commands without words, though." Cedric bent down to get face to face with Jack, "Tell me boy, have you ever seen combat? Do you know the color of blood?"

"That is quite enough," Geller chimed in.

"Yes!" Cedric stood back up, "That is quite enough! It seems this boy has avoided charges by a few mere words in the law; but, nonetheless, the nation of Monarkia will honor our treaty."

With that, Cedric resumed his lead of his group and stomped

angrily up the aisle. By the time he got to the door, the gargoyle was already waiting on its perch inside the room and proceeded to open the door.

Watching the last of the group leave the room, Geller seemed relieved and confused in his voice. "Well, that certainly got interesting fast." He looked at his father and then at Jack. "I don't suppose you know the least about combat, do you?"

"Not really," Jack was relieved that it was all over with Cedric. He felt very on edge about his near captivity. He also felt bad about putting Gubuyis's friendship with Cedric at stake. "I'm so sorry, Gubuyis. I didn't mean to ..."

Gubuyis interrupted him, "No need for apology ... Captain." With that, Gubuyis gave a smile and walked back down to the center to address the remaining members of the assembly.

As his father began speaking, Geller ushered Jack to a nearby bench and motioned for them to sit down. The seats once again formed around each of them, but Jack did not startle, as he was expecting it this time.

Gubuyis spoke with sincerity as he addressed the assembly, "My apologies for the interruption. I want to assure all of you, each and every one of you and the nations you represent, that I fully understand the position we are all in. Each of us must come here and represent his or her nation's views and desires. We all have had times where we have had to bring forth arguments that we, ourselves, did not agree with. It is important you all know your input is crucial to our ability to move forward, regardless of the message. For many millennia, our nations have worked together. Therefore, you should all take care to remember Cedric's message today is just that; a message he was entrusted to deliver to us by his people. It is a tough job we have as diplomats, and he does it well."

He stood silent for a moment before continuing, "I think it would be beneficial for all of us to recess for the time being. Shall we reconvene tomorrow?"

Several clear affirmative responses could be heard along with a general murmur of agreeance. Several members had already stood up and were preparing to leave.

"Very well, I shall dispatch a messenger to inform you each on the time of our next assembly by night's end." With that, Gubuyis snapped his fingers and the doors opened. Within a moment, several members were talking quietly with Gubuyis near the bottom row.

"So, what now?" Jack had many questions stemming from the moment he stepped foot on this planet. But the more he learned and the more he saw, the more confused about everything he became.

Geller had little excitement in his voice as he answered, "You'll have to answer to the Commander of the Valindi Army now. He'll need to train you in ways he has never imagined. You have no powers, none that we know of at least. And, you have no combat training. Plus, you'll need to get acquainted with your duties as a captain." Geller was shaking his head, "I don't know how he's going to do it, but you must be ready before fall's end."

Jack shook his head in disbelief, "You're joking, right? I have to get home. And I would be a wreck to your army. Didn't your father just say that to get rid of Cedric?"

"The only way for him to have saved you from the laws of a nation of our allies, which we must also enforce to the best of our abilities in cases where it applies, is to supersede the law as inferior or inapplicable." Geller was somber and lacked his usual liveliness, "In this case, in your case, he had no choice but to supersede the law by making you a serving citizen of the Valindi, thereby excluding you from persecution under the Monarkia law." Geller laid his hand on Jack's side, "I am sorry, Jack, but you are now a captain of the Valindi Army."

"Can't I just say no?" Jack was becoming worried at the prospect of a more permanent stay on this planet. "Why do I have to accept it?"

Slowly, Geller tried to explain to Jack the severity of not acting upon his father's statements, "I promise, Jack, this was the only way to keep you out of immediate harm's way. At least now … now we have time on our side, if even just a little. You must serve in the army … defection would put you in violation of some of our own laws. Now … we could likely work around those laws … especially in your case. But," Geller hesitated to continue. He watched his father speaking and was visibly unwilling to divulge the information at the tip of his tongue.

"But what?" Jack was becoming a little impatient. He did not want this and did not understand why he had to do it. All he wanted was to get back home and forget about this place. All he could think of was all the danger he had been in since he arrived here, and now he found himself wishing he was still lost in the forest. At least there, he thought, he had more chance of doing things his way and finding a way home. He waved his hands in front of Geller's face, "Hello? What are you saying, Geller? Why do I have to do this?"

Geller snapped out of his trance and looked Jack in the eyes before continuing, "I'm sorry, Jack, I really am. You must understand that I only want you to be safe. You have saved me twice now, and I wish this wasn't the only way to save you."

"What are you talking about?" Jack hated feeling confused all the time.

"If you defect, you will die." Geller said somberly.

"What?!" Jack nearly yelled. Gubuyis looked up at the two of them before continuing on with his discussion. Jack lowered his voice to an angry whisper, "For what? Who's going to kill me? You? Your father?"

"The law," Geller replied quickly, "the code of the law is written as such that you would die if a superseding law is used under false pretenses. You would die upon defection, not by anyone's hand, but by the action of your decision." Geller stood up and was watching his father approach the two of them alone, "Again, Jack, I am very sorry. If there was anything differently, we could have done … I know my father; he wouldn't have made the decision without it being the only option. You must trust me on this."

Before Jack could interject, Gubuyis stood next to them. Geller had already left his seat and was now at his father's side. Gubuyis watched the confusion in Jack's face before extending his hand. "Captain."

Jack stood up. He was so confused and angry now, he could hardly speak. The blood was rushing to his head as his heart pounded uncontrollably in his chest. There were so many things swirling through his head, he felt dizzy from the weight of it all. "Sir ..." he started but was interrupted by Gubuyis.

"First, Captain, before you object entirely, I am sure my son has explained the consequences of deciding not to do this, no doubt. However, something else of importance, we need to confirm your entry into the service before midnight this night. That is why I have recessed the assembly. We must call an emergency service induction ceremony. I will dispatch a message to all department heads and the other elders." While speaking, he wrote a note on a small piece of parchment. Once he finished writing it, he opened the palms of his hands and it levitated slowly from his hands and far above his head. Then, Gubuyis waved his hand and suddenly dozens of stone gargoyles came from the tops of the pillars and flew out the doors, after which, the note dissolved into air.

"T-tonight? We have to make it official tonight?" Jack stuttered in his uncertainty. He felt lost and confused beyond anything he had experienced before.

"If not by midnight," Geller spoke, "you will be considered defected and the law will apply."

"You mean I would die?" Jack asked, even though he already knew what Geller meant.

"That is correct." Now Gubuyis spoke, but not as sympathetically as Geller. "Your ceremony will commence in one hour. Unfortunately, many of our division commanders are already leading defensive campaigns and will not be able to attend. Nevertheless, I am sure you are excited. Geller will take you to the royal blacksmith where you will be fitted with your new armor and weapon."

At that mention, Geller stepped forward without protest and addressed Jack, "Right this way, Captain."

"I will see you two in an hour," Gubuyis turned and walked away.

Chapter 11: Suit of Armor

As Jack began aimlessly following Geller, he continued his arguments. Geller just walked and listened but did not speak. Once they got to the doors, Geller approached the wall next to them. It was the same wall the door gargoyle perched itself in and was intricately covered in stone carvings from bottom to top and side to side. Some were large carvings, and some were barely the size of Jack's hand, but all were different. He watched as Geller placed his hand on a carving of a shield with two swords crossing in front of it. The stone sank into the wall after a moment and he heard a clanking from inside the wall. The gargoyle came down from its perch and walked past them. It went to the corner and climbed up to the top of the wall. It pressed its talons into holes that matched its claw on a carving of a door. Within a moment, part of the wall moved and made a doorway for them to walk through. Jack was amazed at how this all worked and reached his hand out to touch a stone carved like a star.

"It only works if you're a Valindi. And..." Geller was walking through the door already, "...it only works if you have rightful blood."

Jack pulled his hand back and looked at the carvings for a moment more before following Geller down a dark hallway. Once the door closed behind them, a fiery globe similar to the ones that lit the Council Room slowly lit up on the wall. As they walked, the sphere followed them down the hallway.

"What do you mean, 'rightful blood'? What is that?" Jack had pondered the thought for a few moments and could not help but ask.

Still walking, Geller explained, "To put it simply, if one were a diplomat or of diplomatic blood, he would have rightful blood."

"So, Cedric would be allowed to use the wall?" Jack asked in disgust.

"He has the right bloodline. However, he is not Valindi. It only works if both are true. Anyway, it's just a shortcut to many of the places in the city. There's not much else to the wall. Plus, not all the stones work, I've tried. Many of them do nothing. I figure they're probably there for future expansions."

Before long, they came upon a small wooden door, not large enough for Jack to walk through.

"Sorry, Captain, like I said, it was designed for Valindi only. You will have to crawl through."

Geller opened the door and walked into a bright shop filled with metal and leather armor and weapons made of steel and some other metals Jack was unfamiliar with.

Jack nearly crawled through the door. It was not too bad, as the door was oversized for a normal Valindi, it made the fit for Jack a little easier. Once in the shop, Jack could see Geller speaking with the blacksmith. Looking around, Jack only saw armor and weaponry made for small hands and body sizes. There was no way he could find something in time for the ceremony.

"Ahhh!" The blacksmith approached Jack with enthusiasm. "I received the message not moments ago! We have a new captain. How exciting!" He did not seem concerned with Jack's size or the fact that he was human. "Come. Come. Let me see your size." He pulled out a string and began walking around Jack and making quick measurements from head to toe.

"Excuse me, sir. But, do you think you can forge me armor and a weapon by the ceremony?" Jack asked concerned. He did not want this at all, but even worse, he thought, was what would happen if he appeared to be weak and incompetent because he did not even have the most basic of armor. He would be addressing top military officials soon, and he was now concerned about what they might think.

"Why of course, Captain. I have many weapons and armor here in my store. Many of these weapons and armor are enchanted and forged for the mightiest and bravest heroes! All you have to do is let the armor and weapon select you and you will be on your way. The payment has already been covered. So, please, shop away." The blacksmith made a small bow and backed away.

Geller walked over to a rack of small swords and motioned to Jack. "Here, Captain, we'll start here."

"Why don't you just call me Jack?" Jack was a little unnerved that everyone was now addressing him as a captain. He could not tell if it was a sarcastic joke or if it was really a formality.

"I can call you Jack, yes." Geller smiled.

"Then do, please!" Jack was a little happier now that Geller would stop calling him Captain.

"I have been hoping to one day use some of these," Geller was looking at some of the swords and axes on a different rack.

Jack examined the undersized weapons on the first rack of swords. There were many racks filled to the brim with weapons. He did not know what to choose, so he just looked for a while. One sword finally caught his eye. It shined brightly with a hint of blue in the metal and curved from side to side. The handle had several blue jewels embedded into its hilt. Jack reached out to grab it, but it did not move when he tried retrieving it from the rack.

"Sorry, Captain," the blacksmith called from behind his counter, "it does not choose you."

Jack looked over at Geller, who could see this concept was not understood by Jack.

"What he means is, you may only wield a weapon that matches your skills," Geller explained. "Without much experience, you will not have many choices. When a weapon fits your skills, it will sound out a hum on the rack."

The concept was completely foreign to Jack, who was more accustomed to building skill with a weapon, not the other way around. However, he continued to search the racks, moving from swords to axes to daggers and sabers. Finally, he came upon a rack of older swords and one of the daggers hummed when his hand moved over the handle. He rolled his eyes at the tiny weapon, but grabbed it in desperation.

"Before you pull that off," Geller walked over to him, "be sure you want it. Once you pull it, it will be yours and cannot be properly wielded by any other."

Jack nodded and hesitated for a moment. He did not know if this was the weapon he wanted. He did not understand how he would know without holding it in his hands. He held on to it for a moment more and decided to take it.

"One more thing," Geller interjected once again, "you may only wield one weapon at a time. Until it breaks or you discard it, you cannot choose another."

Jack hesitated again. He looked at all the other racks stuffed with hundreds of weapons. Most of them looked much more appealing to him than this one, but this was the only one that gave him any indication of working right. So, he decided again to pull it, but before he pulled it all the way off the rack, he looked at Geller.

"Any more important information I should know?" He asked.

Geller smiled and shook his head, "This will do you just fine."

Jack finished pulling the dagger off the shelf and it slowly became longer. Its hilt filled Jack's hand just right, too. And, despite its larger size, its weight was still as light as it was when he pulled it off the rack.

"Ah, a fine dagger sir. Made from light Valindi steel. Strong! And that one has a sprinkling of Valindi energy dust within its blade. You may find that your foe is troubled by an electric shock on occasion." The blacksmith smiled at this as he pulled out a small box from the wall behind him. "This should do," he had opened it and pulled out a small leather object and tossed it to Geller who handed it to Jack. "It will sheath your weapon, sir."

Jack took a few moments to look over his dagger. It felt right in his hands as he tossed it from hand to hand. He felt like it would work well in both hands and its weight was nothing like he had known before for a weapon.

"It kind of looks like the one from the forest the other day," he said as he sheathed it.

Geller's brow furrowed some, "What dagger?"

Jack reached under his belt and grabbed the cloth covered dagger and unwrapped it. Geller looked at it with wide eyes.

"That's mine!" he grabbed it out Jack's hand. "Where did you find it?"

"It was stuck in the body of a creature that was chasing me and Anna," Jack watched Geller as some excitement filled his eyes.

"The body? So, it did die from my blow," Geller was smiling now.

"Yeah, I think so. This looked like the only thing that hurt it."

"It doesn't look like much," Geller waved it in the air, "but it has been enchanted with a very powerful poison." Then he stopped and starred at it again very seriously. "Jack? Is this the same dagger you used to kill the dragons with?"

The blacksmith lit up, "Killed dragons did ya?"

"Yes." Jack did not seem to understand Geller's concern.

"How is that possible? This is my weapon?" Geller looked at the blacksmith. "I attained this dagger in this very store. How could he use my enchanted dagger?"

Jack did not understand what Geller was getting at, so he asked, "Am I not able to use it? I'm sorry, I didn't know whose it was."

The blacksmith walked from behind his counter and looked at the dagger himself. "You could use it, yes. But only as a dagger to cut and stab and kill."

Jack was still missing something, "That is exactly what I used it for."

"But, Jack, you were able injure the dragon by the poison from its blade. I am sure of this. No dragon would be so easily disabled from such a small blade." Geller then asked the blacksmith, "Will I still be able to use it?"

"I would certainly think so," he said confidently, "no weapon can change owners."

"Why shouldn't I have been able to use the dagger?" Jack asked.

The blacksmith held the dagger as he explained to Jack, "Ever since the age of enchanting metal came about, the specialized metal could only ever be used by one being. When an enchantment is put upon an individual, it is unique to that individual. Much like when someone is cursed, they do not simply spread the curse just because someone else touches them."

"I don't think I understand," Jack tried to comprehend what it was he was saying. "Are you saying enchantments aren't contagious?"

"What I am saying," the blacksmith tried to clarify for him, "is that once the enchanted metal has chosen and been accepted by an individual, all of its enchantments become the property of that individual. No other individual can use the enchantments, no matter how hard they try. Even if you were to have the most powerfully enchanted sword in your possession, if it were stolen it would only be a large blade to the next person. That is, until you were able to use the General's weapon here. It has a very strong poison enchantment, but you were somehow able to use the dagger and its enchantment, even though it did not belong to you."

"This is very strange. Never has this been heard of before. An enchantment for armor and weaponry is designed to fit the skills of the possessor. Only one person may ever fully possess these things. Any other person would simply have a sharp piece of metal or heavy armor if they were to come across another's items." Geller took back his dagger and inserted it into an empty sheath on his belt. It shrank some once he began sheathing it and fit perfectly in the small leather binding.

"Then how did the dagger work when I used it?" Jack asked out of curiosity.

The blacksmith looked into Jack's eyes, "That is a very good question, sir. Until now, I would have simply told you there is no way and that would have settled that. Now," he returned to his position behind his counter, "I will need to read some of the ancient metallurgy documents and cross reference them with enchantments. I don't know yet the seriousness of this issue, but, rest assured, I will inform you immediately of my findings, Captain."

Just then, a small metal bird flew down from a hole in the wall near the corner. It landed on the end of the counter and tweeted several times and then flew back. The blacksmith jumped at this.

"Well then, sir, it seems we are running out of time." He began hurrying the two of them over to an area of racks and dummies dressed in various armors.

"It is the same process, Jack. This usually takes a while. Many times, the armor doesn't accept one in full. You may find a perfect suit, but the boots won't accept you or the dang helmet refuses to sit over your head." Geller tapped his knuckle against the side of a steel helmet, and it rang out a tinny sound.

Looking at all the small armor, Jack expressed his concern, "Will these also reshape to fit me?"

"Yes sir," the blacksmith said. "Come now, Captain, look here." He was rolling a dummy covered in heavy, solid metal and chain mail. "It is perfect and will protect you for years of heavy battles."

Jack felt the plates of steel that were to cover his chest. He noticed it did not feel warm or move or make any noise and asked, "Will I know?"

The blacksmith began rolling the dummy back into its spot, "You will know." He was already pulling another one over and then another and another.

Nothing happened for any of the plate mails or chain mails they looked at. Finally, they had looked at all the full armors made of steel and other metals. The blacksmith seemed a little distressed, but not as much as Jack.

"Does this mean I won't have any armor?" Jack asked exasperated and worried at how foolish he would look without any armor.

Geller chimed in to try and cheer him up some, "You'll need to simply choose each piece of armor rather than a set, that's all."

"I am very sorry sir," the blacksmith said as he quickly ran off to grab several different items of armor.

"Why's he so sorry," Jack asked Geller when they were alone for a moment.

"This is his life. Armor and weaponry that doesn't accept someone of such a position in the services is embarrassing to him. It is considered insulting to the buyer that he has not made good enough armor."

"That's just ridiculous," Jack said just as the blacksmith returned with several more gauntlets and leggings and placed them on the counter for Jack.

Again, nothing worked as they continued to search for suitable armor.

"I ... I just don't get it," the blacksmith scratched his head, "this never happens. Usually something has worked by now. We've just about tried all the metals now."

Jack looked around the shop. It was packed full of weapons and armors stuffed on racks and shelves. Some items looked like they had not been touched for years and others looked brand new. The overall condition of the shop was that of an old room, like an oversized, long forgotten dining hall. It was hard to believe the blacksmith could find anywhere to work. At one end of the counter, there was an open doorway that glowed orange from open flames in another room. Behind the counter were wooden storage boxes of many sizes and shapes, all haphazardly stacked on each other on dilapidated and dusty old shelves. In one corner, Jack saw several old racks full of leather items, none of which looked new or so much as disturbed for ages.

"What about something from back there?" Jack asked.

Geller scoffed, "HA! You'd be better off wearing nothing!"

Both the blacksmith and Geller were laughing at the suggestion.

"If nothing else will work, I should at least try." Jack approached the racks, "Besides, I am familiar with wearing leather armor."

"Forgive me sir," the blacksmith had stopped laughing, "but leather is for those more likely to be ahead of the army. Hunters would be more appropriately dressed in such attire, as it is more agile and suitable for stealthy combat." The blacksmith was much more serious now, "These old things were made long ago, when service volunteers were much higher in numbers. Now," his eyes glazed as he spoke, "we have seen our numbers severely diminish over the past few years. I don't believe we're losing, mind you, but we are in some need of reinforcements. I have not had to make anything leather for too long," he smelled the shoulder of one of the vests, "I do miss the work."

Just as Jack was abandoning his efforts with the leathers, one of the suits set up on a wire frame jumped some, like a strong magnet catching the attention of a piece of metal from across the floor. All three of them watched for a moment in disbelief.

"I don't understand," the blacksmith was more confused than before, "this day is definitely a first in several ways."

Geller excitedly approached the leather armor, "Well, it seems we may have found you some armor after all!"

"And from the looks of it, the whole ensemble agrees with him." The blacksmith was still befuddled.

Jack grabbed the leather cap off the rack and it resized itself as he placed it upon his head. "It doesn't seem like it would really stop a lot from getting through."

"It's only leather," Geller agreed, "it will hardly stop a pebble lobbed at your head."

"Yes," the blacksmith was holding his finger up in confirmation, "but this suit is very unique."

Geller laughed, "Aren't they all smithy?"

The blacksmith grabbed a sword, jumped up and swung it at Jack. The blade struck Jack squarely on the back of his head and clanked out of the blacksmith's hands.

Geller, not laughing any more, yelled, "What are you doing, you crazy old man?!"

"I know my armor," the blacksmith was smiling as he picked up the sword.

Geller turned his attention to Jack, "Are you okay? Is there any blood?"

Jack was standing wide-eyed. He was not sure if he was hurt or not, but he knew he was not dead. He raised one hand behind his head and felt for a cut in the leather. As his hand searched the cap, he slowly replied, "I think I'm okay."

"My dear boy!" the blacksmith was nearly jumping with joy. "I've always wanted to see this piece in action!"

"What are you talking about, you fool?" Geller was still angry, "you've probably already damaged it."

"Have you found a cut?" the blacksmith asked Jack matter-of-factly.

Jack pulled the cap off his head and visually scanned the back of the cap. "I see none," and he felt his head, "and I don't feel any pain, either."

Geller grabbed the cap and scanned it over. "That's amazing," he was much less angry now. "I wanna try! Jack put this back on!"

As Geller grabbed for a nearby pike, Jack protested, "I'd really rather not!" He backed up some as Geller situated the pike in his hands. "Besides, aren't we pressed for time?"

Geller slowly lowered the pike and agreed in disappointment, "You're right, we need to meet the Council soon."

Jack quickly tried the rest of the ensemble on as the blacksmith explained how the armor worked.

"This piece is stronger than most plate mails, chain mails, or dragon scale armors. And it's only made from leather! I was able to come across a rare enchantment ingredient from a trade long ago. It requires the coupling of several rare ingredients to perfect, but it most obviously is a jewel. This piece hasn't so much as quivered at another in all the years I have had it here."

"What rare enchantment makes this armor so strong?" Geller was intrigued.

"I can't divulge the whereabouts of the rarest ingredient, but let's just say the Reign were quite distressed over its absence from their inventories."

Once again, the small bird came into the room and tweeted. The conversation quickly changed to business as the three of them rushed over to the counter.

"Payment will be made by my father this evening." Geller stated.

"Yes, yes," the blacksmith was waving them off. "With your father, I have no concern about when to expect payment. You must hurry, though, the Council is convening."

Chapter 12: A New Comradery

J ack and Geller made their way back through the small door and up the long, stone passageway. When they emerged from the door into the council room, hundreds of Govilians, the name given to the collective group of allies against the Reign of Karakaziem, filled the benches. It was not like before when many seats remained empty. Jack could not believe his eyes; never had he seen anything like it. There were people of all different sizes, and some of them hovered above the others. The room was filled with noise, and no one noticed the arrival of him and Geller.

"C'mon," Geller motioned to Jack, "we need to find our seats."

Jack followed him down the main aisle to a pair of empty seats on the lowest level of benches. As he passed the seats, he could hear whisperings. He was sure they were about him. He sat down and noticed Valindi generals and officials were suited in metal armors. Suddenly he felt stupid and like a sore thumb. It was obvious he did not belong there, but now his battle attire accentuated that fact.

An abrupt shriek filled the air from behind them and the room came to a quiet. Jack looked and saw the gargoyle from the wall tucking a timepiece into his pocket and then called out, "All are accounted for!" He then closed the doors one at a time and climbed back onto his stoop and back through the wall where Jack first met him.

"Very well, then," Gubuyis started.

Jack turned and saw Gubuyis standing on the center stage.

"Once again we amass our forces to stave off annihilation. Fall is upon us, and the suns pull their favor from our lands." Gubuyis was not speaking loudly, but it was not hard to hear him either. "Gentle Govilians," he raised his hands, "our numbers have diminished greatly in the last few years, and we have little hope of maintaining our defenses this year. We are here to determine our strategy, and strategy is exactly what we'll need to make it through this winter."

A voice called from the back, "We need numbers! Our defenses depend on numbers!"

The room filled with the noise of hundreds of Govilians talking all at once. Some loudly agreeing, others shouting ideas, but most chatted amongst themselves.

"We cannot control what we do not have," Gubuyis continued, "but we can control what we do have." The room fell silent again, "Yes, my friend, we need more fighters, I think we all can agree with that. But we have exhausted as many resources as we have sought to exploit. The simple, undeniable truth is that we have very little power left against such a formidable foe." His face was somber as he spoke, "We have lost so many to the tragedies of war, not in the name of peace, but in the name of survival. And, we have lost many to corruptive powers we seek to end."

Another voice yelled out, "Traitors! They are all traitors and deserve to die with their soulless brethren!"

"Traitors, indeed. But to whom?" Gubuyis stepped off the pedestal and paced the inner circle. "Our brethren have watched their fathers and brothers and sisters and mothers and children die. We have all seen horror in our lives that we would never want our children to have to see. These wars grow more devastating every year and these 'traitors' have found themselves hoping for a better future for their young. We must seek to recapture our lost brothers and sisters and reunite them with our nations."

"This is absurd!" A stout, elfish man stood from his seat and addressed the room, "We have no strategy, no idea, not even enough soldiers to fend for our borders. However, we speak of reuniting our traitor brothers in arms back into our borders. These Govilians have chosen to abandon our virtues and ways of life so they may fight against us and cause us the very anguish they ran from. We are losing! By forgiving them and allowing them back into our homes, we allow the enemy an open eye into our secrets. Our secrets are the only way we've survived thus far."

Once again, the room filled with the shouts of opinions and

disagreements.

"Govilians," Gubuyis returned to his post, "please, I implore you to know what is right. Do not forget what it is we stand for."

The elfish man spoke again, "And what is it that we stand for?"

Without a pause, Gubuyis responded, "Peace. We stand for peace and that includes forgiveness. If we expend our time seeking ways to punish our own, then we have lost the simplest meaning of our ideology. Of all others in this room, I would think you might have an appreciation of those virtues, Nothrip."

With that, the man returned to his seat without another word.

Gubuyis motioned for Geller to come to the stand, "Gentle Govilians, please lend your ears to General Geller. His insights may prove a powerful emissary in this dark hour."

Geller met his father at the stand and gave him a small nod of acknowledgement. From the room came murmurs and whispers.

"My fellow Govilians," Geller looked more serious now than Jack had seen him. "I have been gone for a while, as many of you may already know, I was being held captive by Frinkul. However, many of you probably do not know, we are now rid of him. With his leave, we have one less problem here. Unfortunately, that also means the attack this year will likely be stronger and sooner than ever before. The Reign will seek to replace his position in his outpost. If we can hold back Ghowla's forces, we will hold the advantage for the winter."

There was a small wave of general agreement from the assembly.

"But," Geller stood up straight, "I believe I may have a strategy that will prove more effective than before. As I lay captive, I learned things about Ghowla's foothold. All trees need water, and Ghowla's foothold is no exception to this fact. He commands his tree to use as much water during growing season as possible. He seeks to gain strength in his foothold's size. The name of his tree is Ezjuin, one of only a few dozen Arbolion remaining. It may seem like useless information, but it is greater than even Ghowla would know."

Jack thought about how weak an old wizard must be to control a simple tree as a foothold. He even smirked a little as he pictured an old wizard standing in the branches of a tree and yelling at it to grow. Then, he recalled seeing the word Arbolio before. It had been in the library book, the one about the map. Although surprising, Jack quickly realized there must have been some kind of relationship between that book, the symbol he found in it, and everything that was happening to him. Now he found himself wishing he still had the book.

Geller continued as the assembly eagerly awaited his reasoning, "By commanding Ezjuin to grow much more rapidly than normal, the tree has no reserve water for the winter. Ghowla knows this and releases the tree from growing at the end of summer."

Nothrip chimed in, "I still don't see what you're getting at, General."

Geller gave him a glance and continued, "Ezjuin needs water. She must drink nearly ten times as much water in fall than she normally would; in doing so, she cannot only replenish her reserves, but build enough inventory for her inhabitants. And there are many inhabitants dwelling within her roots."

There was silence in the room as Geller awaited any response.

"Please continue." Gubuyis beckoned.

"What I am getting at is that we could poison her." He said flatly.

Suddenly the room filled with angry protests and shouts of horror.

"What have the Arbolion ever done to us!" Nothrip protested. "Peace is killing the neutral nations now?"

"This climate has no neutrality!" Geller's face was red with anger. "By all means, she is a rare breed and we will find ourselves looking for forgiveness from her relatives but removing her from the equation will give us strength and position. We would not only gain peace of mind for this winter, but when spring comes, we would have a weakened foe!"

The room fell silent as Gubuyis stood and raised his hands. "We must hear all possibilities. Our survival depends on it. I challenge all of you to bring forth your ideas, so that we may all consider them."

No one stepped forward or made any suggestions. The room was as quiet as if it were empty.

Then a voice shouted out, "We could try renegotiating with the Frost Birds."

"Ha! The idea of poisoning Ezjuin would come to fruition well before the Frost Birds took a side. Their neutrality is very dangerous, and they know it." Nothrip retorted.

"Still, though, their alliance would prove a turning point in our fight, to say the least," Gubuyis nodded.

Nothrip responded again, "And how might we gain their favor? They aren't interested in our gold or weaponry. We have nothing they need or desire to have."

"If we can find diplomacy with them, then by all means, we should explore the idea." Geller was much calmer now and his face was his normal color, "The Frost Birds have declined our invitations to alliance in the past, but maybe they may still be swayed."

"The trick," Gubuyis said from his seat, "is to make them want to assist us. They feel they have nothing to lose by remaining neutral, at least not directly."

"We could trick them somehow," another voice rang out.

"And risk our treachery discovered. And through such discovery," Nothrip had begun walking down the main aisle to the inner circle floor, "lose a powerful ally to our enemy. We would have done our enemies a favor and done all the work of gaining their alliance for them." He scoffed, "We are better off with our current situation."

"You have an idea, Nothrip?" Gubuyis asked.

"I believe we might be able to find their willingness to help us if we could prove to them that the Reign is working against them, even as they are neutral. If we expose the Reign's exploitation of their lands, we may find ourselves incidentally shaking hands with them."

"What exploitation do you speak of?" Geller questioned Nothrip.

"Last week I received news from our scouts in the East that the Reign needed more water for their main stronghold. So, the Reign devised a way to pull more water from deep underground. They dug deeper than one should ever have to dig to find water. And they found water, lots of it. Rumor has it, though, they weren't simply digging for water. They were searching for relics of an ancient power from long ago. And, as rumor also has it, they may have found their relics."

"How does this affect the Frost Birds?" Geller asked, confused.

"All their digging emptied a vast network of underground water channels. The same underground water supply that lies under Wyvergia, the home of the Frost Birds, is fed by these channels. The nesting trees there have begun dying in recent months and the hatchlings have been dying from dehydration as the Frost Birds can no longer drink from the trees."

"That's absolutely awful," Selini called out from the top of the main aisle. She stood there with Anna by her side, they looked like they had just come in.

"Yes," Nothrip continued, "and that is exactly why we should carefully and tenderly enlighten them."

"Just because they are neutral doesn't make them friendly," Selini marched down the aisle. "They have proven to be inherently moody creatures. What makes you think they'll want to listen to us? We have exhausted our diplomatic approaches with them already."

Nothrip looked right at Jack. "That is why we will send him."

The room filled once again with murmuring and Anna ran to Jack's side. He was just beginning to understand a little about the struggles the Govilian were facing, but now it seemed he may very easily become a part of that struggle. He stood, but he did not intend on speaking. He could not think of any reason why he stood, but to at least acknowledge the fact that he was singled out.

"Are you mad?" Geller stepped off the stage. "He doesn't know the slightest thing about Frost Birds; let alone where to find them."

Jack finally had to say something, "I have to agree with Geller, er, General Geller. I don't have any clue about Frost Birds. I would probably make things worse."

"Do not worry, my young companion, harm will not befall whilst my dear friend is with you." Nothrip said, trying to sound reassuring.

Anna finally spoke up, "The Frost Birds would eat you both alive, if you give them the chance. And with their recent lack of water, their lands hold much less food. You would be a meal walking right into their den."

Jack whispered to her, "How do you know anything about the Frost Birds?"

"Selini and I have had a lot of time to talk," she replied back.

"She makes an excellent point, Nothrip," Geller was speaking with one finger raised in confirmation. "Their already grumpy demeanor will be coupled with the fact that their young are dying to their dismay and their food sources are becoming scarcer by the day."

"I admit," Nothrip chimed in, "I have little to offer that I might myself hold back the Frost Birds. However, I do carry with me a short sword of flames." He pulled out his short sword and swung it with skill as it burst into flames with intense heat.

Geller, unimpressed by the display, broke in, "That sword will prove useful against the freezing blasts of frost from the beasts. How many, though, do you think you can hold off with that dagger? Because I can assure you, every last one of them is hungry and cranky."

Replacing his sword into its sheath, Nothrip spoke again, "I have a good friend who is willing to go in my stead."

Jack looked around for someone who might be much larger than everyone else. He hoped this other person could hold back a dozen of them without trying.

"And," Geller asked sarcastically, "who might this companion be?"

With a devilish smile on his face, Nothrip answered, "Cedric."

An uproar of voices came from the assembly, some were even laughing. Jack felt his knees become weak and he sat back down with a sigh. The inner circle quickly filled with diplomats from several nations arguing with one another on the validity of the plan. He could see Geller yelling at some of them, making a point to express his severe disapproval. Jack looked over to where Gubuyis was sitting and watched him sit quietly, with his arms folded in his lap. Jack felt that Gubuyis was actually getting some enjoyment out of the chaos that ensued in front of him.

Anna sat next to Jack, and began to shout over the noise, "I hear you've had quite the day."

"Yes," Jack replied, "and it seems to be getting worse."

"Selini told me about your situation. She also doesn't believe there is anything that can be done to get you out of it."

"If we go back home, I won't have to care about this anymore." Jack said in exasperation.

Her face fell some, "Jack, you can't. If you abandon your post, you will die."

"What do you mean? Who would kill me?" He asked defiantly.

"It would be the power of the oath." She retorted.

Jack smiled, "Well, I'm in luck! I haven't taken any oath!"

"You are to take it tonight," Anna was not smiling the least. "And if you don't take it by midnight, the temporary status you hold now will expire and you will automatically become a captive of Cedric's again."

Jack slouched into his seat. He had almost forgotten about that small fact.

Anna continued, "You have no choice, Jack. You must do it if you ever want to see home again."

Geller had made his way back to the stand and shouted, "THAT IS ENOUGH!"

The room slowly returned to a still and everyone began returning to their seats. Anna and Jack were now watching him eagerly, hoping for some good news.

"There is no way we can send Jack with him. Cedric has made it a point to inform us all humans would be arrested on site." Geller was obviously annoyed at the actions of the last several minutes.

"Ah, General," Nothrip interjected, "he has informed you that it is his solemn duty to arrest all humans of the human nation. Being that your Captain Jack is not of the humans, but indeed of your army and therefore a human of the Valindi nation, there shan't be a problem."

Geller's face remained still. Jack could tell he was thinking. But it troubled him that Geller could not think of anything to say.

"Gubuyis," Nothrip addressed, "I believe you understand my position. The boy will have an advantage. If we exploit that position, we can then inform the Frost Birds of the means to their impending demise. We can gain their favor. And, with their lot on our side, we can hold our borders this season and live to fight another day."

Jack was confused about what he had that was so special the Frost Birds would give them a chance.

"It is true." Gubuyis stood.

"We can't just throw him out there. What if they encounter the Reign?" Geller looked concerned.

It was becoming obvious to Jack that this was no longer a proposal, but that he was being recruited to do it without his opinion.

Gubuyis spoke softly, "Nothrip has a valid point. We have vital information the Frost Birds should be aware of, regardless of their choice to be our allies. They are our neighbors, and they deserve to know the facts." He approached Geller.

"Father..." Geller was lost for words to argue with.

Gubuyis continued, "Jack gives us a very unique chance to reopen talks with them. It cannot be merely chance that he has come to us at this time. We would be foolish to ignore this possibility."

Geller stood silent for several moments, Jack watched his face become grave and then give a look of submission. Jack looked at Anna who was also aware of the same thing Jack was thinking. Geller was about to agree with Gubuyis and Jack had to say something.

"Excuse me," Jack inched forward some as he spoke, "but I don't believe I am qualified for this. There has been some mistake, Nothrip, sir, because I have no familiarity with the Frost Birds in the least. You are mistaking me with someone else."

Before Nothrip could respond, Geller spoke. "Nothrip is right. You do provide all our nations with a unique position with the Frost Birds. And, for that reason, you must go on this mission. It can prove very beneficial for us all."

"You're kidding right?" Anna protested angrily, "He's in no better position to talk with Frost Birds than he is to travel with Cedric! This quest is surely meant to be his end!"

"You have saved me twice, Jack. And for that, I thank you with my life. I cannot so simply allow you to enter a hostile adventure without ensuring you are protected."

Jack was feeling a little better with this comment. Maybe Geller had come to his senses after all and realized Jack could not possibly make it out of this alive.

But, after letting out a sigh, Geller finished his statement, "That is why I will go with your camp."

With that, he stepped off the stage and began talking to his father quietly.

"Well then, I will go as well!" Selini had stepped forward and looked proud to make her announcement.

"Me too!" Anna shouted. Quickly, though, she drew back some as she realized she had no clue about what to do or what she was getting herself into.

"I think we shall call that a deal," Gubuyis was taking his position on the stage. "It seems we have camaraderie. It should be finalized before the whole room joins in this quest."

As Gubuyis was about to tap his staff, another voice called from the assembly. Jack could not tell if it was words that were shouted, or just simple squeaks of sound. But, before Gubuyis finalized the group, the voice called out again, but a bit clearer than before.

"I will also go," a small, high pitched, squeaky voice called.

Jack could not tell who had said it, and he did not recognize the voice at all. Then a small, winged creature much like an oversized bat mixed with the looks of a gargoyle flew over his head and landed in front of Gubuyis.

"Gibble at your service," he bowed as he spoke.

"I had hoped you might be," Gubuyis smiled and then tapped the staff.

As far as Jack could tell, nothing seemed to happen. Except that everyone accepted the motion as final.

"On a different note," Gubuyis continued, "we have an oath to administer."

Gubuyis motioned for Jack to come down to the center. The newly formed group sat back down, making way for Jack to stand in front of Gubuyis. Jack felt reluctant and walked slowly, almost shuffling along, as he made his way to him. He looked at Gubuyis, hoping for some sign that this was all just an elaborate hoax or that something would cause another distraction. He just wanted more time to think.

Lifting up his staff, Gubuyis began, "Lift your right hand, Captain."

Jack slowly obliged. A small stream of purple left the staff that Gubuyis was now holding above his own head. The magic fluttered slowly to Jack's chest and splashed against it like smoke crashing against a wall. After a few seconds, the magic absorbed into Jack's chest. He did not feel anything except a slight bit of warmth.

"Congratulations, Captain!" Gubuyis said with a large smile on his face. "You are now a ranked member of the Valindi army. Know this, peace is above all else. The abundance of life is only through peace."

Chapter 13: A Poisonous Plan

L ater that night, Jack and Anna returned to their dwelling at the end of the hall in an odd building. In tow behind them were Selini and Geller, who were discussing how to speak with the Frost Birds without somebody getting killed.

Once they got into the house, Jack sat at the table. There was a good deal of food prepared and waiting, but he did not have any appetite, despite his long day.

"When do we leave?" Jack asked Geller.

"The morning after tomorrow, so we must get good rest and feed well. The journey will take several weeks, and we are not likely to be blessed with an easy path."

Selini began describing the journey to Jack and Anna. "Once we leave our borders, the land becomes barren. Since fall is upon us, the lands will be slightly cooler, but you will find it hard to believe. No matter what you do, you will seemingly always have sand in your eyes and find it gritting between your teeth. The winds will blow against us."

"And once we get to the mountains," Geller continued, "we will no longer deal with the unbearable heat and dusty winds."

"This is true," Selini spoke as if they were taking turns, "the winds will no longer blow dust and the heat will surely subside. However, the mountains are more unforgiving than the desert lands. The air will be as dry as the barrens but will blow blistering cold winds at your face and flow through even the smallest holes in your clothes."

"For that reason," Geller chimed back in, "we will have to carry heavy clothing through the desert. That will only add to the pain and misery in our desert travels. Selini, however, can work her charms some to reduce this burden"

"I feel sorry for Cedric," Selini smiled, "he has much more cloth to fair."

Anna broke her silence, "So, after we get to the mountains, how much traveling will be left?"

Selini answered, "The mountains are considered the beginning of the journey, my friend. It will take more than a week to traverse them. You'll have forgotten the color of the world and only know shades of white and grey."

"That sounds miserable," Jack slouched some in his chair as he thought of being stuck in snow for more than a week.

"Oh, it is." Geller confirmed matter-of-factly, "The water in your canteens will freeze before you ever get a chance to take a drink. For that reason, we'll empty our water upon reaching the mountains and drink melted snow. This will reduce our weight some as we continue through the mountains."

"Tell me it gets better on the other side of the mountains," Anna demanded.

"Well," Selini looked at Geller with a pause before continuing, "it won't be as cold anymore. Plus, it won't be hot like the desert either."

"The other side of the mountains will be the hardest part." Geller and Selini held up small wands and flashes of small lightning bolts shot between them. "We'll be walking through something like this."

Jack's jaw dropped open. He knew not much good could come from walking through an electrical storm. "What happens if we get hit?"

"You're most certain to die." Selini responded.

"And how exactly are we supposed to not get hit," Anna looked annoyed that such a journey could even exist.

"We could run," Geller stated matter-of-factly again, "but you'd have to run for more than a day. On the other hand, we'll be in better luck if we travel as close to cliff walls in the lowest lands the best we can, but the rest of the time we'll have to hope for the best. That will take us nearly four days."

Jack put his head down on the table in despair.

"What!" Anna shouted. "There's no way we're 'hoping for the best,' that's ridiculous. What kind of strategy is that?"

Ignoring the question, Geller continued, "After all that, we'll arrive to the borders of Wyvergia. It will be mostly easy from that point, but don't expect to be out of danger."

Selini decided to chime in at this point, "Yeah, this is the trickiest part. We don't want to be seen by patrolling Frost Birds before getting deep enough into their lands. The patrols will more than likely see us as their next meal. In this case, the closer we are to danger, the less likely we are to be killed."

"This is getting confusing," Jack said with his head still buried in his arms on the table.

"Zarx'l will be too curious to command the Frost Birds to kill us," she explained. "He's the leader of the Frost Birds, and he'll want to know why we ventured so far into his lands that he'll have us captured. We'll let that happen."

"Okay," Anna rebutted, "let me see if I have this right. We're going to make this awful journey through deserts, mountains, and lightning storms and then sneak far into the borders of the enemy just to let them capture us?"

Geller spoke, "Remember, they are not our enemy. The Frost Birds have declared neutrality but will defend their lands if they feel threatened. And they pretty much always feel threatened when others enter their lands."

"It will be better that we be captured than if we managed to make it all the way to the nesting forest undetected." Selini continued, "If we were to get all the way in without them noticing ..."

"Which we could," Geller was smiling.

"Yes, which we could," she continued, "It would hurt their pride as masters of detection. It would also make Zarx'l question our real motives for being there and be much less willing to hear our position. Not to mention the fact that he would almost certainly issue an order for our deaths."

Jack raised his head, "If they are so moody and sinister, why in the world would you want to fight by their side?"

"It would be a tricky situation," Geller explained, "however, our dwindling allies and troop numbers call for tough decisions. It would be better for us to have them on our side and deal with the pain of their menacing presence than it would be to have them as our enemy."

The few of them spoke for some time into the night. Anna asked most of the questions as Jack felt a growing sense of unease with the whole plan with every explanation of it. He could not find a silver lining to anything they said. It all sounded like doom from the beginning. Eventually, though, they all retired for the night and Jack was shown to a room with a bed just right for his size.

Early the next morning, Jack woke to the sounds of talking in the main room. He changed into his clothes, which were washed and pressed and laying at the foot of his bed. When he came out of the room, Geller was talking to several other generals from the Valindi army and various other armies. From what he had heard already, he could tell they were discussing a strategy to poison Ezjuin.

"That's an awful lot of poison to come up with," one officer said.

"Getting it won't be the hassle," Geller explained to him, "administering it at the right time and in the right river is the key."

"When is the right time?" Jack spoke out.

The room turned and watched him as he found a place to stand near the fireplace.

Geller spoke, "Right now is the right time. Fall is upon us and she is thirsty from her aggressive growing season."

"Then what river?" Jack asked. He was curious and hoping he was not asking things that were considered common sense.

Pointing to a large, heavy leather map on the table, Geller said, "This is what we must determine. If you look here, her root system is most definitely in this region," he pointed at a large red circle that had been hand drawn on the map. "This part we have confirmed. We can probably assume that her water collection system runs to about here," he drew another circle a little ways outward from the original one. "That puts these three rivers moving through her."

Jack watched confused as Anna came up by him. She had also just woken up and came to see what was going on.

He leaned in and whispered to her, "How big is this tree if three rivers can run through it?"

She looked at him and grabbed his arm. Pulling him across the room to a bookshelf near one of the windows, she whispered, "You're going to want to see this."

She pulled a book off the shelf and opened it to a very complexly drawn tree. It looked similar to the one he had seen in the library, but much grander. She began to explain, "These trees are collectively called Arbolion. There are only a few dozen left on this planet. Once they take root, it is extremely difficult to remove them. One tree will look like an entire forest to the untrained eye. As the tree grows, it becomes larger underground. And don't let the term 'tree' fool you." She turned the page and showed an illustration of different growing stages of an Arbolio. "The root system is the greatest thing about the Arbolion. They are massive. They are so massive, entire cities were sometimes built in them by other nations. And I'm not talking about small colonies, I'm talking about entire nations. Ezjuin is the home of the entire army for Ghowla. They dwell within her roots and they are growing stronger every year as the Valindi and their allies grow weaker."

Jack picked up the book from her and studied the illustrations for a moment, "This is fascinating; just absolutely amazing."

"Jack," Anna said with concern, "if this is right, I don't think this Arbolio is simply a foothold. They could be housing an entire…"

"Legion!" One of the generals was looking right at them from the table across the room. His voice was stern as he continued, "Perhaps even two!" A smirk washed across his brazen face before he returned to studying the map.

Jack knew then that a victorious outcome with this plan had more damaging effects to the Reign than simply holding off an inevitable win until the next spring.

Anna's eyes expressed their worry as she continued, "Ezjuin is controlled by Ghowla, a powerful wizard. She has little ability to fend for herself. But, the sheer size of her takes most of Ghowla's power to control. This may be an advantage to them. Because of this, Ghowla cannot freely leave the tree and must rely on his scouts and messengers to keep him informed of the outside world, at least beyond the sight of Ezjuin. What they are hoping for," she pointed at the group still huddled over the map and arguing over which river was her main water supply, "is that she will drink enough poison to kill her. If she dies, her roots will not provide warmth and light. There would just be this huge root system that lay beneath the forest above that would be dark and freezing cold."

"And that would force Ghowla's army out," Jack concluded.

From behind them, Selini spoke, "That is part of the strategy. But simply forcing them to leave the confines of Ezjuin's roots will only work to our disadvantage if she hasn't been killed."

"Why? What happens when she isn't killed?" Anna asked curiously; Jack wondered the same things.

"If Ezjuin is still alive, even if her roots are dying, she will prove to be a formidable foe. Her tree, or the forest that you will see, is impenetrable. The above ground part acts as a defense, and it does so with great skill. There's little she can do as far as offensive maneuvers, but that's what Ghowla's army will take care of. As long as she is still alive, she will defend herself and they will attack mostly from within the confines of her canopy. They always win defense for this reason, and this is why we cannot attack them there. We have to wait for them to get to our borders, which is tricky because we have to mobilize our troops all over the place and scatter across the region. Without being able to concentrate our efforts in one localized area, we remain weak."

"So, what will happen if the poison doesn't work?" Jack asked louder than he intended.

Geller spoke from the table across the room, "Then we will die."

An awkward silence filled the room as the other officers studied the map more intensely.

"It has been decided," Geller jumped off the bench at the table, "we will poison the river of Anub. We believe it runs the closest to her central intake."

"Why wouldn't it work if you poisoned any of the rivers she drinks from?" Jack asked curiously.

"She would surely be poisoned, yes." Geller sat back down in the main room and watched the fireplace as he spoke softly, "but she would realize she was being poisoned well before it did enough damage to the whole of her. The Arbolion may be trees, but they aren't stupid. She would stop drinking from the rivers altogether and analyze the poison. Then she would report it to Ghowla."

Anna lit up some, "Maybe she wouldn't realize it was intentional."

"Oh no. She would most definitely know." Geller continued speaking softly, "One would not find this poison idly flowing down a river, especially in such great quantity. She will assume the worst. She will adapt to its qualities and develop a filtration system that would block it in the future."

"In other words," Selini spoke, "it is a onetime operation. If it doesn't work, we don't get a second chance."

"If we fail, all the nations of the west will begin to fall one by one." Geller's voice trailed off as he spoke.

"Then why take the risk?" Jack asked, "Why not fight to hold them off and develop another plan?"

"Haven't you been listening?" Geller spoke much clearer and louder now.

"We don't have the power to defend ourselves anymore. We have lost so much in the last several years. When I was captured, we were still very strong. Every nation in the west was allied together and Ezjuin was still small enough to take on. Ghowla's forces have grown tremendously. And let's not forget, he's only one of six. There are five other armies just as large or larger than his. Even if we succeed, which is slim, we will still have to face the wrath of the remaining Reign."

After several moments of silence, one officer spoke up, "We are confident in the choice of Anub as her main river, sir. And we will fight or die by your side with pride."

Geller sighed heavily and dismissed them from the room. After they left, Selini proceeded to roll up the map and set it in front of Geller.

"These are indeed desperate times, sister, but those men trust me too much." Geller spoke quietly.

He was slouched fully into the chair and spoke with despair in his voice, "They cannot possibly have entertained what it really means if we fail, or they would not so blindly follow me."

"They believe you are great. You have proven this before, and they know you would not lead them astray from victory." She tried to comfort him.

"If we don't have victory, their wives and children will be mercilessly killed in the name of the Reign's evil intent. This is not as simple as losing today and fighting tomorrow, this is not a battle. This is the war we have been fighting so hard to prevent from entering our lands. And," he paused for a moment before continuing, "I'm not sure we are prepared."

The thought of knowing their loss could be the end of the Valindi and the death of the little ones he had seen running through the streets so happily playing in their innocence, filled Jack with a courage he had not expected.

"I will fight with you until we win," Jack blurted out.

They all looked at him and Anna gasped, "Jack," she whispered loudly, "if you put yourself in harm's way, you may never return home."

"He has no choice," Geller spoke up, "but, nonetheless, it is reassuring that you will put forth an effort. I am comforted some by your determination, and I know you are destined for great things."

With a clap of her hands and a small jump, Selini exclaimed, "Well! Let's get to start'n the day before tomorrow is upon us."

Chapter 14: A Recipe and a Box

When the four of them arrived in front of the small house with the long hall, Jack could see hundreds of Valindi parading the streets in celebration. There was loud music and the smell of freshly baked breads and meats filled the air. Flower petals were floating above them and songs from many different singers met his ears.

Anna shouted over the sound of the street, "What are they doing?"

Geller and Selini were already beginning to dance with strangers on the road, but Selini managed to yell back, "We're celebrating the victory we will have soon!"

With that, she and Geller had disappeared into the crowds. An old Valindi woman came dancing up to Jack and Anna and sang drunkenly and loudly as she passed them. She grabbed a handful of flower petals and threw it at the two of them. Jack ducked, but it was just flower petals and he felt foolish for doing so.

"Look," Anna smiled and pointed at his shirt.

Jack looked down and saw the flower petals had formed into real flowers that lined his neck. Nothing held them together, but they would not come off him either. He smirked a little at the oddity of his new look.

"Why would they ever celebrate a victory before they have one?" Jack shouted over to Anna. Even though they were standing next to each other, it was increasingly harder to hear one another in such commotion.

"Here," Anna shouted back, "let's go in here!"

She pulled his arm and they ducked into a tavern. Not too many patrons were in it and the noise was definitely much less. Most of those that were there were with others and talking loudly and happily.

There were a few tables, however, that belonged to individuals who had much less to say. The bartender was wiping out some glasses when he looked at the pair of them and smiled.

"Good day to ya!" He was very enthusiastic, "I haven't seen yer kind in here fer some time!"

A lone Valindi at the end of the bar mumbled, "You should keep it that way, Bolar."

"Ahhh, ya ol' bag," Bolar said, still holding a smile on his face and gazing at the two of them, "yer never hold'n on ta yer happiness."

The Valindi mumbled incoherently back and slammed his fist on the bar.

Bolar excused himself from the two of them, "Give 'em a bit, he'll light up like a ray of sun." He spoke as he walked over to the lone Valindi and poured him a glass of something. "This'll cheer y'up and right yer day!"

The bartender returned to Jack and Anna as they took seats at the bar. The seats changed to match their sizes and part of the bar heightened to fit their legs under it.

The man at the end of the bar let out a humph as he watched the seats resize.

"So," the bartender was excitedly smiling again, "What can I do ya fer?"

"I'll have water, please." Anna said.

The bartender's smile shrank for a moment before he smiled again, "Well you betcha, miss lady, I got some of that here." Bolar was now looking at Jack and waiting for his request.

"I don't have anything to pay with," Jack shrugged.

Bolar raised his hand before Jack could speak any more, "Nonsense! Me good Cap'n, I git paid fer ya by the head o' the court."

"You mean Gubuyis?" Anna asked.

"Yes ma'am." Bolar had filled a water glass and put it in front of her, "Wouldja like someth'n else then?"

"I don't know," she said earnestly.

Jack could not think of anything either, they did not know much about the food and drink in this world. Jack was surprised at how good the food was, but he did not know anything by name. As Anna asked Bolar for recommendations, Jack squinted and began reading the labels on the largest bottles.

"I really don't want anything with spirits," Anna was explaining to Bolar.

He let out a laugh, "Me dear friend, I thinks ya've come to the wrong place." He laughed some more. "But I do have this."

He walked back to a small kettle floating above a flame and picked out a bottle. He opened it and smelled its contents with his eyes closed and returned to her with a large mug and the bottle.

Anna smelled it and backed away immediately. "Ugh, it's that same stuff from the cabin in the forest."

Jack remembered she was not too keen about it, but he suddenly remembered how good it was for him.

"I'll take a glass as large as you can fill it!" Jack found it hard to hide his excitement.

Bolar looked a little taken aback, "Ah, ya've had some then?" He began pouring it in the mug, "'Cuz dis here is not fer a weak tongue."

"I love this stuff," Jack remembered how good it made him feel when he drank it before. It made him feel like he was sitting at home on a cold wintry day, snuggled into a heavy blanket and sitting in front of the fire with a freshly baked slice of pumpkin bread and a hot piece of pumpkin pie.

"I thought you were just being stupid about it before," Anna was upset, "but now I see you want to be a jerk about it."

Jack just finished a large gulp and set the glass down, "What are you talking about, this stuff is great! I'm not kidding, it is probably the best drink I've ever had."

"I hope so," Bolar butted in, "it takes a lot o' skill and preparation to git it right. 'N not many people want it either."

"I can't imagine why," Anna said sarcastically, "it's oh-so delicious."

Bolar scratched his head and furrowed his eyebrows, "I thought …"

"She doesn't like it." Jack confirmed for him.

Bolar looked more confused, "Well, I better be git'n to me other patrons. Why don't you two enjoy a bit 'o conversation." With that, Bolar began making his rounds.

Anna shook her head, "I really don't see how you can stand that stuff."

"I'm going to see if I can get some of this for the journey," Jack said.

"Suit yourself, but you'll have to drink it by yourself."

Changing the subject, Jack asked, "Do you think you're ready for the trek to the Frost Birds?"

"No," Anna quickly stated. "Do you even know anything about them?"

"I heard quite a bit about them during the assembly last night," he smirked a little, "But how menacing can a pack of birds really be?"

"That's what I'm talking about." Anna scooted in toward him a little, "I was reading about them last night before going to bed."

Jack rolled his eyes, "How many books are on that bookcase? Cuz

I'm willing to bet you've already read half of them."

She sneered at him, "That bookcase is connected directly to their library here. Just think of the subject you want to learn about and then pick up a book. That book will show you everything you need to know related to that subject."

"What? That's awesome!" Jack was listening more now, "How did you find that out?"

"Selini and I had a lot of time yesterday while you guys were at the assembly and picking out your armor. Which, by the way, is leather. Did they have nothing in your size for steel?"

"It's a long story," Jack shook his head a little. He knew he was going to be the laughingstock of the entire army when he presented himself in full leather armor in battle.

"Anyhow," Anna continued, "the Frost Birds aren't birds at all."

Confused, Jack asked, "Well, then what are they?"

"They fly alright, but the name 'Bird' insinuates a much smaller creature than they really are."

Jack asked slowly, "How big are the Frost Birds?"

Bolar had just been returning to the bar and overheard them talking.

"Ahem," he cleared his throat and looked at Jack.

"Can we help you?" Anna asked.

Bolar approached the pair of them and looked around the room as if someone should not hear what he was about to say. He then leaned in and spoke quietly, "Ya're darn lucky never ta h've met the likes of a Frost Bird."

"Have you met one before?" Jack asked him.

He nodded and responded back, "Me fatha used ta work with 'em. When I was a lad, our farm sold food to their lot. Grumpy li'l buggers they are."

"Why are they called Frost Birds?" Anna asked him.

He stood up straight again, "Well, they blow a lot o' frigid cold air! They'll freeze ya right up, they will. I never could figure out what use there was in freez'n everything when ya was mad at the world. They just plain freeze stuff with their breath. It takes but only a moment ta completely freeze som'thin with them"

Jack nodded his head, "It does seem rather useless to freeze things."

Anna snapped back, "Oh come off it, Jack. You could do a lot of harm if you could instantly kill someone by freezing them to death."

Smiling, Jack responded, "But how long would it take for a bird to freeze someone?"

Anna and Bolar both stared at him and Jack suddenly felt like he was uninformed.

"Ya ain't never seen one, have ya?"

"I can't say that I have, no." Jack's smile was completely gone. The way Bolar had spoken made Jack realize what Anna was trying to get at. The name 'Bird' was probably misleading.

"Jack," Anna explained, "you fought dragons and remember their size, right?"

"They're as big as dragons?" Jack remembered what he had gone through and suddenly imagined walking into an entire land filled with dragon-sized 'birds' that liked to breathe frost. "You would think someone would have mentioned this before."

"They ain't no size o' dragons," Bolar blurted out and poured another glass for Jack. "Most of 'em birds are a little smaller than a dragon, but some are much bigger."

Jack's eyes widened at the mention of the Frost Birds' size. He could not think of anything to say, but half-heartedly raised his glass in thanks to Bolar instead.

"May I ask why ya're gonna make that kinda journey at this time o' year just ta talk with a bunch o' misfit, no good fer nothin' oversized chunks o'ice."

Jack said unenthusiastically, "We're going to try and convince them to fight with us in battle."

The three of them sat in silence as Jack felt a new kind of burden fall upon him. Before, he had imagined dealing with large birds with an attitude. Now, however, if anything were to go wrong, he could not see how they would make it out alive. Now he understood why nobody else wanted to speak with the Frost Birds. And it was even more confusing that all the others in his group would even fathom going, knowing what they were about to get themselves into.

"Well, it's a noble reas'n." Bolar had been leaning on the counter in front of them but was now walking away.

"It's obvious he thinks it's a suicide mission," Anna observed out loud.

"Maybe I should've ordered something with spirits," Jack grumbled under his breath.

"I'm sure the others wouldn't have wanted to go if they didn't believe there was a chance that this could work," Anna was trying to comfort Jack.

He thought the same thing, but it did not help. The pressure of knowing that they were counting on him to be able to pull this off was becoming unbearable. He was sure he had no ability to reason with the birds.

In the far back of the tavern, beyond the bar, was a large fireplace that held some meat on a rack. The back room had many spices and ingredients and dirty dishes all over the place. Jack watched Bolar walk up a set of stairs with a small scroll in his hands.

"I can't believe I'm doin' this," Bolar said as he brought them the scroll, "but these times are a callin' for desperate measures." He handed Jack the scroll with gust.

Jack began to open it, "What is it?"

"Not here!" Bolar whispered frantically. "Follow me."

Bolar walked back into the butcher-style kitchen and down the large wooden staircase. Before going down, though, he gestured for the barmaid tending the fire to watch the tavern in his absence. Jack and Anna followed him into a dusky, dark cellar full of barrels of many sizes. The floor was made of dirt and the only light was from several small balls of light similar to the one that lit the secret passageway in the council room.

As they walked into the cellar, the lights grew brighter and scattered throughout the room. It was not a very large cellar, but it held several dozen different barrels and boxes of supplies. Bolar walked through a maze of these until they reached the back wall, where there was a small door. Bolar grabbed a key from his pocket and opened it. As Jack attempted to fit through, the door became large enough to fit both him and Anna comfortably.

"Okay," Bolar said.

The room was dimly lit and the door shut behind them. It was packed with smaller boxes of odd items and what appeared to be a desk under most of the heap.

"Now I can open it?" Jack asked.

"Now ya can open it," Bolar motioned for him to unravel the scroll.

Jack and Anna peered at the scroll once he got it open and saw what looked to be an ingredient list and a recipe.

Confused, Jack rolled it back up, "I think you have given me the wrong thing, Bolar. This is some sort of recipe."

Pushing the scroll back into Jack's hands, Bolar explained, "It is the recipe of my family. It took me fatha and me motha most of their lives to git this right."

Jack looked at the scroll again, and hesitatingly said, "Thanks. I'm not sure how much cooking we're going to do on this journey, but it may prove useful."

"No," Bolar said emphatically, "yer ta give this ta the Frost Birds. Oh, me fatha would kill me if he knew what I's doin' here."

"Why exactly are we giving this to the Frost Birds?" Anna was about as confused as Jack.

"Them birds love Prunklesnider mo' than good ol' Jack here does."

"Prunklesnider? Is that what I was just drinking at the bar?"

"Yep." Bolar replied.

Remembering that he had had this before, Jack became curious, "And this is a family recipe?" He asked.

Standing proudly, Bolar stated, "It sho is!"

"We've had it before, though." Anna stated. "And it wasn't in any tavern."

"Anyone can make it," Bolar explained, "but few can make it right. And if ye have the skills ta make it proper, ye can charge a fine bit fer it."

"So, why would we give it to the Frost Birds? Can they even make it?" Jack asked.

"Prob'ly not." Bolar smiled. "But as much as they love this stuff, they'd be sho to figure it out one way or anotha."

"They'd probably appreciate it more if we just brought them a batch." Anna said.

"Ye have to keep it hot once it's made," Bolar explained, "else it'll taste 'orrible. And they wouldn't much appreciate that. Plus, they've never been giv'n a recipe fer it before, so they'd really love ya for it.

Just don't be let'n ev'ryone see that recipe. I still needs to make a liv'n here."

"I'll see what I can do," Jack said.

As Bolar shuffled them out the door, he finished by saying, "And if ya find they doesn't need it, try 'n destroy the scroll. I don't much need it, I have Prunklesnider all put together in me head."

Once they reached the top of the stairs, Jack could see Geller speaking with the barmaid as she was pointing to the kitchen.

He made his way toward them, "Jack, Anna, we must leave today." His voice was hurried some.

"What's happened," Jack asked him.

"We've received word that a major windstorm is coming from the northwest in the Desert of Gillia, the one we are to cross. Once it hits our group, we'll be slowed tremendously by its force and blinding power. We won't be able to beat it, but we can make some ground before it meets us." Geller was already walking away and out the tavern door.

Jack quickly turned and thanked Bolar for his help and they followed behind Geller. He was making his way through the loud streets still in celebration. Soon enough, Jack and Anna spotted Selini coming down another street and she had Gibble in tow. It did not take much effort to see Cedric. Jack and Anna were already taller than most of the people in the streets, but seeing Cedric was as easy as seeing a tree in a prairie.

Jack walked as briskly as he could but only found himself just barely keeping pace with Geller who was still a half block ahead of them. It did not matter too much to him; he could tell where Geller was headed by the looks of his general direction. It seemed as if they were all about to meet at the Panthyun. Cedric, with his massive strides, made it there first and looked much more pleasant than before.

"Geller, good friend, what a fine day for such a journey," Cedric said happily.

Geller met him with a kneeling hug and handshake. "We'll be off in only a moment."

"Ah, Selini," Cedric's arms were wide open again for another hug.

Excitedly, Selini hugged him, "It's good to see you outside of the council room."

Jack and Anna were now standing on the steps but were not sure how to greet Cedric.

It only took a second for Cedric to see them and he spoke directly to Jack, "Captain, it is good to see you again." His voice was more formal now, but still much less threatening than when they first met.

"Um, yes, it's good to see you too, Cedric," Jack did not want to start the journey on worse terms. He figured as long as they could fake it, they had a chance.

"I must apologize for our first meeting," Cedric sat down so that he could face Jack. Even with Cedric's big voice, he still had to shout a little to overcome the music and festivities from the streets. "I am, or was, the ambassador for Monarkia, until yesterday evening. I had to follow through with the request of our government, even if I didn't agree with it. That's part of the job. I have had to act upon many requests over the last several hundred years that I did not agree with, but I cannot sit idly by while our forces are about to meet their toughest battle and argue a point that would have us waste resources and gain nothing. For that I am sorry. But I can assure you, there will be no more problems, as I am no longer an officer of the embassy. I still hold my position in our army, however, and will assist you in any way I can."

Jack felt better, but could not help wondering, "If you're still an officer in the army, don't you have to arrest Anna for being human."

Cedric stood up, "Yes I do."

The group stood there for a moment, nobody saying a word. Jack contemplated grabbing Anna's arm and running as fast as they could down the street, but he could not see how they would outrun Cedric.

Then Geller began laughing, followed by Cedric.

As he laughed, he spoke, "It is my duty as an officer of our army to carry out such a task. But it is merely frowned upon that I would choose not to obey that order. And, I choose not to follow through with that command." His laughter had subsided, "As ambassador, I had to follow through. I had to lead and be the example. Being that I am no longer the ambassador, I have the right to ignore such an order without penalty of death."

Anna's face had gone pale and was regaining color. Jack's heart had been pounding and he felt the need to breathe a little harder, as if he had to catch his breath.

"Ah, the rest of our party," Geller was looking to the doors of the Panthyun.

As the others approached, Geller and Cedric made more greetings.

"Ouch!" Jacked grabbed his side. He quickly turned around and noticed Anna had jabbed him.

"Really?" Anna huffed as she mocked Jack's words, *"If you're still an officer, don't you have to arrest Anna?"*

Jack smiled as he rubbed the pain in his side. "Sorry, I didn't think."

She sneered at him.

"Right then," Geller spoke as all the individuals in the group came in closer. "It looks like we are all here. I am saddened this journey even has to happen, but times are desperate." Geller was speaking as if he was speaking to friends. "Be that as it may, we must embark with haste."

"Wait!" A voice cried to them from the Panthyun. Everyone looked and watched as the blacksmith hurried toward them. He had somewhat of a clumsy hobble in his walk and he seemed annoyed at the sun. It was evident that he seldom left the confines of the Panthyun's catacombs. "This belongs to you!" he said. His voice was straining to make his words heard over the excitement of the streets.

"To whom?" Geller inquired as the blacksmith finally made it to the group.

"To him." He was pointing at Jack and holding a small octagonal box in his hand. It had a slight glisten in the sunlight but looked fairly aged and dirty at first glance.

Jack held his hand out as the blacksmith gave him the box and explained, "It goes with your armor." He scanned Jack and looked around a little, "You do have your armor, don't you?"

Jack nearly forgot. It was in the room near his bed. He had not expected to leave today, so he had not seen any need to bring it along while in town.

Patting a bag, Selini spoke up cheerfully, "Everything we'll need is in these bags."

Jack felt a little relieved. He knew things would certainly make a turn for the worst if it was learned later that he did not have his armor. Albeit, he did not feel much more protected by it than when wearing the clothes on his back.

"What is it?" Jack was examining the box. It was covered with small, raised figures similar to the ones on the wall of the council chamber. Although it looked like a dingy copper, Jack could tell it was something else he was not familiar with.

Before the blacksmith could answer, the box's top quickly unfolded in such a way that it melded into the sides of itself.

"By Zaglar's beard!" Geller exclaimed. The others were also looking in amazement. "Is that what I think it is?" He asked the blacksmith.

The blacksmith smiled as he sat down on the steps, apparently tired from his unusual excursion away from the shop. "I had almost forgotten about it. It was made with his armor. As I was recording the sale in my books, I noticed an item still existed in my inventory as it pertained to the collection. That's when it hit me. I had to search for some time through all the little trinkets I have before I found it."

"Well, what is it?" Anna asked.

"It's a box," Geller replied as he looked at it closer.

Impatiently, Anna snapped back, "Yes, I see that. But that thing looks like it could only hold a small trinket at best."

Selini smiled, "More importantly, it's a Cerilian box. Not many exist, and I've never known one to be so small."

"It is really quite amazing," Geller replied. "Does it function just like its larger counterpart?" He asked the blacksmith.

"I would imagine so," the blacksmith was less breathless now. "It seems your journey may not be off to such a bad start after all."

Anna and Jack exchanged confused glances.

Just then, bells began to ring from the city walls. The excitement in the streets lessened as the people turned their attention to the northwestern wall. The bells kept sounding and guards could be seen scrambling for the gates and shouting orders at each other.

"We must go now!" Geller set off toward the fountain's gargoyle statue.

The others followed and Jack could see they were going to use the same door he had come into town from. And, with a flick of his wand, Geller summoned the gargoyle to open at the base as it did before. They all made their way through the doorway as some of the city's people waved them off amid the confusion of the streets.

Jack turned to the blacksmith and held up the small box and called back to him, "Thanks for this!" He then quickly shoved it in his satchel that had been repaired by Gryan the night before.

Selini was the last one in and she gave a flick of her wand as she walked down the narrow steps. The door closed and the cavern became as dark as midnight. Jack remembered this room well as the roots that hung from overhead filled the cavern with a faint glow from the speckles of flowing, glimmering light. He looked down at the steps and could see they were made of a roughly cut stone. They went on for some time, much longer than he'd remembered them from before. And the farther they went down, the more the shimmering roots overhead began to look like stars in the midnight sky.

Except for the voices of the group members, the cavern was vastly quiet. Jack also remembered that this was the place he had slain the dragon before. Although he did not care much for meeting them again, he felt more confident taking them on with a group. And, although he was still not sure about Cedric, he felt comforted by the presence of such a large individual on their side.

Chapter 15: The Darkened Way

The six members of the group continued through the cavern for the better part of the day. Gibble had taken to occasionally flying above the group and Cedric spoke loudly and boastfully of past battles he had fought in. Selini answered Anna's constant questions about all there was to know.

Jack, on the other hand, remained quiet and observed the cavern intently. He could not help but fear something was watching and following them. He kept remembering how quickly this very cavern had changed from a serene nightscape to a war with dragons. He could still hear the shriek of the dragon when he thrust Geller's dagger in its side. The fear that quickly grasped the other dragons as one of their own lay dying by his hand still perplexed him.

He wondered, "How could they believe I would be able to take them all on?" He shook his head as he thought.

"We haven't had a chance to meet," a small voice filled Jack's right ear. "I am Gibble, son of Aldar."

Gibble landed next to Jack and walked with him. Jack smiled, "I'm honored to meet you, Gibble, son of Aldar."

Gibble's voice became slightly higher pitched as he spoke again, "No, sire," he gave a slight bow in his step, "it is I that is honored. I am witnessing a miracle sent to our armies by Zaglar himself." He puffed his small chest out with pride and his wings gave a flutter.

Jack was not accustomed to anyone feeling honored to meet him, so he gave a quick, silent "Thanks" and changed the subject.

"So, how much longer do we have until we get to the desert?" Jack asked.

Jack looked around the cavern and could only see the darkness that surrounded them, broken by the small shimmers of twinkling glows from the roots. He did not remember seeing any pillars along the way and wondered how such a large underground void could support itself like this. Then he wondered if he would even be able to see a pillar if it was just off the path. The only way he knew they were on a path was by a faint glow of blue coming from cracks in the stone, like water seeping slowly through the cracks in a levy. It only flowed along the path they were taking.

"I'd say about another day, if all goes well." Gibble spoke matter-of-factly, like nothing would go wrong on this part of the journey.

Jack felt some confidence by Gibble's nonchalance, but he still recalled the terror of the dragons and how quickly the serenity of the cavern had nearly become the last thing he would have ever seen. He felt the side of his hip and his fingers ran down the hilt of the dagger he acquired at the blacksmith's shop. He knew he did not have much skill with a weapon, but it still provided some comfort to know he had at least something with him.

Then he realized it was only him and Anna that were not wearing their armor. He realized the others had not prepared once they learned of the necessity of their early departure, but, instead, were almost always in their armor. He felt foolish and considered asking them to stop so he could quickly put it on. He decided against this idea, feeling it would just draw more attention to his feeble preparedness.

Seeking to draw his mind away from his embarrassment, he uttered out ahead of him, "Anna, do you have any armor?" His voice was much louder than he meant it to be and the group came to a halt. His voice echoed for a brief moment.

Anna, surprised by the suddenness and oddity of the question, managed to sputter out a sound of affirmation. She pointed to the pack on her back and had a small smile on her face that made him suddenly feel stupid for asking.

Selini chuckled, as did Gibble, but Cedric gave a burst of laughter. "You might want to check your packing list slightly sooner, Jack!" His laugh was big, along with his smile.

The group soon began moving ahead again. Jack smiled at his naivety, but quickly realized he had done exactly what he did not want to do. He had drawn attention to the fact they were both walking without their armor. Now his face was red with embarrassment, and no one was even taking notice.

Several hours had since passed and some canteens were beginning to run dry. Cedric's stories had become much more silent and Anna was no longer asking Selini questions. The loudest sounds were now from their feet scraping loose gravel and dirt across the hardened stone pathway and the occasional clanking from numerous pots, gear, and various other items shuffling around in their packs.

Jack was pleasantly surprised at the lightness of his pack for its size. He had only packed some of it before they had begun the day, but someone had finished it for him. He figured it was probably Selini, since she had also taken care to ensure his armor had made it. He also figured it was better that someone with knowledge of what they were embarking upon packed for him, especially since there was easily more than double what he thought he would be taking.

"Let us take leave for the night," Geller had stopped by the side of the path. "We will need to gather some more water for tomorrow. Then, before we enter the Kanayabe Steppe, we will fill all the canteens."

Jack moved to where Anna was standing and leaned in, "How are we going to make it through a desert if we have to get water already and then again tomorrow?"

Anna smiled and pointed at the oversized bag on his back, "They didn't fill all the canteens so not to slow us down more than we needed. There's plenty of water here, so they packed only a little water for this part."

Jack slumped, "I'm carrying a bunch of empty canteens?" His face looked suddenly stressed, "How am I going to carry them all when they're full?"

"Right then," Geller grabbed a small bag out of Selini's bag on her back, "we'll pitch camp here." He held the bag upside down and shook the contents onto the ground.

Cedric already had a tent up and was sitting on a stone next to a small but growing fire. He leaned back and groaned as he put his feet on a small log. Gibble was fussing at the roots as he attempted to attach a cloth to several of them above their heads. Jack watched in humor as Gibble's small arms could only reach two or three of the roots at a time. For a while, each time he got a hold of a couple, he would lose one while he attempted to reach for another. Eventually, though, Gibble was successfully able to attach a cocoon-like tent roughly twenty-five feet above the encampment.

"We should probably get started on ours," Anna was slipping her backpack off. It landed with a heaviness that sounded like much more than she should have been able to carry. She began digging around for a tent.

Jack followed suit and found a bag similar to what Geller had pulled from Selini's bag. He opened it up and gazed inside for anything that would resemble the assembly of a tent. He decided to also dump it out like Geller. Several small poles clanked on the ground and a light, but strong cloth landed atop the pile. He gestured to Anna to look for a similar bag and she soon found herself dumping the contents of a tent on the ground.

After fiddling with the poles for a few moments, Jack asked her, "Are you having any luck? I can barely see anything in here."

Before Anna could reply, Geller stood between their two feeble attempts at pitching their tents. "It works better if you have this." Geller gave a small flick with his wand and both tents sprung to their full attention in a flash. He smiled, "Make sure you get your rest. You never know when the night will prove short." He turned and disappeared into the darkness before his tent filled with light.

"Well, that beats reading directions!" Jack was still sitting on the ground where he had been trying to pitch the tent in the first place.

Anna turned to her bag and began searching for something to sleep on.

Selini stepped out of her tent, which was also lit up quite well. She looked at Anna, "You'll find everything you need is already in there." She pointed at Anna's tent.

Jack watched her as she entered her tent with awe. He turned and followed suit, entering his tent, hoping to find something soft to sleep on. The interior was brightly lit from several small orbs whimsically afloat above his head. Outside the tent was a cold smell of damp rock, but within the tent, Jack felt warmed by the inviting smell of warm bread broken in a small wooden bowl on top of a small table to one side. Several amenities existed throughout; including a small dresser and a large, soft bed smothered in thick, white blankets and oversized pillows. Jack felt like some kind of royalty.

Jack did not mess around with the details of the tent's furnishings. Instead, however, he grabbed a few pieces of the bread, took some water, and quickly jumped into bed. He instantly felt a sense of warmth and rejuvenation. As sleep overtook him, the glowing orbs began to fade until they dissipated into thousands of small flutters that looked like gold flecks floating on an invisible, rippling pool above him.

When Jack woke hours later, the dimly lit flutters of light returned to their orb states and the tent felt awake like the morning sun. He could hear Selini chatting up a cheery storm with Geller. And, he could hear Geller, drearily moaning meaningless affirmations to her words. He stepped out of his tent and waited for a moment for his eyes to adjust to the cold dark of the cave. He saw Geller sitting upon a rock, not far from a small cooking fire in the center of the ring of tents. Selini was just how Jack imagined her, walking around the fire, shuffling through belongings as she prepared meals for the group, looking for anything to serve food on.

"… and I'm telling you now, there's no way the Captain would have let that man go without concessions. I mean, think about it, where do you think he got all those booze for his imbibing partygoers …" Selini stopped immediately upon noticing Jack standing there and quickly rushed over to him with a cheery smile. "Good morning,

Jack!"

She tossed a small hand cloth back towards Geller and grabbed Jack's hand. "Come. Come. I've made some eggs and... various other items I could scrap together." Her face was radiantly lit with her smile.

Geller, on the other hand, was still slightly slouched over a steaming tin with both hands eagerly clasping its sides. He looked up at Jack and gave a slight nod of his head before watching his drink again.

"Don't mind him, he's just little mister grumpy-poo."

Geller adjusted his posture some but remained inactive. Jack grabbed the plate Selini was shoving eagerly into his chest. She then returned to chatting away to Geller as if he cared about what she was saying.

Although Jack had had a good night's rest, he still felt a little groggy. And, while Selini went about with her story, Jack felt it hard to follow since he had not the slightest idea what she was going on about. Whatever it was, she certainly felt it was amusing, as she let out a number of quick laughs.

It was not long at all before the other members of the party trickled out and gathered around the fire for their fair share of Selini's meal. Jack was rather impressed that it tasted so good. Everything was so full of flavor.

"What's she all excited about?" Anna plopped down on a small boulder near Jack.

After thinking for a moment, Jack replied, "I'm not sure."

Anna shook her head and rolled her eyes. "How long have you been out here listening to her?"

"I've been out here for a good ten minutes, but I only listened for one of them." Jack smiled and scooped another glass of his drink, which was something similar to a strong tea that made him feel warm down to his fingertips.

"It's an old story from a long ago quest we were on." Cedric was watching Selini as she walked back and forth from bag to bag, repacking items from the night before and spouting out her story to a continually uneager and equally disinterested Geller. He smiled and looked at the two of them, "It is truly a long story, but it involved a poorly informed strategy based on all sorts of social misinterpretations." He chuckled, "Let's just say Geller was the pun of the seas for decades. Some say the Captain even had one such pun engraved on his tombstone, wherever that may be."

"What did it say?" Anna was definitely more excited than Geller.

Cedric grinned from ear to ear, "I could only guess, but the Captain was buried in an undisclosed location centuries ago. I'm not even sure there's one on it, but I wouldn't put it past him to have had one last jab at Geller."

"Were they enemies?" Jack asked.

Cedric hesitated while searching for his words for a moment, "I'll put it as easily as I can. Geller was certain they were, but in the end, they became comrades with an unbreakable alliance."

Anna was watching Geller, "Poor Geller. Why is Selini making him so miserable with it?"

Gibble fluttered down from his quarters in the roots, "He only looks miserable. Truth is he probably enjoys that story the most." He was scooping his meal into a small, dirty looking bag and slung it around one of his small shoulders and across his chest.

Not long after, all the bags had been repacked and the tents dismantled. Everyone was grabbing their items and the group quickly set out again. The cave remained dark and cool, and without the glow of the fire, the roots above were again glowing and swaying like drifting stars in a snow globe. The path was once again an iridescent blue from the lazily trickling water between the rocks. Conversations began like the day before as the trip progressed, but with less enthusiasm. Their echoes seemed distant as they reverberated throughout the deep and expansive cavern. And as more time passed, the air began to feel thicker and warmer.

Other than the glittering of the path and the roots above, the only light available to them was coming from lanterns hanging from Gibble's and Cedric's necks. Gibble's lantern was much smaller than Cedric's, and when he would take flight, the light would cast shards of shadow and light across the ground and the group. Although it did not prove very useful, it did make it seem like they were moving faster when he flew. Cedric's lantern was much larger and hung by a sturdy chain that looked like it could hold many times more weight than that of the lantern. And Jack could not tell, but it looked as if the same floating lights from inside the tent were the same lights Cedric was using in the lantern.

Jack began to think about where he was just a few days ago, the library in Stonevue. It was hard for him to remember, though. It was as if he had simply forgotten about anything from that afternoon. He could not help but feel this was all his doing, though. Usually his actions had a tendency to get him into some sort of trouble, but nothing he had ever done before got him remotely close to this outcome.

He looked over at Anna and watched as she chatted with Selini. She seemed to have accepted the predicament they were in, but he still felt terrible that she was here. He did not really know much about her, except that she was a quiet girl that worked for the library sometimes. He knew she lived with her mother because her father had died when she was just a few years old.

He looked all around him, wondering why he was there. A sense of fear fell over him as he thought about the confidence everyone had in him to help them win their war. The best he could figure was that he was a good hunter, but that was of animals. He had never fought in any battles before and certainly had no warrior training. The town's militia, which consisted of roughly a hundred men and teenage boys, had even looked him over every year during their annual, drunken recruiting ceremonies. Even then, the militia had little formal training and mostly existed to give its members something to boast about at the taverns.

Jack was concerned there had been a big mistake about who he was and what he was capable of. The wizard Frinkul's and the dragon's deaths were by accident. And he had not even been the one to kill Frinkul, that was done by Geller. Plus, the dragon died by Geller's weapon and the fire of a bigger dragon. Besides Anna, the rest of the party was comprised of people of this world who had experienced many years of combat. Jack knew his self-discouraging thoughts were the last thing they needed right now, but he could not help feeling the whole thing was heading for disaster.

"I think we're getting close to the end of the cave," Anna was now beside Jack. "Selini told me the warmer air is a good sign."

"That's good," Jack's previous train of thought was interrupted, and he gladly switched to a new one. "I can't even tell if it's still day and I keep expecting to walk out into a starry desert. I relish the idea of seeing the sun again."

"Near as I can tell, we're somewhere in the late afternoon." Anna looked like Jack felt, "I'm getting tired of walking in the dark, it feels depressing and I hate the ..."

Clink.

Chapter 16: A Storm in the Darkness

The heaviness of the surrounding darkness and deafening quietness that filled the cavern was suddenly shattered with an abrupt and short metallic clanking sound that came from all their weapons.

All talking ceased immediately and Geller, who was heading the group, stopped and held his hand up to signal for the rest of them to as well. The lanterns quickly faded and became as dark as the night. Before the lights had completely gone out, Jack saw Cedric and Geller grabbing the hilts of their weapons. Then he could hear two small movements of metal against their tight leather wrapping, which he figured must have been Geller's daggers. That was quickly followed by a similar and much longer sound, presumably Cedric's sword. Then there was silence.

After Jack's eyes adjusted to the darkness, he could begin to dimly see the silhouettes of the other members from the light of the path. It did not look as if anyone had moved except for the weapons now in the hands of Geller and Cedric. A small gust of wind blew through Jack's hair and he could feel goose bumps creep up his back and neck. He had felt this feeling before.

Selini whispered, "We need to get off the path, now!"

A small flash of light came from ahead.

"Agreed! Get off the path!" Geller spoke with urgency and loud enough for anyone else in the vicinity to hear. "And get into the darkness."

Jack followed Anna as best as he could see. More flashes came from several sides now. He put his hand out to hold the back of Anna's bag in hopes of not losing her or the group. His hand felt nothing and all he could see was the pitch black in front of his eyes. He began fumbling hurriedly for anyone or anything else. His foot caught something hard and small and he fell to the ground with a loud crash as his bags lost some of their contents across the rocky floor. Several more flashes came, and they were nearer to each other in distance and time. He clumsily attempted to grab his belongings from all around him, shoving various items in as quickly as possible. He stood up but could not tell if he was turned around now.

"Jack! C'mon!" Anna's voice was much farther away than he had anticipated, and he did not know which direction it came from.

The wind was much stronger now and growing every moment. Jack felt overwhelmingly lost and feared this was the same thing that happened before. The flashes were coming from all over now and thunder began to ensue. Now he had no chance of hearing Anna or anyone else's voice. He knew he would struggle hearing her if she had been right next to him.

Jack tried spinning around, looking for anything that might catch his eyes. Then he noticed the path about a hundred feet in front of him. He could not believe how easy it was to see with all the lightning, but he figured he would take what he could. Knowing the path was behind previously, he turned and set off as quickly as he could in the opposite direction. It was easier this time because he could see the ground with some concentration.

Then, small iridescent raindrops began falling slowly. As they hit the rocks, they splattered little crystals of light and the cavern started becoming illuminated. He could hear the sound of rushing water from behind him, so he turned and saw the once quiet path was now spewing water high into the air. Its light illuminated dark, swirling and rapidly moving clouds that shot lightning from all directions.

Suddenly he felt his arm being pulled and he swung around in a startled scare. It was Gibble. He was shouting something to him, but he could not hear anything over the monstrous thunder and rushing water. He followed him as fast as he could, but the water on the ground was rising fast and his legs were tiring as they worked their way through it. Everything was lit as far as he could see now with the same iridescent blue from the water in the path. Only about fifty feet ahead were the others getting into a rowboat.

The wind was howling so loudly now, Jack could hardly think. The water was rising fast and the wind driven rain felt like sand blasting the back of his head. Numbness was overtaking his legs and feet. The howling of the wind turned to an all-out roar that filled his ears and it carried a strange sound like thunder, but constant against all the other sounds.

Lightning flashes were making it difficult to see anything and he was beginning to feel a sense of hopelessness. The light of the water was no longer a dim iridescence, but had become like the noon sky, bright and blue. The thrashing waves became stronger and stronger and he could feel the water pulling him against his will. The rain was hardly visible anymore, overtaken by the bright flashes and sky-blue waters. And, although incredibly well-lit now, the cavern became a confusing mess of lights and sound that overtook his senses. He no longer knew what he was trying to do, except to try and stay alive in that very moment.

At this point, Jack could hardly move his tired legs anymore. There was a strong undercurrent that fought Jack's every move in any direction. The water was just above his shoulders now. Gibble was furiously pulling on Jack while fighting against the raging wind and cresting waves that were overtaking them both. Water was now making its way into Jack's mouth as he gasped for air. He could no longer keep his head above the waves and his feet no longer found refuge on the rock below.

It was then that Jack realized Gibble was no longer holding on to him. He did not know when, but the two had now become separated and he was sure there was no chance he could find him again. Another wave crashed over Jack and the undercurrent swept him back and under the water. Any attempt to kick against the water was now futile.

When each wave subsided and before the next was sure to ensue, Jack allowed himself to sink to the bottom and used his best effort to kick against it. He shot straight up as hard as he could and broke through the surface. Under the water had been a muffled version of the air above, and as he broke through the water's surface, the noise once again took over his senses. He flailed as best as he could, hoping against all odds that he would be seen by Gibble. Only a second later, the next wave crushed him back into the waters below and the current pulled him much farther this time.

All hope was gone from his thoughts. He tried again to rise to the surface, but the water was deeper this time and it took longer. As he gasped for air once again, another wave overtook him.

Struggling with all he had, Jack gave another effort to push against the bottom and into the air. But this time was different. As he rose to the surface, his trajectory was intercepted by something massive. The flashes of lightning were for a moment blanketed out by a dark figure. Jack opened his eyes and could see he was blocked from resurfacing. He panicked. He did not know where to go. If he went down and tried again after the object passed over him, he might lose his chance to get around it. If he tried going around it now, he would surface just as another wave came crashing down and would only get a mouthful of water as a reward for his effort.

Assuming this was a log or some other piece of cave junk, he tried going around it. But as he neared it, he could see a distinct shape he knew very well. His field of vision was now filled with hundreds of large scales, like those of the dragons he had encountered before.

Turning as fast as he could, Jack swam downward. He did not know what he was going to do, but he did not want to just give himself over freely without a fight, or what little fight he could put up. There was little time. He had now missed air for three breaks in the waves and was feeling an overwhelming need to open his mouth and take in whatever he could to appease his aching lungs. He fought the urge to do this and instead grabbed onto a large boulder on the bottom and anchored himself to it the best he could. He smashed his face into his arm to keep himself from opening his mouth. His body was becoming less willing to follow his direction and was now beginning to try anything to get him to open his mouth and take in some air.

Jack was fading and his thoughts were panicked and incoherent. There was little he could do to get the surface now, which was higher up than he could guess. The water at the bottom was becoming much quieter, even with the loud crashes of thunder still shaking the floor of the cavern. As he watched the dark figure of a dragon above him swim in methodical circles with little negative effect of the fast-moving waters, he noticed several more coming in. He watched as a dragon made its way to the bottom and began swimming above and between the very boulders Jack was hiding in. It was quickly approaching, and Jack looked down at the boulder, looking for anything to hide under. His lungs ached and he was feeling despaired. He was trapped and there was nothing he could do to prevent his being found.

Then, Jack saw a small stream of bubble coming from a crack in the boulder next to him. He scanned it intently, looking for any kind of cavity he could duck into. He saw one. Without thought, he thrust himself away from his current anchor and into the small cavity. He struggled hard to squeeze in and knew this would be the place he would last know. There was no turning back at this point, regardless of the dragons. His last breath had been too long ago, and his senses were nearly gone. He could hardly keep his eyes open at this point and everything was becoming dark. He was still fighting against the urge to breathe in the water and his chest was beginning to convulse.

The dragon was now almost on top of him just as he got his feet to finally fit in. He squirmed in the rest of the way into the interior of the cavity and found the top of his head was above water. He struggled against the tight walls of the boulder's interior and situated his mouth into the air. He gasped as hard as he could. Never had air felt so good entering his lungs, which were now on fire in searing pain even as life filled them anew.

He continued to gasp over and over. He felt tired. His body was numb, but he could feel it reviving as he panted in the air. He knew this was going to be short lived, though, as the water was slowly creeping up past his chin. The air had been leaking from a crack in the rock, but Jack still felt a sense of euphoria as he sat there with his body twisted oddly to accommodate the fit of the cavity.

Within a few moments, the air was just about to be impossible to retrieve. Jack was scared that he was about to endure lack of breath all over again. He tried to prepare himself and calm his mind, but the tightness of his position just added to the feeling that he was about to drown. Before he could take his last breath, however, the boulder smashed into a hundred pieces. His body was now freely floating in the water and the last of the air he clung to so desperately was making its way to the surface in a hurry. He was confused. He did not know if he was hurt or what had happened, but that quickly became evident. He had been found.

The dragon had used its tail to smash open the boulder and was still swinging it violently about. Another boulder smashed open, then another. Some simply bounced around like pebbles in a stream and others disintegrated like the one he was in. He realized the dragon had not known which boulder he was in. He took cover as quickly as he could amongst other boulders. He watched more boulders get smashed with the same fate as his. Then he realized that there must be dozens of these rocks with air pockets in them. He felt excited and simultaneously fearful. It would not be long before all of the boulders in the vicinity were destroyed, leaving him nothing to hide in. But, if he tried swimming away, he would surely be noticed. Whatever he was going to do, though, was now too late. Another dragon had spotted him.

Now dozens of dragons were swirling in. He had nowhere to go, so he decided to do the one thing he could do. He swam up as fast as he could, toward the belly of another dragon. He grabbed onto its scales and clung on as tightly as he could. Another dragon breathed a fireball toward him, and it hit his dragon just feet from him. He felt a sudden flash of heat in the water and the cool water quickly takeover once again. His dragon, however, was now thrashing about and swimming directly upward. It flew out of the surface of the water and several other dragons began throwing fire at it. Jack was airborne now as he held on to the burning dragon.

He did not know what to do, but he was now in the air, which gave him some hope of getting away. It was not long before his dragon began to falter in its flight, the damage from the flames to its body was too much for it to overcome and his body was losing its rigidity.

The other dragons did not care they were killing one of their own. They were willing to sacrifice it for the life of Jack. The roar of the air outside of the water was again too much for Jack. The thunder was constant, and the wind was louder than he could bear. Then, he lost his grip and fell back into the water. The dragon crashed not far from him and the others were swooping, looking for any sign of Jack. It was not long before they found him and he ducked into the water, trying to avoid the extreme heat of the ensuing flames.

Once under water, he saw dozens more coming from every direction. He knew now there was nothing else he could do. He swam to the body of the dead dragon and hoped to use it as a shield for as long as possible. Once his head popped back above the water, his ears filled with a roaring sound like none other.

Several balls of fire flew at him from everywhere, but suddenly changed direction. The fire swirled around and around before disappearing into the storm. Some of the dragons were now frantically flying away, with some going the same way as their flames, up and around until they also disappeared. But Jack could not see what it was. The constant lightning made it difficult to distinguish rain and clouds, all of which were swirling violently around them. Before Jack could do anything else, the dragon's body began to pull out of the water and, despite any effort of his, so did Jack.

In only a few seconds he was now far above the raging water below and was part of something more horrific. All the air in his lungs seemed to be pushed out and it was increasingly difficult to replenish them. Some of the dragons must have kept close, though, because Jack found himself in the midst of a firestorm. Fireball after fireball lined the sides of the funnel wall. Lightning strikes were just barely missing him as they shot through the center and the thunderous roar overtook all other sounds. He could hear no thunder or dragons' wings or the fireballs that were so narrowly missing him. His head was filled with a singular sound of confusion. It was then that he realized he was being sucked up into an immense waterspout.

Jack was sure he was about to lose consciousness and fought his hardest to stay awake. The changing pressures and rapid spinning made it hard to keep a clear mind. Jack struggled hopelessly against the winds to do anything to get out of the funnel. He did not have the slightest clue as to what he needed to do or what he would do if he was able to free himself. The dragons would surely be waiting to finish the job if the twister had not already.

Suddenly, the roar around him began to fade and other sounds penetrated his senses. He could now hear the thunder of the lightning and the thrashing of the waves below. He could also begin to see the cresting waves. Something was even more wrong now than before. The twister was fading, and Jack was left a hundred feet in the air amongst high winds and lightning. He could feel the relief in his lungs as he filled them with air once again. And then, it was over. The twister was gone. Nothing but remnants of its existence remained. And he fell.

Plummeting back down, he was again surrounded by fireballs. He dodged them the best he could as he fell to the maddening water below. Another fireball shot from under the water and straight up to him. He grabbed a silver object which was once part of the twister's plunder and used it to shield himself from the fire. It was only about half his size, but he managed to curl up enough to stave off the brunt of the blast from hitting him directly. He screamed as the metallic object heated in front of him and the blast stopped momentarily. Another was surely on its way, and Jack knew he could hardly stand the heat another time. He was hoping the object did not melt or shatter on the next blast.

Another flame was coming right at him and he ducked again behind the object and winced as the intense heat mostly deflected past him. Once the flame stopped, Jack could hear, over all the winds and constant thunder, the raindrops boiling away as they hit the object from all sides. That is when he noticed that he had not fallen very far from when the twister ended a few moments prior. His descent was much slower than he expected. This brought a new worry. He was not going to get into the cool water in enough time.

Jack now feared he was going to fry before he drowned. He could not think of which was worse but knew he would prefer another choice. Again, another flame smashed into his makeshift shield. This time he had to push away from the object. Its radiant heat was now too much to bear being close to. He kicked it away and watched as his only chance of staying alive drifted slowly away. As it spiraled, he noticed the raindrops were now flash boiling. Several fireballs were coming at him now from different directions. He curled into a ball, squeezed his legs into his chest and closed his eyes. The inevitable was about to happen and he knew there were no more options.

The moment before the blasts found him, he could feel the air suddenly become intensely hot. The wind-driven rain no longer felt cool, but instead was like boiling droplets of water on his skin. But, the most incredibly unexpected thing happened. The fireballs all dispersed at the very moment they should have disintegrated him. He felt the sudden coolness of the air and the rain and he opened his eyes in surprise.

Expecting to see Selini or Geller, he opened them back up and looked in every direction. The flashing lightning and bright rainwater made it difficult to distinguish most of the shapes. He did see, however, that the fireballs initially intended for him were now blasting the very dragons that had shot at him. Unable to do so before, he could now make out the locations of each of these dragons. They flew violently and rapidly through the air, seemingly unaffected by the turbulent windstorm they flew in. He heard a searing noise below him and saw the metallic object from before now gliding into the water. He was almost to the water's rough surface as well.

A dark object was making its way up from below him and he expected to see another blast of fire any second. But it kept rising without shooting. After seeing what just happened, Jack was not surprised it might just try eating him or impaling him with its barbed tail instead. As it got closer, though, Jack made out a shape that was different than the dragons. Then it surfaced directly below him and a sturdy, metal hatch popped open. There stood Geller yelling something to somebody in the vessel. Gibble flew out and clumsily fought through the wind and grabbed Jack. He assisted his dissent straight into the hatch and Geller slammed it shut.

Jack laid on the floor for a moment, noticing just how weak he had become from the ordeal. Anna rushed over to him along with Cedric and they quickly propped him into a small cot along one of the walls. He gazed around and saw Selini steering the ship under water as she sat in front of a very large, protruding window. The view was clear as day and he recognized the landscape very well from only minutes before. They were making their way over the smashed rock field where Jack had most definitely been before. There was a large spherical window on the floor as well and he could see the rocks passing below them.

In only a moment's time, he watched as the path they had been following for more than a day was still intact and Selini adjusted her course to match its heading. He now noticed just how quiet the inside of the underwater boat was compared to the outside. His ears were throbbing, and a loud ringing sensation had taken place of all the wind and thunder.

Anna was bent over Jack yelling something at him, but he could not understand her over the deafening ringing. He watched as Cedric's mouth was moving as well. It looked like everyone was yelling, but he could not tell to whom or about what. Jack attempted to sit up on his own and quickly fell flat onto the floor. He watched several pairs of feet as he felt his body being raised back into the cot. Then, the floor began to spin, and darkness surrounded his outer vision. All the color faded away from everything and the last remaining light finally faded into oblivion.

Chapter 17: The Kanayabe Steppe

Jack awoke to sunlight breaking through the fabric of his tent. The glittery light was once again reforming into small, drifting orbs above him. He lay still for a moment and wondered if this was real or if he had died. He struggled to remember what happened. But flashes of it were filling his thoughts erratically and were mostly incoherent. He felt warm and was surrounded by the softness of the tent's oversized pillows. The sunlight, though, made him feel safe.

He pulled himself out of bed and instantly felt all the soreness of his endeavors aching in every bone and muscle. He sat at the edge of his bed for a bit while he tried to muster the energy it was going to take to get up and walk against this physical drain. He took a big breath in and winced at the pain in his chest. His hands were covered in heat sores and his legs felt as if they were the weight of anvils.

There was bread once again in a small wooden bowl sitting on a small table. He reached and grabbed a chunk. It was still warm and had a light crisp as he bit through its crust. The taste filled his mouth with delightful sensations and the empty feeling in his stomach suddenly took over all other pains. He ate quickly, trying to appease his growling stomach. After a few chunks, he took his fill of water from a jug sitting next to the bowl. It was refreshingly cool for the environment. Then it hit him. The air in the tent was surprisingly cooler than he was expecting, too.

A mirror that stood atop the dresser reflected back Jack's swollen and bruised face and chest. He looked awful, and he felt it too. He saw his clothes hanging from the back of a chair and started putting them on. They were cleaned and there was noticeable stitch work in several places. Other places still showed signs of searing from encounters with the dragons. And, as he put his mended clothes back on, he began wondering just how they were able to escape. He finished putting on his shoes, which was no easy task with burned hands and unforgiving leg muscles.

Walking outside, Jack was greeted by the beating sun. It blinded him and its heat felt much worse on his weakened skin.

"Ahhhhh!"

A voice called from nearby. Jack squinted, trying to adjust his eyes better. He could see several figures sitting around the remnants of an old fire.

"Jack!" He knew Anna's voice well. She ran to him and greeted him with as big of a hug as she could give for her slender arms. "I was … I thought you'd … Well, you're okay and that's what matters!" She was tearing up, "I'm so glad you made it."

His eyes were now mostly adjusted, and he could see all of them surrounding him, each giving their bit of relief.

"What the heck happened?" Jack meant for his first words to be more eloquently spoken but did not regret the question.

Selini grabbed his hand and led him to a position near the fire pit. "Sit, sit. You'll need to continue resting for a few days before you've regained your strength." She looked him over, "You've gotta be feeling pretty sore still. How's your pain?"

Jack did not know how to answer. He wanted to say exactly how he felt, but he was not sure how. He also was not sure if he should let them know that he felt a few days would not cover it. He felt like it would take months to undo his damage. He did not want to give the group any more despair than he was sure they had already encountered themselves.

Before he could answer the questions, Geller chimed in, "How do you think it is?" he asked Selini. His tone made him sound as if he was annoyed for Jack and not himself. He put his hand on Jack and looked up at him in the eyes, like he was trying to read their stories, "We're all sure whatever happened to you was no mistake, no freak accident."

"You guys don't know what happened?" Jack felt like he was all alone in his pain. He now noticed how none of them had repaired clothes or bruising like his. "Dragons?" He gestured to the seared edges of his cuffs and his burned hands. "Anyone?" No answer ensued. "Nobody?"

Anna spoke softly, "Jack, we all made it to the boat before things got real bad."

Jack put his face in his hands. He was relieved none of the others were hurt badly, but it was unsettling how everyone else made it out unscathed.

"Jack," Cedric spoke as softly as his booming voice could, "The whole thing appears to have been set into motion to kill you. Until we picked you up, we didn't have any problems navigating the waters or the air, besides the storm itself."

"We could see dragons everywhere," Selini spoke informatively, "and I mean everywhere. There were dozens, maybe even hundreds, and they were in the water and in the air. We just couldn't find you." Her voice dropped at the last comment, showing her sympathy for not finding him sooner.

Still cradling his face, Jack asked, "Why didn't you guys just start with where the fire was?"

At this point Geller chimed in, "Jack?" He again held Jack's shoulder, "It was a confusing string of events, even we were caught off guard. I assure you; we are ashamed of the outcome. In hindsight, I'm sure we could have handled things better, but we're here. We're alive. We can still prevail." He sounded confident in his words, but Jack could not help but remember all the anguish he endured.

"Not to mention they were breathing fire pretty much everywhere and at anything." Gibble's voice squeaked as he tried to defend their position.

Hushing him, Selini motioned for Gibble to keep quiet.

"Well then, how *did* you find me?" Jack's curiosity overcame his anger. He remembered how difficult it was to see or think in the storm.

"Well," Cedric responded, "we were looking hard. We tried following every dragon's breath we could, thinking one of them may have been aimed at you. But then we saw something that really stood out..." he looked to Geller for further explanation.

Geller took the cue immediately, "Like Gibble said, they were breathing all sorts of fire, like they were moving in on something. The whole thing was strange, but what we saw, what led us to you, was incredibly out of the ordinary." He paused, apparently stuck on what to say.

Selini had no problems with taking over as she continued for him, "Out of nowhere, we watched as dozens of fireballs instantly scattered from one singular source and struck dead as many dragons. It wasn't a hard decision to at least check it out."

"And there you were, slowly falling from the air into the water." Anna finished for the group. "How you got there is still a puzzle to us, though."

"I think the whole thing will need some explaining" Geller looked at Jack inquisitively.

Jack was no longer cradling his face but was feeling very tired. His sudden exhaustion must have shown because Selini began grabbing some food and water for him to eat.

"That's a story for later," she said speaking to Geller. "For now, you need to replenish your body and get plenty of rest."

Jack ate what he could and laid down on the ground next to the firepit. When he woke again, he was watching the desert move away from him in a slow and methodical up and down motion. He was puzzled at this new view and was unsure of where everyone was. Then he heard the familiar voices of Geller and Selini from behind him. They were deep into conversation. After a moment, he figured he was riding in a makeshift sling on someone's back. He had no doubt it was Cedric's. He still felt tired and his body still ached, but it felt better than before. He pulled a hand loose and glanced at it. The sores showed signs of advanced healing.

He spoke out, "Hello?"

Cedric stopped and turned so the others in the group could see Jack.

"How long have I been out?"

Selini responded, "You've been in and out for several days. This is the first time you've spoken since we last talked, though. Which, I think is a good sign."

Anna looked relieved, "You're looking much better, Jack." She smiled and Jack felt better with the gesture.

"Can I get down from here? I've gotta be slowing us down."

Cedric spoke, "It is better to be slowed momentarily than to be slower the whole time."

"He's right," Geller affirmed, "It will be nearly impossible to carry you through the mountains. You should gather as much strength as you can to return to a normal state before then, else we will be impossibly pressed to complete the mission at hand. We only have fourteen days left."

Jack was surprised to hear this news, "Fourteen?! I've slowed us down too much already! Have we even made it through the sandstorms yet?"

"At this rate, we shall be greeted with that tomorrow afternoon." Geller spoke nonchalantly.

"So, we're almost out of the Desert of Gilia?" Jack asked. He was slightly impressed with himself for remembering the name of the desert.

Geller flashed a faked smile, "We're still in the Kanayabe Steppe, the barren land before the desert."

Jack looked around, "You've gotta be kidding. This isn't a desert?"

He could see little semblance of life and the little vegetation that existed were dry and coarse.

"Jack," Anna spoke now, "the Gilia Desert has no vegetation and almost nothing lives in it. It will be difficult."

Jack felt overwhelmed by how far behind they were, "I don't see how we're going to make it in time. And all I've done is slow us down tremendously."

"We must remain committed to the outcome," Cedric spoke up.

Gibble's voice broke in, "If we fail, everything we know is lost. And if we stop now, if we start questioning our ability to succeed... we can't fail, we can't stop. We will prevail."

Jack did not feel any better but did not want to be a drag on their committed efforts. He simply nodded in agreeance.

"We must not hesitate any longer," Geller began walking ahead, "if we're to make up ground. Cedric, if you please, could you walk ahead?"

Cedric made his way to the front of the group so that Jack was now facing the remaining members.

Geller then asked Jack, "Now then, Jack, do you feel up to recollecting for us the events that transpired in the cavern?"

Over the course of the next hour, Jack retold his account of what happened during the storm in the cavern. It took a while to get from the beginning to the end because of all the questions they all had at various points. Once he was finished telling it, though, he had a question of his own.

"You've been asking me questions about the color of the dragons and sounds I heard," Jack was asking Geller, "but why are you concerned with these details over others? And where did you get an underwater boat?"

Anna quickly jumped at the opportunity to answer the question about the boat. She seemed excited and amazed at the possibility of it.

"That was Selini!" She said happily. "She has a small boat in her bag that she can make bigger!"

"I *had* a small boat in my bag. It was an enchanted boat made to be the size of a trinket. It's only good for one use, though." She sounded a little disappointed. "I was hoping we could use it later, but I really didn't see any other way."

"I thought you all were getting into a rowboat." Jack seemed a little confused.

"It was a rowboat at first, but it was enchanted to adapt to what was needed. It wasn't designed to be shrunk back down, so I couldn't bring it back with us. Which is why I said it's only good for one use." She sounded a little concerned now as well.

"Are there other details you feel I should know?" Geller asked unfazed by the conversation about the boat.

Jack shrugged, "I didn't even know you wanted the details you wanted, so, no, I don't think so."

"We're concerned with the details for two reasons," Geller responded to the original question, "the best account of what happened for the record keepers in the Panthyun and to attempt to ascertain who or what caused such chaos and for what reason."

"I thought you said it was because someone was trying to kill me."

"Yes, that much seems clear as day, but why you were the target is still a mystery," Geller stated.

Anna spoke, "Maybe it was out of revenge for Jack killing one of them before?"

She seemed proud for a fleeting moment for having deduced the motive.

"If that were truly the case," Selini was adding her thoughts now, "what caused the storm? Plus, they seemed more in disarray than in an organized revenge. I think it's pretty clear they were there for Jack, but I don't think they were there on their own recognizance."

Not caring about the current discussion, Geller asked, "The metallic object you used as a shield, what did it look like?"

"I really don't know. Things were spinning around me, the lightning was striking right past me, and fireballs were just missing me. I didn't take a good look at it." Jack was puzzled as to Geller's sudden interest in it and he saw Geller looking through a small book.

Selini also took interest in Geller's question and noticed his little book, too. "You aren't thinking it's...?"

Geller didn't answer.

"It's what?" Anna asked.

"We've got something on the horizon!" Gibble had been flying just over the group.

"Everyone down," Geller spouted out in a loud whisper.

He quickly stowed his book and hurried to a nearby boulder. He watched for a moment, then motioned for something from Selini. She rummaged through a bag and pulled out a small magnifying glass, which she tossed to Geller.

Without looking at what landed in his hand, Geller raised the magnifying glass to his eye and looked through. Quickly he jerked his head back and looked at it. He rolled his eyes and snapped his fingers, causing the magnifying glass to form into a spyglass. There was silence for a moment, then Geller turned and faced the rest of the group.

"I can't make him out yet, he's too small and my view keeps getting blocked by the rocks. But he's running right towards us."

"Do you think he's coming for us?" Anna asked.

"I don't think whoever it is knows we're here. He's only a few hundred feet now, close enough to have cast a damaging spell if he wanted."

Cedric drew his sword slowly. Selini watched as Geller did not motion otherwise. Taking note of this, she drew her weapon as well. Jack felt trapped. If anything happened to Cedric, if he were to be pierced through, Jack would be killed as well. He did not have his weapons or armor on him either.

Ducking back down, Geller motioned for silence, "Here he comes."

Within the moment, Jack could hear festive, but bad singing from two different voices. He could not tell what they were singing about, but they did not sound like they were there to do harm. Although the others still remained at the ready, he felt relieved. Then the voices could not have been more than twenty feet when Geller, Selini, and Cedric jumped from behind the rocks.

Jack could not see what was happening while Cedric faced the two who had been singing. But he heard Geller's angry voice loud and clear.

"YOU TWO!" He exclaimed with familiarity.

Chapter 18: Gink and Fink

Obviously startled, one of the singing individuals let out a high pitched, "AHHHHHH!!"

Jack smirked at the sound of it. He imagined a barmaid seeing a large spider in an empty pint glass.

Geller spoke sternly, "What are a couple misfits like you doing all the way out here?"

Cedric answered for them, "Up to no good is what they're doing. Nobody comes this far out without good reason."

A small but hearty voice replied back, "We might ask you the same."

Anna and Gibble had now appeared from behind the rocks having determined the situation was not as dire as they thought. Jack saw Anna's face as she came out and watched an oddly contorted look turn into somewhat of a smirk. Now, Jack really wanted down. He wanted to know just what they were dealing with.

"We're asking the questions here!" Geller responded swiftly to the remark.

One of the individuals must have noticed Anna, "Well looky 'ere. You've been roundin up the pigs have ya? They've got a human, Gink."

The two laughed and chuckled in a maniacal sort of way that made Jack feel uneasy.

Anna's face clearly showed disgust toward them now, "I'll have you know I most obviously bathe more in a week than the two of you probably have combined."

Jack felt Cedric chuckle quietly.

The two gasped and one quickly retorted, "Wh....?! How dare you speak to Gink and Fink!" Now he was obviously speaking to Cedric, "Why aren't you controlling your bounty? It is disgusting, filthy, and absolutely abhorrent!"

Cedric replied coolly, "She is not my bounty, she is my friend with whom I travel. And, it is you that I will not tolerate speaking with that foul tongue. Anyway, she is right, I believe we could've smelled you coming well before seeing you."

There were some muffled murmurs between Gink and Fink before a reply was made by Fink, who had done most of the talking, "A friend, eh? Since when does the Ambassador, under threat of death for such a travesty, carry in his company a human?" Some smirking took place between the two, "We would very much like to live today and see your fate tomorrow, than to take up swords with you now."

Jack could hear a small sword returning to its sheath, which must have been pulled when they were surprised. Then, he felt Cedric's body relax some and the motion of his sword returning as well. Selini and Geller followed suit.

Anna asked, "Do you all know each other?"

"Ehhh..." Gink and Fink were still unsure of how to respond to a human and were obviously bothered by her nonchalant manner of addressing them. "Is it obvious?" Fink replied.

Selini spouted back hastily, "Cedric has informed you that our guests are our friends. I will not remind you again, else you will lose your tongue. And, from the looks of things, you're running low on body parts to lose. Be mindful of your words."

"How do you know each other?" Anna restated her question.

Geller spoke, "He is Fink and his back rider is Gink, whom we like to call Gimp. If you'll notice there, Gimp is missing his legs."

Jack could not tell, but it sounded like Geller was pleased to point that fact out.

"IT'S NOT GIMP!" A high pitched, screechy-like voice yelled out. Jack was sure it was Fink who said it.

Again, Cedric's body shook with a silent chuckle. It was clear to Jack that the group did not care much for the visitors and were not afraid to show it.

"Alright, that's enough. It's not Gimp," Selini spoke, "If we'd like them to show our guests some respect, I think we can give them a little."

"And who might you be carrying, Ambassador?" Fink snapped.

Cedric turned around to show Jack to them and he finally got to see the singing visitors.

A large grin from ear to ear filled the small face of a man that stood only three feet off the ground. He was covered in gritty rags and numerous pouches that were attached to his belt, legs, and chest and many pockets adorned his clothes. They also appeared to be filled with many items. His hair was frazzled badly and quite unkempt. It also appeared as if it could be the home of some nesting creature.

His eyes were overly large, and the surrounding skin showed signs of prolonged goggle wearing. His nose was also larger than would be expected, along with his ears. His hands had long fingers and the skin on them was thick. His skin was covered in wrinkles, caked with dirt, dust, and sweat. Jack could now see why Anna made her comment earlier regarding his bathing. Attached to his back by custom-made leather straps and a large sack, was another man similar in looks to Fink. It was Gink.

"What happened to you?" Fink asked.

"I might ask the same." Jack responded back.

Fink's hands were suddenly being surrounded by a purplish glowing strand of what appeared to be chain.

"You're coming with us," Geller said. He then returned to their course.

Geller was really pressing on, and Jack knew they must be further behind than he led on before.

Struggling to not follow, Fink protested, "I THINK NOT! WE ARE VERY BUSY!" But, no matter how hard he resisted, the chain, not visually attached to anything from what Jack could tell, pulled Fink with the group when he got more than a few paces behind.

Selini walked next to them, holding an open scroll and reading from it:

> *It is hereby declared that the Sle'indo pair, known as Fink and Gink, self-proclaimed bombardiers and merchants of magical enchantments, must be captured dead or alive upon contact or shall be revealed by those with information regarding their whereabouts or reveal to the Valindi those who may have such information. This is under order of the Valindi and its Allies for treasons against the Great Alliance of the Govilian Council for colluding, cooperating, and informing the Reign in matters considered to be a threat to the overall security of the Great Alliance and all those who oppose the Reign.*
>
> *Bounty for their living capture is a pardon for a previously committed crime (treason not withstanding), and capture by death is for any previously committed crime including one count of treason and 10,000 valins.*

She continued, "So, you see Fink and Gink, you two are going to travel with us and we have every right to make you. Seeing as we cannot bring you in immediately, we will bring you with us. And, don't you think about slowing us down. It sounds like the bounty is higher if you're brought in dead."

Eyes as wide as they could get, Fink screeched out, "Wha... we've never done those things."

Gink shouted out, "Intentionally!"

Fink elbowed him and continued, "This whole thing is rubbish an' we aim to contest it for all the Valindi to see in the Court of the Panthyun."

"It sounds like you have some sort of show ready to put on already," Cedric shouted back without turning.

"I believe that is why the bounty is higher if you're dead. Less show, more justice." Geller sounded delighted to point that fact out again.

"We take care to ask all our … purchasers … if they're working for the Reign before we make any deals," Gink called out.

"That sounds like a fool-proof method, doesn't it?" Selini asked rhetorically. "I don't see how anyone could possibly get past that ironclad *security* question."

"We're law-abiding citizens, and I don't think we should have to answer to anyone for the unfortunate misuse of our products," Fink sounded resolved with this expression.

Gibble stopped in his steps and turned to the pair of bombardiers, "Try taking that snobbish, arrogant, idiotic response to the people of Brookenvale. Or maybe have it inscribed on all their headstones, since they were massacred by the Reign last fall by the use of your so-called 'product'!"

Gibble was shaking in anger and Geller had stopped the group. Fink looked as if he was going to respond, but Geller spoke first.

"I would recommend holding your tongue, Fink. Else, your last words will be a mockery of your crimes." He reached out to Gibble, "Come. Walk with me, my friend."

For a moment the group waited in silence while Gibble glared at the pair with his hand held firmly to his short sword still in its sheath. Then, he turned and walked in front of the group with Geller and they resumed their course.

The bombardiers whispered some words of disdain, but were

quickly hushed by Selini, who had taken to giving a rather painful looking flick to one of each of their ears without uttering a sound.

It was hard for Jack to not look at them. He was being carried on Cedric's back and was facing right at them. Fink kept a watchful eye on him and would occasionally make a childish face. Jack returned the favor several times.

Now the group walked in silence and dusk was slowly setting in. Jack stopped caring if Fink saw him staring, and really started to examine their prisoners.

It was evident Gink was missing both legs, but more damage seemed to have been done to his head. Part of his scalp was hairless and scarred up. His left ear was mostly gone as well. The remaining hair was long and thin, revealing most of the remaining scalp. Fink did not appear to tire from carrying the weight of his brother, despite his short legs having to move twice as fast to keep up with the rest of the group.

Jack could see all sorts of trinkets bulging from a variety of pockets on Fink. He also had a couple thin, long containers slung over a shoulder that contained a number of scrolls. There were potions hanging and clinking together around his waist and hanging from the bottom of Gink's carrying bag, some were tiny vials and others were nearly the size of jugs. It seemed impossible that anyone would so readily and willingly carry so much junk in the middle of this landscape. Some of his pockets had feathers and others had various odd items, like small animal bones and roots. More pouches existed on Fink's clothes than Jack could count, and they were as varied in size as the vials. He noticed a short sword hanging off Fink's belt, but no other weaponry.

Jack could not resist asking, "What *were* you two doing way out here, anyway?"

Without a pause, Fink replied, "Looking for business, of course."

Jack pondered out loud, "Seems like business must not be doing so well if you're out here looking for sales."

Cedric chimed in, "Don't let him fool you. What he means is that they were selling to someone who didn't want to be seen buying from them."

Fink did not reply or attempt to make a correction to Cedric's statement, but instead shrugged in affirmation.

"What do you sell?" Jack asked.

They both replied simultaneously, "We've got everything you need."

Then just Gink, "From a quart of mead..."

And finished by Fink, "To a magical creed."

And together again, "Gink and Fink's Wondrous Feed!"

"Feed?" Jack asked.

The two tried explaining their name, but Fink finally admitted, "It's a work in process. 'Creations' didn't rhyme well and threw the whole thing off."

"Ha," Selini laughed, "More like 'From a weak mead to a magical misdeed, we've got nothing but greed.'"

"Ha ha." Fink did not look amused.

"How about," now Cedric chimed in, "'We'll take your money and give you crap, Gink and Fink's Stupid Stuff.'"

"Now you're not even trying," Gink shot back. "Besides, who would buy from us with that kind of tag line?"

Fink elbowed him again.

Jack smiled, but he could not tell if Gink was serious or not.

Fink replied back, "Say what you will. Say what you will. Business has been good to us."

"At least it has been to you," Selini gestured at his legs.

Holding a finger up to affirm his coming remarks, he stated, "Now, now. What happened to Gink could have happened to anyone."

Correcting his logic, Geller shouted back, "Anyone experimenting with explosives, fire, and magic in the hopes of making a few extra valin."

"It could easily have been me that happened to." Fink responded back, still holding his finger up as he spoke.

"Of course, Gink was made aware of all possible outcomes of just such an experiment," Selini was smiling.

"He wouldn't have done it if he thought it was more dangerous than normal," Fink quickly retorted. "I don't like what you're getting at."

"What am I getting at, Fink?" Selini asked.

With a heavy sigh, he replied back, "All I'm saying is that he knew what he was doing, and it was a freak accident."

"Really?" Selini sounded surprised and amused at the same time, "So, you're saying Gink knew the compound he was constructing consisted of one of the most volatile exploding fairy sands known?"

"Yes!" Fink retorted back.

"No!" Gink sounded surprised.

"Well, maybe not entirely aware, but, like I said, it could have easily happened to me had I been the one experimenting that day."

"I think you made sure it wasn't you doin' the experimenting that day," Cedric commented.

"Again, I don't like what you're getting at here," Fink shot back angrily.

Selini, still smiling, replied back, "You don't have to like it to make it true."

"Is this true, Fink?" Gink asked.

Fink looked bewildered and flat out mad now, "I love my brother and would never have intentionally put him in harm's way. What happened to him is the nature of our business. We make a livin' doin' things others aren't willin' to do! Sometimes that puts us at risk of gettin' all sorts of messed up!" He was puffing and red in the face, "So, no, Gink, it's not true. These fellas are just trying to get us all bothered!"

Selini looked pleased at Fink's dismay. "I guess time will tell."

Looking at Jack, Fink said, "We're good folk, we are. Just trying to make a livin'. That's all."

Cedric whispered back to Jack, "Just doing it illegally and at the expense of everyone else."

Fink looked embarrassed at his show of anger. And Jack felt a little sorry for him. Even if he had been responsible for Gink's accident, Jack figured he must have felt bad since he carries him around.

"Could you make a remedy to regrow his extremities?" Jack asked.

"Maybe someday," Fink said sadly. He did not look too hopeful.

Gink spoke out as well, "Someday we'll get that one right. And I'll be just as useful as before. You'll see."

Fink's eyes glossed over hearing his brother's words. Jack could see Fink had lost hope of finding or creating any such potion or magical device for fixing Gink's situation.

"Well, I wish you well in your attempts," Jack said lightly to Fink.

Fink shot a small smile up at him, but his eyes showed the despair and hopelessness he felt about it.

Chapter 19: Potion Masters and Enchantments

Fink looked like he was concentrating on remembering the whereabouts of a particular item as he patted his pockets. His bound hands searched over his clothes until one came to a stop and his face lit up.

"Ah," he took out a small sack containing a tiny vial, "you'll find this may be somewhat useful for the both of ya." He tossed it to Jack, who caught it with his free hand.

Jack looked at the vial, which was half full of a dark red liquid. It did not look appealing and he was not sure what Fink wanted him to do with it.

"Go ahead," Fink gestured, "drink it."

Jack looked at Selini who gave a slight nod of affirmation. He looked back at Fink and watched him gesture a drinking motion. He popped off the small cork and smelled it. His stomach turned in disgust, it smelled like some kind of old blood. There was no way, he thought to himself, that he was going to keep this down.

"Is he smelling it?" Gink sounded annoyed. "Tell him not to smell it."

Fink's face was smiling from ear to ear again as he continued his drinking gestures.

With his face winced, he drank the liquid and swallowed it as fast as he could, trying not to allow himself to taste it. His nostrils filled with the sensation of burning and his throat felt ice cold. He must have shown his discomfort all too easily, because Fink was now laughing at the sight of him.

He did not feel the need to expel it from his stomach, but he wished he did. His whole body was experiencing variations of hot and cold and he felt like he was covered in bugs. His fingers cringed and folded in. He gritted his teeth and looked at Selini. She did not look amused like Fink, but she also did not appear to be bothered by his reaction, almost like she was expecting it. Now his joints felt swollen and sore and his feet were heavy.

"What's happening to him?" Anna was concerned.

"He'll be over it in a moment," Fink replied.

"Why?" Anna asked frantically, "What did you do to him? It's killing him!"

"Relax," Gink replied, "He's fine."

"You can't even see him! How do you know?" Anna replied angrily.

"Anna", Jack called, "I think he's right. I feel fine now." He pulled out his other arm and looked over his hands, "I think I'm better than fine."

"It's a healing potion," Fink stated.

Cedric let out a grunt of approval and delight. He kneeled down and unloaded the straps off his shoulders that held Jack. Jack stumbled to the ground as he tried unwinding his wrappings. After a moment of pushing, he finally got them to come loose and Cedric stood back up. Several loud cracks and pops filled the air as Cedric leaned forward and sideways, his back still mostly covered with his normal baggage.

Geller had not stopped and neither did Gibble. The pair of them were already many paces ahead and the rest of the group quickly set off to catch back up.

"You're heavier than you look!" Cedric smiled at Jack. "That's one reason I'm overwhelmingly thrilled you're back on your feet."

Jack, curious what other reason there might be, asked, "What other …?"

But, before he could finish, Cedric shifted around some of the bags he was carrying and dropped two of them to the ground.

"These are yours; I believe." Cedric let out a quick chuckle and went on his way, content with his new circumstances.

Jack threw on his bags as fast as he could and caught back up with the group. He walked beside Anna now.

"These feel heavier than before," Jack struggled with one of the straps, which was frayed and weakened.

Anna slapped his bag from behind, causing it to adjust enough for Jack to get comfortable with its final resting point.

"That's because we filled the canteens before making it into the Kanayabe Steppe, which didn't take long at all, considering its availability at the time."

Jack gave a gesture of affirmation to her comment, then quickly replied with a sense of genius in his tone, "My tent always has fresh, cool water. I'll just fill what I need for each day and leave the others empty! That should get rid of a great deal of this!" He smiled. He was proud that he had concluded what should have been such an obvious solution.

"You have been out of it for a few days," Anna said sympathetically, "but there are some tricks to those tents."

"Are you going to tell me the water turns to dust upon leaving the tent?" Jack asked disappointedly. He was sure that was not the case, but the way Anna spoke made it seem like he was going to be catching up on a number of these little instances.

"The water provided to you in the tent is cooled by its magic, and the bread is warmed by it, but you only receive those, and some other items, if they are included with your baggage. Think of it as a sort of timesaver for unpacking and repacking. What you do not use just goes back into your store, and if you do not have any to begin with, the jug and bowl will be empty."

Mumbling under his breath, Jack uttered out, "Sounds like someone could have worked the enchantments for a little longer to include those small details. That could have been a great benefit."

Fink, who had been walking near them, replied, "Water and food are considered life magic. The enchantments for those require a great deal of expense and some rare ingredients. I'd offer to sell you the necessary ingredients, but I'm all out and it ain't easy replenishing those stores."

"Even in a world of magic, we still need to use conventional means of doing things. Just our luck." Jack was disappointed.

Selini spoke up at hearing their conversation, "Magic is not as easy as it may appear. What Geller and I can do may seem like something big in the eyes of a magic-less being, but we have our limits. We drain our internal energy when we use it. If we use small amounts, it's easy for us to replenish that energy. But, if we do something beyond our normal capabilities, we run the risk of being drained for days, months, or even succumb to death.

Some creatures are more energized for certain kinds of magic, while others have near limitless stores of energy capable of producing massive quantities of magical spells and actions. Take the Sle'indo," she motioned at Fink and Gink, "their kind are specialized and apt for doing great magic in enchantments, like the potion you took. But a healer would have been able to simply flick her wand and you would have been repaired just the same. They hardly have the ability for such magic, and if they tried, it would surely drain them for days at least, worse if you were in real bad shape."

"What magic are you and Geller made to do?" Anna asked.

"The Valindi are unique because each individual within our race is born with a specialty that must be discovered and trained in the early years of life. We have the ability to do a little of everything for the most part, but at varying costs to our energy, sometimes unpredictably so. For that reason, as individuals, we stick to what we know we specialize in and only do minor spells, if at all, in other magic."

"You humans have proven little in the way of magic," Fink said lightly, "and those who attempted always seemed to be putting on some sort of show of it. Humans aren't considered much of a threat to any creature other than the fact the human population grows too quickly and so much food is eaten, and the filth they leave in tiny houses mounted over holes..."

"I get the point," Jack cut him off, "we have a few small flaws."

"I wouldn't say *small* or only a few," Gink began saying, but Fink elbowed him again. "OW!...What's wrong with your wretched arm Fink?"

"Like I said before, we've never really figured out what makes humans special or unique," Selini stated. "Humans aren't from this planet originally, though. Maybe they were something special where they came from, at least they act like it."

"How'd you know they weren't from here?" Anna asked quickly and anxiously.

"They were brought here by the Vampire nation to be harvested like a crop. The Vampires were under pressure from their allies and enemies alike to reduce their consumption of the natural wildlife. Eventually, they found a way to open the Bridge of Kardun, which was previously thought to only be a mere myth, a tale among the nations to speak of as the ultimate quest. It was only thought to be a tavern's story for the highly unintelligible storytellers. Somehow, the Vampires figured it out."

Anna and Jack shot each other excited glances. They were both thinking the same thing; there was a way back to Earth.

"How did they do it?" Jack asked almost too excitedly. "Is the bridge still there?"

"No," Selini said flatly.

"Those blasted Vampires made a dang mess of the whole thing, using it like a walkway of sorts," Fink explained. "Something with that kind o' power needs to be treated like a thing o' beauty."

Sorrowfully, Gink replied, "Oh, the wondrous things we could have accomplished with power like that."

"You mean the profits you could have turned," Cedric snapped sarcastically.

"Nothing wrong with makin' a little profit off something like that," Gink replied.

"You'd have destroyed it yourselves had you gotten your hands on it," Cedric again replied.

"It was destroyed?" Anna asked, sadness and disappointment obvious in her tone.

Selini spoke again, "'Fraid so. Like Fink said, the Vampires overused it. Using something with such magnificent power can have all sorts of outcomes, many unpredictable at best. It began weakening over the years. They only had it opened for a few decades, though. The nation of Vampiria used the bridge as a corridor for simply gathering food stores."

"That's repulsive," Anna stated in disgust.

"What," Gink began, "if you were a goat or a deer, would you understand your demise any better?"

"What he's getting at," Geller shouted back from his position with Gibble several paces ahead of the others, "is that humans were thought to be a more complicated being just above a goat-creature, but nothing worth losing sleep over. And from what the Vampires had said, they weren't showing much promise as a self-sustaining nation on their own planet either."

Furious at the notion that humans were considered to be unsophisticated beings just above livestock and wildlife, Anna started to reply angrily, "I'll have you know; we humans have a..."

Jack shook his head, motioning that her attempt would fall on deaf ears with the group. She stopped and gave him a dirty look for not trying to defend humankind.

"We don't all believe that," Gibble called back, "but it has been hard for those of us who do think otherwise to prove so. Every time we think we have proof of higher intelligence; something gets in the way."

Cedric chuckled, "It's usually pride!"

Fink added to his comment, "Humans are so prideful, it's darn near blinding to them!" He was laughing as well.

Jack gave a confirming look to Anna as if to prove her point would have fallen on deaf ears had she tried.

Fink continued, "It's great for business, though. If we come across one that has something worth trading for…"

Gink chimed in, "We can usually talk 'em out of it by saying any smart human would do the trade, and we give 'em somethin' along the lines of a bag full 'o *magical* rocks." He started laughing as he was remembering something that must have happened like this before. "And then tell 'em what they 'ad was so easy to use, only an idiot wouldn't be able to figure it out. They're too prideful to come back and say they don't know how to use 'em!" He was laughing again. It was obvious he was remembering a specific incident. Even Fink was smiling and nodding.

Jack could see Anna was about to retort something, so he quickly butted in, "So, we never figured out why humans showed up here, though."

Selini spoke up, seeing that Jack was trying to change the conversation's course, "Yes, we didn't. Vampiria was thin on allies, and the alliances it did have were in place to enhance trade amongst its bordering nations. The Vampires had lost allies and strength in the last alliances throughout the years because of their overwhelming thirst for blood. Vampiria had a land barren of anything other than plant life. They had been sneaking over borders and illegally paying for lifts on sanctions on other hunting grounds. Their allies were beginning to take notice, and once the treacherous acts were discovered, friends became enemies. Soon, Vampiria was faced with all-out war. The Vampires also faced a power struggle from within over which brother was to take control of the crown after their father was killed, by a spy, nonetheless. They also encountered countless battles against those from the outside who wished to take control of the Bridge."

"By a spy?" Anna asked.

"Vampiria keeps its affairs closed." Cedric announced. "There's not much known of the happenings behind the fall of the crown, just that its undoing was by a spy."

"Who else would want to use the bridge?" Anna asked eagerly.

"I would!" shouted Gink over Fink's shoulder.

Fink smiled and nodded in agreement.

"Imagine coming across a discovery of a whole new world." Selini explained. "All those uncovered riches and resources untapped and unclaimed. There were even those in the Govilian Council that wanted to seek control of the bridge for the gain of our nation."

"What about humans?!" Jack exclaimed. "Did anyone consider that this other world was already spoken for?"

Tenderly speaking, Selini replied, "I don't think humans were considered … advanced enough to …"

Anna and Jack could tell she was attempting to choose her words delicately. It was obvious humans were not considered intelligent enough to be anything special. After all, everyone kept pointing out how uninteresting they were without powers.

Shaking her head, Anna stopped Selini. "It doesn't matter. What was done was done. Now there's no bridge and no way home."

Cedric stopped. The others followed suit. Now the whole party was staring at Jack and Anna.

"What do you mean … no way home?" Cedric inquired slowly.

Anna had just revealed what Jack was so careful not to. He was not sure who to trust with this information but felt Selini and Geller were probably the best choice. Now, though, they had little option left but to divulge their story to the party.

Selini stepped forward, tilting her head inquisitively, "Jack? Where did you say you were from?"

Chapter 20: The Journey Continues

Jack and Anna explained the events that led them to Lunia. Once they started explaining, Jack found it easier to tell than he imagined. He covered as much detail as he could, and Anna filled in the other parts. Gink and Fink were obviously enthralled with this tidbit of information. Jack figured this meant the possibility of new profits. Cedric looked stoic through much of the presentation. Gibble was nervously excited. And, both Geller and Selini showed signs of bemusement.

"We need to tell father," Selini said to Geller after all was said and done. "I think someone knows you made it through from the other world and that's why they keep trying to kill you."

"It has to be something to do with the Reign! It just has to!" Gibble was all aflutter at Selini's comment.

"How would they know?" asked Anna.

"Frinkul likely had a spell on the whole forest." Geller tried explaining as he thought. "If he knew there was a portal in that boulder, he would have had it guarded more closely."

Jack replied back assuring everyone in the group, "There was no way back out. I looked, trust me. I'm not even sure how we were able to get into this world."

"You've got a key, you do!" Gink exclaimed from behind Fink.

Fink elbowed him again to shut him up.

"Ow! I seriously want to know what's wrong with your stupid arm!"

Cedric chimed in, "It sounds like some sort of key to me."

"I think we can all agree you *may have* found a key in that bag from Frinkul's cabin. What does that mean, though? Does it work on that same rock or is it for something different? My father might know." Selini was pondering aloud while looking over the small trinket Jack had discovered in the forest. She was looking at the symbol intently and whispered, "Might know indeed."

"We've got incoming!" Gibble had been hovering slightly higher than Cedric's head and noticed the dust storm was on its way.

"Everybody buckle down and be prepared." Geller commanded. "This is going to slow us down a bit. We need to get moving!"

With that, the group shuffled clothes and bags, tightening straps and pants. Then, they set off almost immediately toward the storm. A low rumble could be heard in the distance as it moved closer.

Selini handed the trinket back to Jack. He glanced at it again. It began glowing ever so slightly. He slid it back into his repaired satchel that he had attained from Frinkul's dilapidated cabin.

Gink and Fink both almost simultaneously put on goggles that had been resting on their heads. Jack got the feeling the goggles were a part of their everyday ensemble. Selini covered her mouth with a scarf-like cloth and Geller had a funny looking type of mask for his nose and mouth. Cedric did the same as Selini and Gibble landed next to the group and walked with them. With a quick shutter, his face poofed out a large tuft of hair that guarded his face naturally from what was in store.

Jack began to panic. He did not have anything to cover his face. Anna had tucked her mouth and nose into her shirt, so he did the same.

It was not long before the dust storm reached the party. It pounded at them with a steady howl. The day became dark and it was hard to see anything ahead. Jack followed Cedric, who was still leading the pack without showing any signs of hesitation. He seemed to know exactly where they were going.

Fink had pulled a small, golden compass from one of his pockets and was watching it as he walked. His hands were still bound together by a purple haze that lit up like a smoke in the dust.

Everyone was closer together now and their pace had slowed noticeably. Each member of the party was intently watching where he or she was going except for Gink. He was still strapped to Fink's back and was fidgeting with several vials of liquids. Jack figured it was Gink's way of passing time – he just got to fidget with potions all day.

Gink noticed Jack watching him and smiled menacingly. After several mixtures of different liquids and a few shakes, he handed Jack a vial with a bright blue liquid in it.

He shouted over the wind, "Take it!" His smile was that of a slight level of insanity. He looked so pleased with himself and Jack was not sure he could trust him. But, remembering the healing potion, he reluctantly reached out and grabbed the vial.

"Drink! Drink! Hehehe!" Gink's excitement made Jack all the more nervous.

Jack did not feel like he needed another healing potion or anything else for that matter. He studied the vial for a minute and politely declined, trying to hand it back to Gink.

"Just drink it!" Fink called over to Jack. "It'll help with the storm!" Fink also had a menacing smile on his face.

Jack glanced over to Selini for approval, but she was too busy watching the way ahead. He then looked over at Anna expecting a look of disagreement, but she was also intently watching the path they were on. He decided to drink it.

He expected it to taste awful like the healing potion, but it was not that bad. It tasted like pine tree needles and water. He shrugged his shoulders. He looked around his arms and fingers expecting to feel something, but nothing was happening. He suddenly felt like he had been fooled into drinking nothing in particular, like Gink had just played a practical joke on him.

Jack felt lighter now, though. He felt an overwhelming sense of safety. His fingertips began turning blue like the path from the cave with strings of light swirling around them.

Worriedly, he shouted to Gink over the sound of the wind, "What did you give me? What's happening?"

Gink just smiled. Normally Jack would feel more anxious about the whole ordeal, but he could not help but feel safe. He felt for sure it had to be something about the potion.

Suddenly, the blue swirls of light exploded like a ring of flames away from his body in every direction. The wind died immediately, and the dust settled. Everyone in the party had stopped and was looking at Jack. He could see they were now in a shielded bubble that was stopping the storm from getting to them. It was about ten feet in every direction around him.

"Told ya it works on humans!" Fink stated matter-of-factly to Gink.

"What did you give him?" Selini asked

"Jack, what did you do?" Anna snapped at him.

"He took a protection potion." Gink laughed excitedly. "It shields him from danger ... for a bit."

Cedric looked at Geller and Selini in disbelief, "I haven't seen a protection potion like this before."

"It's designed for humans," Fink stated. "Normally it works like a shield right next to your body, but with humans it works like a bubble. It's way cool! I've never actually seen it in action except on that one guy." He nudged Gink as if to gesture for him to remember something about it from before.

"We sold a small bit once before to a human. He just wanted to be able to win a fight." He laughed as he remembered his story, "He won for sure, but got the crud kicked out of him the next day for cheating!"

"Jack," Anna interjected, "remember these two are under arrest.

You shouldn't be drinking their potions."

Geller, obviously pleased with their newfound ease of travel, then commanded, "We need to keep moving. Jack, since you're our shield, you should walk up front with Cedric."

Jack gave a quick glance to everyone in the party to make sure everyone was ready to go and proceeded to walk with Cedric.

The potion lasted for the rest of the day. The group was able to make good ground with the shield in place. As an added bonus, they were not being scorched by the sun either, which was still blacked out from the storm all around them.

Anna had taken to walking behind Jack and was explaining to him more about the Frost Birds. Jack got lost thinking about how much safer he would feel if the Frost Birds were on their side. He had heard in the Panthyun how few fighters the Valindi had left and he was growing more and more nervous about the idea of fighting Ghowla. It made the Valindi nervous that the Frost Birds were not fighting on either side. They knew they would be in big trouble if they had to fight them as well. And without being on either side, there was a chance the Frost Birds could suddenly pick the side of the Reign.

Jack remembered a winter several years before that came too early. He remembered how devastating it was to the crops and trees. The night was long and loud with the sound of crashing tree branches and booming tree trunks as they froze prematurely. He also remembered how Geller and Selini spoke of how terrible the winters here get. So bad that not even Ghowla would wage war during this time.

Through many of her explanations, Anna had mentioned that the seasons and years on Lunia were longer. Each season lasted about two months longer here. As far as Jack could figure, fall was almost done, that meant they had only weeks until winter. That did not seem like enough time to get this deal with the Frost Birds out of the way and to find a way home.

Night was coming and the shield was beginning to diminish. The storm had not passed yet, but they made good ground. They had come across a pile of large stones.

"Here's a good place to stop for the night," Selini said.

She pulled a small container from her bag and fiddled with it for a moment. She then set it on the ground and tapped it with a small wand. A small stream of light slowly made its way above them and formed a bubble similar to the one they had travelled under. Selini smiled and dropped her bag from her back and began unpacking. A shield formed around the group just large enough to allow them to sleep under it without their tents.

"We can use that tomorrow!" Anna was excited.

"No, it's only good in one spot." Selini explained. "Once I close this back up, it'll be done. It's also only good against the weather. If you haven't been able to tell yet, I'm pretty good at enchantments."

"We've got so much to learn." Jack said to Anna as they laid blankets on the ground.

The whole party got situated in their tight quarters as Selini started a small fire in the center. It was not long before Geller was working on something to eat. Without the wind, the smell of food permeated the bubble and filled everyone's noses. Soon after, Geller announced he was done making dinner.

"Time to dig in!" Geller exclaimed.

Jack saw the pan floating over the fire, but its contents seemed too little to feed the lot of them. He did not protest, though, knowing they had to ration their food and water as best as possible. As he ate his first bite, he felt comforting warmth come over him and it tasted much like a rabbit stew from back home. Then, he noticed after a few bites that he was getting full.

"How am I already full?" Jack wondered aloud.

Selini giggled, "Geller is pretty good at making food. That's one of his specialties. It wouldn't seem too useful in the army, but it has worked to our advantage many times."

"I used to hate the fact that I was good at this," Geller held his plate up as he prepared to take another bite, "but I've come to enjoy it some."

It was the same for everybody else. They all could only eat a few bites before feeling full, even Cedric stopped after only four bites. Not long after eating, the party was fast asleep. Their day had been full of walking in heat and sun and then a dust storm. As Jack nodded off to sleep, he wondered how they would get the Frost Birds to fight side by side with the Valindi. He also could not help but think of all the events that had happened in just the last few days. He was fascinated by the magic he had seen and experienced – the swampees, the healing potion, the storm shield, the royal blacksmith – it all began swirling around in his head at once.

Jack drifted off to sleep.

The group spent another couple days in the Gilia Desert before coming upon the dreaded Carvoonian Mountains. Jack remembered that they would have to travel more than a week in the mountains.

Anna and Jack spent much of the time during their walk in the desert learning about different creatures and ways of Lunia. Gink and Fink remained bound by Cedric's magical cuffs, but they joked readily as if they had been a part of the group all along. Gibble spent more time traveling on the ground with the group because the scorching suns burned his wings if he flew for too long. Cedric had so much hair, the sun stood no chance of reaching his skin. Selini had a small, ornately decorated umbrella that floated above as she walked. And, Geller fussed about the heat on numerous occasions. Jack and Anna benefited from small potions and enchanted foods meant to ward off the intense heat of the suns, but they were still uncomfortable.

The Carvoonian Mountains were dreaded because there was only one way through, and that was to go over them. Snow and blistering cold plagued the way. It was a path rarely taken and sat just beside the border of Wyvergia, the land of the Frost Birds. The Frost Birds were very temperamental and had little liking towards visitors, invited or not.

Jack's party knew they were in for trouble. They had planned for it. But that did not ease Jack's anxiety. Even though the plan was to intentionally get caught, he was afraid it would all go wrong. Indeed, very little about his trip had gone 'right' so far. Someone or something was trying to kill him and had nearly succeeded on a couple occasions.

As they made their way to the top of the first mountain, they all added extra layers to their clothes. Jack and Anna put on their armor, not because they were expecting a fight, but because the extra layer would benefit them in the frigid cold. Geller had prepared some extra spiced bread on the last night of camp before the mountains. The consumption of this bread made everyone feel warmer. And, as the group travelled through the snowy mountaintops, they would take the occasional bite to rewarm.

There was much talking while they traversed the mountains. It was so bitter; all they could do was talk to pass the time and keep their minds off the snow and wind. Gibble flew for most of the trip. Sometimes he flew ahead as a scout and other times he flew with the group. He rarely walked in the snow as his feet got cold quickly.

Jack noticed Gibble's wing flaps did not match his flight like that of a bird. His wings looked like that of a very large bat, and they only flapped on occasion.

Curiosity finally got the better of him and Jack asked one day, "How do you stay in the air when you don't flap your wings like a bird?"

"It's just how it works for me" he replied nonchalantly, "I only have to beat my wings every so often to stay afloat. Sometimes, I can go several minutes between beats. It just depends on the air. If it's windy, then I have to work harder. If it's calm, I can kind of float without much work."

There were so many mystical and magical things Jack was learning about, it made his head spin at times. All the happenings since he arrived on Lunia, a completely different planet, were almost too hard to fathom. He wanted to learn more about it, almost as badly as he wanted to get back home. It was easy to forget about how home felt at times, especially now. The freezing cold kept his mind occupied on his body. He was so cold. All of his body ached in the frigid temperatures. His legs felt like they were working against him and his arms felt like he was carrying around logs. Even with the all the extra layers of robes, the bitter cold still found its way through every fiber and snaked through every opening.

Other than the constant state of cold and wind, the mountain journey seemed to go fairly well. The party got behind schedule a little when Fink made a whole fuss about having to traverse the mountains with his brother on his back the whole way. When he dragged behind everybody knew he was doing it on purpose. He spent half a day complaining and stumbling around before Cedric, fed up, finally gave in and offered to carry Gink for him. Not to be left out, Fink then made a fuss about not going anywhere without his brother. Cedric eventually caved into this as well and carried the pair of them on his back. They both gave Jack a maniacal grin from ear to ear after they got situated, which had become all too familiar with the two.

With Gink and Fink both positioned side by side and facing the rest of the group, Jack got plenty of time to ask them all sorts of questions. He found the two were both rather willing to talk about anything. They sometimes spoke in riddles, which irked Jack to no end, especially since much of the time the riddles referenced events or things on Lunia for which he had no knowledge.

On an especially cold day, Jack asked for another shielding potion like in the desert. But they simply replied they did not have enough ingredients like it was no big deal. It had become obvious through talking with the pair of them that they were masters of potion making and had a particular fondness for the kinds that exploded.

Jack had remembered Selini explaining to him and Anna about how different Valindi had unique powers they were good at. Selini was good at enchantments above all else. She said she learned at an early age that she could enchant things with ease. She had once enchanted a small doll when she was a kid and it turned into the size of her entire bedroom. It walked on its own and destroyed half the house as it made its way out the front door and down the street. Geller had learned much later that he was good at cooking. Not just cooking, mind you, but preparing small amounts of food that could literally feed an army. It was disappointing to him at first, but he eventually grew to like it. So did his troops. Jack had already seen both of these skills in action on their trip – Selini with her boat and tent enchantments and Geller's cooking. Geller swore, though, that he had other skills that he just needed to refine. Jack just felt Geller was still not too happy that he was good at cooking. There did not seem to be any reason to be embarrassed, though, Jack had thought as he believed the cooking skill was amazingly wondrous.

As they walked over the mountains, he learned all sorts of stuff about each of the members of the party. Anna was doing the same, but she was much more adept than Jack at getting the participants to share. She just seemed to know how to ask the right questions and kept digging deeper until she was satisfied. There was not too much to do during this part of the journey. All the cold made it hard to do anything but talk. Gibble was good at sight. He could see clearly for miles, which was enhanced by his ability to fly above them. And Cedric's skills had yet to be revealed. Anna tried prying it out of him, but he simply laughed and stated that she will see.

"And how do you know if you've used too much of your, uh, … power or magic or whatever you call it?" Jack overheard Anna asking Selini who was all too eager to answer her questions.

Even though they were cold and numb, the conversation made for a pleasant distraction. Jack could tell, though, that Selini would be happy to answer Anna's questions anytime. Selini was full of answers. So was Geller, it seemed, as he was always nodding in agreement or adding something more.

"You get the hang of it," Selini replied easily, "you just kind of know your own limits."

"If you keep in practice, you can do powerful magic without using much mana at all." Cedric called over his shoulder. "You just have to remember not to try something big that you're not skilled at."

"Mana?" Anna's face seemed confused.

"That's one's level of power – the measure of what and how much one can do." Gink said as he fidgeted for something.

"Like the power level of your soul!" Fink yelled back to them.

"Remember," Selini interjected, "it takes very little mana to do magic that you're skilled at. Like my enchantments, it hardly uses my mana at all. But, if I were to try and perform a healing spell, it'd wipe me out. Not to mention, it would be a weak spell at best."

"Aha!" Gink had managed to find what he was looking for. "Here you go." He handed a small, silvery looking object much like that of a stopwatch to Jack. "Take a look at that."

Jack looked at it. It did not seem too remarkable at first, just a round silvery watch-like object with a small door that flipped open. He looked it over for a moment and then opened it. The inside was like a small smoke storm swirling around under a layer of glass. He looked confused as there was nothing else to see. He looked at it intently, expecting to see something more, something marvelous. After all, Gink and Fink always seemed to be handing him things that were magnificent in power. This just did not seem that way.

"It's a witchle," Fink stated, noting Jack's confusion.

"What is it doing?" Anna asked Jack intently. She was curious, but not enough to shuffle more around in the snow than she needed to.

"A witchle shows you how much mana you have. When it's full, it's bright yellow to the brim." Fink said proudly.

"When it's empty," Gink continued for Fink, "it'll just be all red. No mana means no way to do magic. And if it's bad enough, one might even die."

"What about swirling smoke?" Jack asked while holding it up.

"Doesn't work on humans." Fink smiled matter-of-factly. "Now give it back." Fink grabbed it from Jack and held it for a moment. Quickly, the witchle changed to all yellow. "No need fer something like this in yer possession when you know yer limits."

Fink gave it back to Gink, who packed it back away in one of his many pockets.

Chapter 21: The Cerilian Box

The temperature gradually warmed up over the coming days. The air felt damp and the occasional tree jutted out from the rocks. Eventually they were all walking through a forest on their way back down the final mountain. Jack could not see far ahead of them because the forest was so thick, but Gibble would fly above the treetops and report back to Cedric every so often. Despite the thickening forest and its undergrowth, he felt confident they were heading in the right direction – mostly because nobody else seemed concerned that they might be off track. Then, there was an opening to a beautiful grassland.

Tall tufts of grasses similar to those of the meadow Jack and Anna first landed in swayed slowly in melodic waves under the wind. Large and small flowers alike, some aglow in their iridescent colors of purples and blues and yellows and greens, filled the meadow. There were steep cliffs on both sides far in the distance. The only way was forward and down. Jack could see they were headed for a large lake that spanned as far as he could see. Then he remembered Selini saying she had only one boat. This must have been what it was for, he thought. Now he was left wondering how they planned on getting across, but the group was still pressing on. He figured there must be a backup plan – maybe they were going to have to build a boat now.

"What's that?" Anna was pointing far in the distance to the horizon.

Jack noticed it now, too. The sky flashed again and again. It looked like a storm brewing.

"That's to be expected," Gibble shouted down from overhead.

"I don't suppose you remember that electrical storm we mentioned before, do you?" Geller said cheerfully. It was almost like he was eager for the challenge. "Once we make it across the Lake of A'lurokai, we'll be working our way through that. Then, we head into the lands of Wyvergia."

"Great!" Jack said sarcastically. He gave Anna a glance as if to say, 'Here we go again.'

"Speaking of the lake," Anna blurted out, "how do we plan on getting across? Didn't we lose our boat?"

Jack was glad she asked. He felt with the pace they were walking at, there was already a plan in place. Nobody had mentioned it during the last night when they were having Selini enchant their extra clothes down to a more manageable carrying size. And, the breakfast that morning was full of cheer, but no conversation came up about any kinks in the plan either. He felt such a question would have seemed foolish and was happy that she would take the brunt of criticism for it.

"No idea." Cedric chimed in. He did not even bother to look over his shoulder, he just said it like having no plan was no problem.

Jack and Anna exchanged looks. Her eyes were wide. He could tell she could hardly contain her bewilderment.

"What ... do ... you ... mean, 'No idea'?" Anna asked bemused.

"No idea, no idea!" Chanted Gink and Fink together.

"Woohoo!" Gink added, "This is gonna be fun!"

Fink was back to carrying Gink now that they were no longer in the cold. Jack could tell it was no big deal for Cedric to carry the two of them, but just did not want to on principle. Cedric looked annoyed at the two of them the entire time they were on his back.

"Do either of you have a potion that can get us across water?" Jack asked Fink and Gink. "Or, do you have an enchantment that'll carry us over?" He asked Selini.

The three of them had shaken their heads in a resounding 'No'.

"Are you able to carry us all?" He shouted up to Gibble.

"I can carry quite a bit more than my own weight, but not the whole group." Gibble flew down and walked next to Jack. He could see Jack was getting worried and there was no need to fly right now anyway. So, he walked next to him to try and ease his anxiety.

"I got it!" Anna said suddenly, "Selini can enchant us all to make us very small. Then we could float across in a pot or something!" She was obviously pleased with her deduction and Jack felt like praising her as well. It seemed like a reasonable trick.

"I can't enchant you to be smaller while you're still alive. I can't enchant anything to be smaller that's still alive for that matter." Selini said without slowing her pace.

They were all headed directly for a massive lake, and from the sounds of it, there was no plan on how to get across. The cliffs on either side were nearly straight up for what looked like a thousand feet. Jack could not see himself climbing a steep rock face. And, judging by his reaction to having to carry Gink and Fink, Jack figured there was no way they were going to convince Cedric to let the whole group ride on his back like a raft.

Geller had been ahead of them several paces. He stopped and turned to face them, "There's no plan yet, but that's no reason to not get there as fast as we can. We need to make up as much time as we can." He glared at Gink and Fink for a fleeting moment, "As we lost some during the mountain pass."

It was not until nightfall that the group made it to the shore. Jack had been hoping a solution to their problem got figured out along the way, but much to his dismay, nobody had come up with one. They pitched their tents and Geller made the dinner. All was usual except for the glaringly obvious problem they now all faced. The lake looked much larger and never-ending up close.

There were small waves crashing at the shore. It was dark water with bright blue crests. All sorts of lake life could be seen in the water as Jack walked near the shore. He was carrying his Cerilian box. He could not tell what was more interesting, the lake or the box. He remembered Selini describing how the box works – how it was supposed to be able to hold a lot more than its size. He wondered what he could fit in such a small opening that would be worth holding so much of. He thought maybe food or gold. Then he scoffed at his own thoughts. Those seemed like silly ideas. He could just carry the food they had because Selini had already enchanted it all to be small and they did not even need that much because Geller's ability was magical cooking.

Even though he had no idea what to do with the Cerilian box, he was still fascinated with its ornate design. It was covered in storied images similar to those in the Panthyun. Mostly, though, the images were those of warriors in battle fighting mystical creatures Jack was unfamiliar with. Just as he thought about how to open it, the top swirled open like a mini maelstrom of metal and design all smashing together and then suddenly into the sides. Startled, Jack dropped the box.

Anna jogged up behind him.

"What are you doing?" Anna asked half out of breath.

"Just walking." He was bending down to pick up the Cerilian box. As he picked it up, he vented his frustration, "How are we supposed to cross this lake? Do we wake up tomorrow and magically have an answer?"

"I know. They're all discussing that right now. But it doesn't sound promising so far." Anna tried talking calmly to sooth Jack's frustration. "But they've gotten us this far, haven't they? They'll figure something out."

Her reassurance was not assuring at all. Jack just felt useless. He felt there was something he should be trying to do to help, but he did not know anything about anything. He did not know these lands or the creatures they could come across. He did not know where they were going. He did not know what he was expecting to see when they got to the Frost Birds. He did not know anything about magic. The more he thought about it, the more useless he felt.

Trying to sound as upbeat as he could, Jack responded, "Well, that's good. I'm sure they will, too." He knew Anna needed the positive reaction right now. Jack turned and began heading back for camp.

"What are you doing with that?" Anna pointed at his Cerilian box.

"Just looking at it." Jack brushed off the dirt and sand that had stuck to its side. "I just can't imagine what to use this for." He was obviously still down about the conversation as he flopped the box to its side, and it closed back up the same way it had opened.

"Selini told me all about those things." She said gleefully. She was obviously more upbeat with the change of topic. "It takes an enchantment to make one. She can make them herself, but she says yours is special because it's made from elemental magic which is much more powerful of a magic than she can do." Anna was speaking fast now. "With elemental magic, that box can hold an unfathomable amount."

Jack laughed and held it up in front of him again. "What good does holding a lot of stuff do when the hole is so small?"

"Honestly, I don't know." Anna sounded a little discouraged that she was not making Jack feel happier.

Jack was looking at it again. He thought of it opening and it once again opened. He figured that must be how to open and close it, all he had to do was think about it. He peered into the hole – not quite large enough to fit his head in if he tried – and saw pitch blackness. There was not a bottom, nor could he see any sides, just blackness. Jack's focus had been on the box, so he did not notice a small rock jutting out of the sand. He tripped and fell quickly to his knees. As he fell, the box flew from his hands and rolled into the water. Just then, a tornado of water suddenly appeared above the box and water rushed in. Anna ran over and grabbed it. The box closed.

Jack jumped up. "Anna! Did you say the box could hold an unfathomable amount of something?" He was wide-eyed and excited now as he grabbed the box from Anna and ran toward the camp without waiting for her to answer.

"I've got it! I've got it!" Jack was yelling as he approached the others in the camp. The group was obviously in deep discussion. They all turned from their spots around the fire and watched as he ran up to the camp holding his Cerilian box high in the air.

Jack was out of breath by the time he arrived at the group. He was so excited he could hardly breathe right.

"Yes, yes, it's a very nice box, boy" Fink smiled, still bound and sitting next to the group.

"What have you got?" Geller asked.

At that, Jack looked back at his box, making sure it was still open. He then threw the Cerilian box as hard as he could into the lake. As soon as it hit the water another tornado of water formed. It was bright blue and rushing with a roar into the box somewhere under the water's surface. Soon after several more twisters formed, bending in every direction. Each tornado was bright and blue and swirling around a center. It reminded Jack of an upside-down chandelier.

"Brilliant!" Selini exclaimed. "That's absolutely magnificent!"

Gibble, confused, chimed in, "What am I missing here? I don't understand."

"That box is elementally enchanted! It can probably hold the whole lake in it!" Geller jumped to his feet in joy.

"Well now, it seems we may have found our solution." Cedric was watching the wondrous site in front of them.

The group sat around for hours more as the Cerilian box sucked up all the water it could. The lake was draining faster than Jack would have imagined, it had already dropped a couple feet since he threw it in. He was amazed at how powerful such a small object really was. After a while, though, Geller convinced everyone to get some rest and let the box do its thing. Indeed, the box was no longer even under the water, but the twisters did not cease to bring water to its opening.

Jack woke up in his tent to the smell of meats and breads. He felt well rested, much better than when they were travelling through the mountains where the cold made sleep feel like a nightmare. He lay awake for a minute before he heard the sound of Geller outside, clanking pots and talking. Jack jumped out of bed, remembering the box from the night before. He wondered if it worked.

The sunlight was blinding. Jack had to wait for a moment before he could make out Geller working next to a floating pan above the fire. Without so much as a salutation, Jack's eyes fixated upon the lake. Everyone else had already been up and was standing on the shore in glee. The lake had dried up. Even the water from the lake floor and been sucked out, leaving a dry lakebed for them to now cross.

"You did it!" Anna shouted from the shoreline. She was standing with the others. "It's all gone!" She swung her arms around and gestured at the now missing lake.

Although everyone seemed excited about the newfound route, no one seemed to be in a hurry. They ate breakfast together and shared stories of battles Jack had never heard of. After a while, though, they finally packed up their tents and began back on their journey. Gibble took flight and Cedric led the pack. Jack had picked up the box on their way and he looked inside it expecting to see water. There was nothing, though, it was still pitch black and just as light as when it was empty.

"Put your arm in it" Gink had a large grin on his face again. He always seemed to be up to no good. At least that is what he would have Jack believe. "Go ahead, do it!" He gestured to Jack.

Jack looked skeptical. Would it tear off his arm? He then flipped the box over, half expecting the water to come pouring out, but nothing happened. He flipped it back up and looked in again. There was nothing to see. Jack was amused at the magical properties of such a small object. Then again, all the magic he had seen was amazing to him.

"What are you waiting for?" Gink continued. His face looked like that of a mad man most of time. But he had been right about the healing potion and shielding potion, he figured he would not be telling him to do something that would get his arm ripped off. "Jus' a lil reachy-poo."

Jack decided to try. He slowly reached his arm in. Anna and Selini were back to their usual conversation and were not paying attention to him. Geller was chatting with Cedric, and Gibble was flying ahead of the group. He reached in farther and farther. Finally, he was up to his shoulder and he felt nothing.

"What do ya feel?" Gink asked, a big grin still on his face.

"Nothing." Jack replied.

"What do ya expect ta feel?" he encouraged Jack.

"Water, I guess." Jack had expected to feel water, or at least hear the sloshing of water, but nothing was there. His arm was still shoulder deep in the Cerilian box with his hand waving back and forth looking for something, anything. He felt a little relieved, though, that Gink had not been tricking him.

"Now," Gink continued, "what do you want to feel?"

"Water." Just as Jack said the word, his arm became soaked as the fin of a fish slapped against his hand and he dropped the box flat on the ground. Water splashed out of its sides and then it was gone.

Gink was laughing. Jack picked up the box and looked at it again. It was just as empty as it had been before. He held it upside down and nothing poured out.

"You can only get out of it what you put in it." Gink said cheerfully, obviously pleased with his little practical joke. "And, you can only get something out of it if you want it."

Jack put the box away and briskly walked to catch up with Anna. He joined the conversation with her and Selini. They spent the next few days walking on the highest ground. The lake was slowly beginning to refill from the rivers that fed it, so time was against them if they did not make haste. At one point, Jack offered to put down the box again, but was discouraged from doing so. It was important to the life around it that the lake be allowed to fill as fast as possible. Selini had assured him they had plenty of time.

After a day of walking through the lakebed, the group arrived at the point where the electrical storm started and the lake ended, they camped for the night. The next morning, Selini produced an umbrella for each of them. She only had enough for everyone who was in the group originally, so Gink and Fink had to ride on Cedric's back once again. Cedric begrudgingly allowed this, but not without first expressing his disapproval several times. The umbrellas were enchanted, explained Selini, and would protect them from the lightning. This was counterintuitive to what Jack had learned, which was that umbrellas were probably the worst idea in such a storm.

"These are enchanted to act as a shield," Selini went on, noticing Jack's reluctancy, "they'll attract the lightning, unfortunately, but still protect you."

It was obvious both Anna and Jack were apprehensive to the idea of carrying umbrellas through this. They had both seen some pretty powerful magic, but this just did not make a lot of sense. Noting their reluctance again, Selini gave a demonstration by walking far ahead of the group and into the storm. Not long after, a strike of lightning found Selini's umbrella and flashed loudly against its top. The umbrella glowed bright red for a moment, then back to its wooden state. She came back to the pair of them, looking for their approval. Sparks still sputtered around the edges of the umbrella as she spoke to them.

"Don't worry, they'll hold up!" She shouted. She had forgotten about the thunderous bang that lightning leaves and she was shouting over the ringing in her ears.

Selini then pulled out some hairy rags and handed them to each member, except for Gink and Fink. She motioned for Jack and Anna to put the rags around their heads to cover their ears. She then put hers on. At first, the rags were too big and fell to their shoulders. Selini pulled out a small wand and, having them situate the rags over their ears once again, gave a small flick. The rags immediately adjusted to the proper size. Selini did this for everybody. Gink and Fink, knowing what was coming up, made a small deafening potion and shared a swig each. Suddenly, their ears curled up and covered with skin. They were almost completely gone.

Without much more delay, Cedric set off ahead of the group once again. Each umbrella's size was just right for each member. Cedric's umbrella was the largest, while Geller's and Selini's were the smallest. Each umbrella was made of a strong, light colored wood and had ornate designs. Jack noticed they were similar to the designs on the Cerilian box and in the Panthyun. There were all sorts of pictures depicting figures fighting battles in storms, using their umbrellas as magical weaponry. Without being able to hear what was going on around him now that his ears were muffled by the hair covered rags, he lost himself in thought. He tried imagining the different battles that must have taken place for each of the etchings. He watched as one such etching used its folded umbrella as a staff that shot lightning towards its enemy, a large troll-looking creature.

It did not take long for Jack's thoughts to snap back into focus on the path ahead. Even without being able to hear much more than the occasional dull roaring of thunder, his view was now filled with lightning strikes all over the place. Cedric's umbrella was hit first. A large, white bolt slammed down on the edge of it and the bolt jumped to Anna's, then to Selini's before dissipating. Jack jumped back at the sight of it. The crashing thunder was surprisingly muted, but its shockwave rumbled straight down to his bones. His clothes and his hair shook. He gripped his umbrella tight.

They pressed forward. The lightning strikes continued violently and with more frequency as they got further in. Although the umbrellas were doing their jobs and keeping the group safe, Jack was highly anxious the entire time. Each lightning strike made him jump. He watched as lightning struck the rocks around them, leaving holes where they landed. The whole ground around them had scorch marks everywhere. It was obvious this storm had been going on for a while.

There was not a path in front of them, but Cedric seemed to know his way. Gibble remained on the ground. There was no way he was going to fly in this; he would be fried in the first minute. Jack found himself wishing they were back in the meadow. He dreaded every step in this place. He even felt as if he preferred the cold of the mountains over this.

There were no signs of life. No trees or plants existed anywhere. The ground was a reddish-brown dirt with scattered boulders and rocks throughout. The char marks of the lightning were the only things that added any other texture and color.

Jack found himself wanting to get lost in thought to get away from this place, but the lightning was so frequent it made it difficult. Another bolt hit Cedric and bounced between them. Then, moments later, one hit Gibble and bounced off in a ball of fire and electricity to the ground nearby. The clouds overhead did not rain, they just brewed and swirled like a thousand maelstroms overhead churning in every direction. Another bolt slammed into Jack this time. He nearly dropped his umbrella as he jumped high in the air. His eyes were wide now and his hands trembling. He could see the edges of his umbrella covered in red sparks. It reminded him of a piece of paper slowly burning, red and twinkling. He got hit again. Then, Cedric again. Then, Geller. Then, Jack. All the while, the lightning bounced around like a chain of fire.

That night was the most exhausted Jack had felt since the day he had nearly drowned in the cavern pass. Although he had not been through any physical trauma, his body felt weak from being tense all day. His nerves had gotten the best of him and he could not wait to lay down. They had just made it outside the electrical storm by the time night fell. Even Anna, who was usually chattering inquisitively, was noticeably tired. Everyone else seemed in better spirits than Jack and Anna. Fink and Gink were messing around with various objects in their pockets as they sat aside a growing campfire. Cedric was drinking heavily from a large jug. Gibble was off scouting ahead of the camp. Geller was preparing his usual meal for the group and Selini had taken to unpacking the tents. She had been messing with Jack's tent when Anna inquired about a spell Selini was putting on it.

Jack overheard Selini replying to Anna, "They're not very strong protection charms, but they'll buy some time in the event something happens."

Jack felt immediately queasy. He remembered that someone or something had tried killing him several different times now. He did not want special treatment but was glad Selini was trying to help. He knew she was not skilled in protection charms and that they would be weak ones at best. He figured they might last long enough to wake everyone else up in the event he got attacked in the middle of the night.

The next day brought them to Wyvergia. The land had obviously been lush in the past, but now all that remained were massive trunks and twisted branches of once majestic trees. The dead grass crunched beneath their feet. The winds carried with them the faint smell of rotting flesh. Jack shook his head as he thought about how this place was just as bad as the rest of the journey. It felt like there was no hope here, like life had just given up.

They were not far into Wyvergia before the group stopped.

"We need to be extremely careful not to be seen now." Geller explained to the whole group. "We don't want anything living to see us before we get far enough in."

Selini was fumbling around in one of the pockets of her backpack. Jack had taken notice that everybody seemed to have backpacks full of pockets and pouches that could hold more than they appeared they could. It had turned out that Seliini had enchanted them all with spells that made them act like smaller versions of a Cerilian box. She had explained how she could make a Cerliain box before, but she was not too well versed in that ability yet. She found what she was looking for. It was a shiny, silvery ball. It was a well-polished ball from what Jack could make out. And, it looked like a mirror of some sort.

He wondered what that ball was supposed to do. Everything the others did always seemed to have some kind of magical property to it and now he found himself trying to imagine what this one would do. He glanced at Anna, looking for some ideas, but she too looked curious. Selini placed the ball on the ground and motioned for the group to come in closer.

"Come. Come." She waved to Jack to get closer to her. "This is a Mirror Ball," she explained, "it will act as a giant mirror, reflecting the other side of the ball to its opposite side. It'll keep us nearly invisible. It also makes it so the noise inside the bubble is muted to the outside world."

"It'll only buy us some time," Geller corrected her, "since the Frost Birds have the ability to see the heat from our bodies."

"They'll only do that if they feel like looking for heat signatures." Selini tried reassuring Jack and Anna. "They don't see heat by default; they have to strain their vision to do so. So, they only do it if they have to."

"Won't they be flying around looking for the heat of animals? Like you all said before, they're experiencing a famine." Cedric had chimed in, curious about how this plan might not work.

"Like me, the Frost Birds have excellent vision and can see things from far away." Gibble explained. "They're not likely to be using their heat vision during the day."

"What about at night?" Cedric looked a little anxious.

"We'll just have to cover as much ground as we can during the day." Geller explained.

With that, Selini tapped her small wand against the Mirror Ball and it slowly grew into a dome that surrounded the whole group with plenty of wiggle room.

"Don't wander too far from me." Selini said, "The dome is centered on my wand."

Jack remembered Geller stating how the trip in Wyvergia was going to take at least four days before they were far enough in to be captured. The scenery over the next few days did not change much. There was one day where they crossed through rolling hills, but nothing was alive anywhere they went.

All throughout the trip, Anna was back to her usual questions with Selini. Cedric and Geller were talking at the head of the group. Jack was content on listening to Selini answer Anna's questions. Fink and

Gink had taken to singing to themselves but loud enough for everybody to hear. Finally, Cedric stopped in his steps and motioned to Selini to join him and Geller. She obliged and all the others stayed behind listening.

"I think this is as good a place as any," Jack could hear Cedric muttering. "It's been a solid four days and we haven't seen a thing yet. At this rate, we'll get to the royal den before they even notice us."

"It is a bit strange to not have seen anything thus far," Geller said. "Maybe it's worse than we thought."

Selini nodded and sighed, "I guess this is it then." She looked at the others, "We're going to uncloak. Be ready for the worst. Just remember, the Frost Birds will likely want to capture us now that we're this far in. We can't expect to walk into the royal den all alone; we'd be killed on sight. So, we need to try and get captured as soon as we can."

Jack and Anna nodded in agreement, but they were both quite skeptical of this plan. It sounded too risky. What if a rogue Frost Bird decided to simply eat them? Jack had known this was coming, but he did not feel at all prepared. He hoped there was a plan to defend themselves if they had to.

Gink and Fink were singing more cheerfully now. They mostly sang songs that boasted about the two of them and their endeavors to make a profit. Annoying as it was to listen to all the time, it did make Jack feel a little better to hear their upbeat tunes. Had their songs been gloomy and dark, he figured they would have been shut up by now. Nobody stopped the two of them or even complained about it. The noise was now a much welcome part of the plan. They had to be discovered as soon as they could.

Jack asked Selini, "How do we get caught? I mean, how do we get carried off? Do we ride on the back of one of the Frost Birds? Or, do they carry us in large talons?"

Before Selini had a chance to answer, Geller exclaimed loudly, "Ride on the back of Frost Bird?!" He gave a forced laugh, "Those dragons are so temperamental, I'd be sure they'd throw us off just to watch us fall!"

Selini answered Jack's question, "I have a plan for that." She had just pulled something out of her bag and held it in the palm of her hand. It was a cage slightly larger than her open hand. "It's a cage. We'll 'capture' ourselves for them and make it easy to carry all of us together. This way we're less likely to be separated, too"

"Wouldn't want them to keep only one as a prisoner and eat the rest of us." Geller laughed nervously.

Jack knew by the looks on their faces that this plan was hardly fool proof. In fact, he was sure the plan was relying more on luck than strategy. Before he could get too sick thinking about it, Anna chimed in.

"Well, I refuse to believe we got this far for something stupid to happen now."

Cedric suddenly stopped and motioned for everyone to do the same. He had heard something and was scanning the hills in the distance for movement. Fink and Gink had even stopped their singing. Gink's face grew a big smile like that of a mad man, his eyes furrowed, and his ears perked up. Another sound came from the hills. This time it was evident that it came from ahead of them. Gibble flew into the air instantly. Then again, another sound, this time it was obviously a whooshing sound that roared loudly. Jack could not tell if it was getting closer, but his heart began to pound. This could be the end, he thought. Moments later Gibble landed in the group.

In a whisper, he exclaimed, "It's a Frost Bird! We've found one! He's not too far and it won't be long before he sees us."

"Why whisper?" Gink laughed maniacally. "Don't we want him to hear us?"

Gink and Fink broke out into song once again. Everyone looked nervous, even Gink and Fink, but no one stopped them.

After a moment, Geller lifted his wand and said, "Well, here goes nothing." A shot of red sparks flew from his wand high in the sky. Jack thought the Frost Bird would have for sure seen it. But, before the sparks were done flying into the air, they exploded in one resounding bang with a shockwave to follow. His shirt shook on his chest and his hair laid flat. Jack stopped breathing. He knew there was no turning back at this point.

Another roar sounded in the distance. This time it was louder and longer. Another roar. Jack knew they had been seen. Then another roar, this time closer. He felt panicky. All the feeling in his limbs had gone and all that was left was a heavy numbness.

"Now we meet Zarx'l" Cedric said matter-of-factly.

Chapter 22: Vlagar

In a distance that would have taken most of the day to cover, a single Frost Bird flew in just a few minutes. It landed loudly and proudly in front of the group with as noisy of a thud as it could make. It huffed, and with it came a puff of frost that filled the air around its head. Jack could swear there were small snowflakes for a moment before the air cleared. And in a deep, raspy voice came a slow beat of words.

"Who goes there?" Without waiting for an answer, the dragon continued speaking, "My next meal! I have been blessed this day; I have. I have feasted too long on the slugs of Wyvergia, I would really do well to have some juicy meat once again."

Jack looked in awe at the sight of the Frost Bird. It must have been a hundred feet in length from snout to tail. And, it stood a booming thirty feet high. There was no need for a creature this size to breath fire or frost, it could easily run over its opponent without ever slowing down. Its scales were grey with blue edges. They looked much like wooden shingles or badly kept fingernails. Jack could not decide. He looked at its face with its large, sky blue eyes. Its ears looked much like Gibble's elfish ears, but many times larger. It had a mane of hair like a lion, streaked with blues and greys. And its snout was long with small scales covering it. Its teeth looked like sharp, jagged ice crystals. As it spoke, its breath fogged in the air and ice formed around its lips.

The dragon had mostly focused on Cedric, the largest member of the group, as he spoke. It was clear the Frost Bird intended on starting with him. Geller stepped up from behind Cedric and pulled out his blade.

"We are on a mission from Gubuyis to speak with Zarx'l. You would be wise to let us through."

The dragon pulled its head back suddenly and took a large breath. Jack felt the slightest gust of air whip past him as it sucked toward the dragon's mouth.

"It speaks!" the dragon looked astonished for a moment. "Such a small little thing. How adorable. And, what's that shiny twig in your hand? I couldn't even use that as a needle." The dragon began laughing menacingly. "You need to control your pets better." It was looking at Cedric as it spoke.

Geller was obviously displeased with the treatment he was receiving, but he did not let it bother him as he spoke again. This time he looked at Jack and gave him a wink, like he was signaling all was going as planned.

"I'd like to see what happens when Zarx'l gets word that a convoy on their way to see him never made it because a foolish, half-witted dragon couldn't contain himself." Geller called back to the Frost Bird.

"ENOUGH!" the dragon exclaimed. Jack could see why they were considered temperamental. It only took a few words to provoke him. "I speak only to this one!" He lowered his head down in front of Cedric.

Cedric, having plenty of experience as an ambassador, felt confident that he could convince the dragon to take them as prisoners.

"Good afternoon, er, mister dragon" Cedric began, "I implore you to heed my friend's request to let us live. Maybe you could take us as your prisoners?" He paused and gazed at the dragon who remained silent. "Maybe you might be rewarded for turning us in? Our message to Zarx'l is of the utmost importance. It affects every Frost Bird in Wyvergia."

"How about you tell me the message and I deliver it?" Jack could see a faint smile creep across the dragon's tight lips.

"We have other business as well." Cedric did not miss a beat. "Our mission is secret and can only be shared with Zarx'l himself. This message comes from the Gubuyis of the Govilian Council."

"We Frost Birds have no business with the Govilian Council, nor any other wretched council or faction or army, and we have no business with the likes of your posse either." The dragon remained still and composed but was obviously agitated in his breathing.

"What harm would there be in taking us to Zarx'l? We could share our message and then you could eat us." Cedric said without regard to the death warrant he was signing. "Simple enough, isn't it?"

The dragon huffed a few times as he mulled over what he was going to do next. He finally slammed his tail against the ground, which shook, and then puffed up his chest as if to say he was coming to his decision.

"And how do you suppose I carry the lot of you?" he asked. It was obvious he felt like he had cleverly deduced that only one had to live to get a message to Zarx'l. "I don't give rides."

Without saying a word, Selini took this as her cue. She stepped aside from the group and placed the small cage on the ground. She then tapped it with her wand, and it grew large enough to carry the whole group.

The dragon let out a small growl of frustration. "Very well." He said sternly, "Get in the stupid cage."

Jack sighed a breath of relief. It looked as if their plan was working. Everyone except for Cedric got in the cage. Gink and Fink were much less motivated than before. Perhaps being prisoners of prisoners was confusing to them. Or, perhaps they realized just how much real danger they were in. Either way, Fink reluctantly clambered with Gink on his back into the cage.

"Thank you, good sir." Cedric said to the dragon, "We have shown you that we trust you. We have faith that you are a mighty Frost Bird of your word." With that he also walked into the cage, closing the door behind him.

The closing of the cage door gave Jack the chills. What if the dragon changed his mind and froze them all right there in the cage. There was nothing they could do at this point. Geller and Selini were sitting next to each other in the middle. Gibble was beginning to pace nervously. Cedric stood resolute, watching the dragon's every movement. Gink and Fink were finally silent and focused on the dragon's body. And, Anna made her way over to Jack. The two of them stood at the back of the cage, helpless to the whims of the dragon.

The ground shook with the movement of the dragon as he situated himself on top of the cage. His large talons grabbed the bars and his wings flapped loudly. They were quickly hoisted high into the air and the air sped through the cage. The wind was much like that on the mountains, just warmer. Jack felt uneasy looking down and seeing the ground moving so quickly under his feet. It did not take long for the whole bunch of them to sit down. Jack tried focusing on anything other than what was happening, he felt sick to his stomach. He had never flown before.

Tree after tree after tree whisked by. Then, the landscape changed into rolling hills, then mountains. Oddly, though, even the mountains were bare of moisture. There were snow patches scattered throughout the mountaintops, but it was much less than there should have been. Dried riverbeds meandered throughout the land. Everywhere he looked, Jack saw drought like he had never imagined. It did not look like it had rained in ages. Even the lakes had dried up.

Selini nudged Jack, "We're almost there." She was pointing to a large forest of dead trees. These trees were massive in size, with many standing several hundred feet in the air. Their trunks were forty or more feet across, and their limbs went on for great distances. Jack had never imagined trees so large. As they got closer, he could make out a fortress nestled into the treetops themselves. Branches were bent over in such a way to create halls and ceilings and floors. They were closing in on the grand entrance quickly. He tried imagining how much more glorious it would be if the trees had their leaves, but it all looked grey and dead.

The dragon swooped down and into the grand opening. The entrance reminded Jack of a spider's funnel web. It was then that Jack could really see the greatness of the place. It was like a castle in the treetops. The walls were made of thickly woven branches and the trunks of trees had been manipulated to run from bottom to top throughout the place like columns. Large metallic, vines covered each column. And, where one might expect to see fruit, there were blue lights. It was magnificent in its grandeur, but the color was cold. Hanging from the ceiling were the same metallic vines, adding a twinkling light to the whole place.

Their speed had slowed considerably now that they were in the royal den. They passed halls filled with nest after nest. These nests were extraordinarily large. Some were filled with sleeping dragons, but many were empty. All the dragons looked similar in color to the one that was carrying them, but some were barely half its size. Some had manes and some did not. Even though they were in the heart of the den, Jack felt a little less nervous. Perhaps it was the sheer splendor of what he was seeing that took his mind off the danger they were in. Whatever it was, his fears had been somewhat relieved, and he was lost in astonishment.

Rounding one last corner, they came upon a large room filled with more light than any other. At the end of the room sat a large throne prepared from the same branches that made up the whole royal den. It glowed different shades of glimmering blue and in it laid a glorious dragon. It was much larger than any of the dragons Jack had seen so far. Grey scales were replaced by shades of purples and blues. Its mane was mostly white and grey.

They flew all the way up to the base of the throne, which stood high above them. The dragon carrying them hovered several feet from the floor and dropped the cage loudly. He was obviously quite pleased with himself for causing all its occupants to thrash about.

"Your majesty," the dragon had landed on the floor and was bowing its head, "I have brought you a bunch of misfits who claim they are on a mission to speak with you." He sneered at the group and gave a puff of frost in their direction.

The purple dragon lowered his head and examined them. "Hmm" his voice was deep.

"This is Zarx'l." Selini whispered to Jack and Anna.

Zarx'l was slow to move and his posture was much more trained than that of the dragon that had brought them here. Jack watched as his fear began to slowly creep back over him. The anticipation of whether they would be freed or killed was churning his stomach. Everyone in the group was standing, but nobody was moving. Jack did not move out of fear. Anna looked as if she was about to say something, but Selini quickly nudged her and shook her head.

Then, the dragon lifted his head and spoke gently, "I wasn't expecting any – messages. I can't imagine why anyone would ever wander so freely into Wyvergia and expect my company." He turned his head to the other dragon, "Get them out of my sight, Vlagar."

With that, Vlagar, the dragon that had been carrying them, flew above the cage and grabbed it once again. He began flapping his wings and a grin crossed his face.

"This isn't right!" Fink exclaimed. "We didn't even want to be here."

"What's happening?" Jack asked Geller "What are we doing?"

Geller looked a little disappointed, "I don't think this is going as planned anymore."

Anna shouted out to Zarx'l, "We represent the Govilian Council. We've been sent here by Gubuyis himself!" She was calling out in desperation.

As the cage was being lifted in the air, Zarx'l spoke calmly, "I do not care. I am not a part of the Govilian Council or its petty missions. We have our own business to attend to."

Without thinking, Jack sputtered out loudly, "We know where your water is going!"

Vlagar stopped without command. He knew Zarx'l would be inquisitive at this.

Zarx'l's eyes thinned and he called for Vlagar to bring them back. "Let me see this ... human."

"I hope this works," Selini whispered anxiously.

Vlagar dropped the cage and everybody fell once again. Even though he had stopped them from certain death, Jack felt that he had somehow just made a big mistake. He did not know enough about Ghowla and the Arbolion trees to explain what was happening. He looked frantically at Geller for help.

Zarx'l commanded Jack to speak, "Well, go ahead – human – tell me all about my supposed water problem." He looked angry that Jack had even mentioned it.

"I, er, um, I, it's this Ghowla character, you see" Jack struggled to find the words he needed to say.

"Here we go again!" Zarx'l lifted his head high and breathed a large puff of frost and ice high in the air. He was obviously frustrated at the mere mention of Ghowla. "It's always Ghowla but no proof. Ghowla this and Ghowla that. I've told your council before; we will not wage war for the sake of waging war. There are no sides. There is mighty Wyvergia and then there is the rest of you all squabbling and nitpicking about whose land is whose. We have no interest in a silly alliance."

By the way he spoke, Jack could tell Zarx'l had been approached for an alliance before. Now he was even more nervous. He did not know what to say. He thought about how he started the conversation, telling Zarx'l he knew about where the water was. He took a deep breath and decided to continue.

"He's draining all the water from your land. He's using it to build an army." Jack spouted out quickly.

"AGAIN!" Zarx'l shouted, "Ghowla is my problem you say. But, do you offer proof? Or do you merely expect me to join you on some crusade because he's done you wrong? I refuse to subject my army to a fight that brings nothing but death. There is no glory in your fight, it is impossible."

"I have proof." Selini spoke out. "I have seen with my own eyes what Ghowla has been doing. He has taken over an Arbolio tree named Ezjuin and has been using spells to make her grow much faster than she should. She needs water and lots of it. She drinks from three rivers and an aquifer. Ghowla knows he's killing Wyvergia but he doesn't care. He knows you'll never fight him. He knows he'd win if you did. There are no negative consequences to his actions."

"AAARRRRGGGG!!!" Zarx'l's deep voice raged, "I said I need proof! Not some mutterings of a Valindi! I have had en…"

"I have proof!" Selini had moved to the front of the cage and had pulled out her wand. She gave it a wave and a large cloud appeared in front of Zarx'l. In it were images of Selini's memories from scouting missions. She had seen firsthand some of the actions by Ghowla. She showed Zarx'l all he needed to see, including the decay of his homeland as the ground dried up.

Zarx'l blew the memory cloud away in a fit. Then, after some moments of tense silence, he said, "I want nothing more than to return Wyvergia back to its former glory. But, waging war, even if in alliance with the Govilian Council, would be fruitless. Ghowla is a very powerful wizard. There is nothing we can do to his armies that would win us the battle."

Jack could tell Zarx'l was contemplating multiple strategies and coming up with the same conclusion each time.

"We just need to hold them off until winter. They'll pull back as the temperatures become unbearable and the land becomes unfavorable." Gibble tried reassuring Zarx'l.

Zarx'l pulled his head back in surprise. "Is that your strategy?" Gibble immediately regretted talking. "You don't even plan on winning? What happens after winter? I'm more assured now that we are better off staying out of it."

Geller was annoyed at Gibble for his comment. He interjected, however, trying to repair the damage Gibble had done, "We don't see a viable way to win before winter is upon us. But, the council is amassing its forces as we speak, getting ready for the coming spring.

There just isn't enough time to win this battle for good."

Cedric stopped Geller and spoke, "Since you are not in the Govilian Council, we cannot divulge any more information to you regarding these matters. Our strategy is secret and only to be shared with our council members."

Jack thought Zarx'l would certainly be upset over such remarks, but instead Zarx'l simply replied, "I respect your secrecy, but know this, we are not your enemy. We just aren't your ally."

It had occurred to Jack that the whole reason they were here was to inform Zarx'l of the treachery that was making Wyvergia dwindle away. Now that they had done that, would they be let free? He had hoped for sure that their offering of this news was going to gain them an ally. He had not thought about what would happen if they did not succeed. Then he remembered the Prunklesnider recipe Bolar had given him. He was about to grab for it but thought better of it. What good would that do right now?

"We may be without water, but unless you have some spell to fix that, our business is done." Zarx'l was looking at Cedric for an answer.

Cedric simply shook his head.

"I didn't think so. As usual, I am brought problems with no attempt at providing a solution." Zarx'l's deep voice had diminished in volume as he showed his disappointment. "We already know death here. There is no reason to greet it anywhere else."

"Your majesty," Cedric said, "Seeing as our talks are ended, might I beg of you to let us free so that we may live out our remaining days with our loved ones? You see, we too face death very soon, and we'd rather it not be here."

"You may go." Zarx'l sat back down in his throne and motioned to Vlagar to take the group away.

Once again, Vlagar lifted to cage and began to fly away. Jack's mind was racing. What could they do? If there had been some kind of spell to fix the water problem, Jack was sure someone would have done something about it. Then it hit him.

"WAIT!" he shouted as loud as he could as they were almost out of the great room. "WE HAVE WATER!"

Chapter 23: A Frost Bird Lagoon

Jack had succeeded in stopping Vlagar, but he was not sure what to say now. He had an idea that might work to their favor. He just had to figure out how to elaborate on it, and now was his moment.

Selini's eyes met Jack's in curiosity as Vlagar stopped in a huff. Then she immediately knew what he meant.

"This better not be a stupid trick," Vlagar mumbled as he turned to face Zarx'l. "Should I take them away, your majesty?"

"I'm curious and they're locked up." Zarx'l stood back up and walked toward them. "So, let us continue, shall we? What do you mean, 'you have water'?"

Anna was not so sure what was going on. She gave Jack a little shove of disapproval for his last-ditch efforts. She was sure Jack had simply said it as a trick to talk with Zarx'l more.

"Oh ho ho ho ho!" Gink smiled his wide smile, "This one's smart he is."

Fink was smiling, too. The pair had figured out what was going on.

"Tell me, boy, what do you mean?" Zarx'l sounded impatient and frost shot out of his nostrils. "I do not like to be lied to!"

"It may not be a permanent solution, but it'll help." Jack started. "I have a lake of water I can give you."

"He lies!" scowled Vlagar. "Humans have no power!"

"It's true," Selini chimed in. "He has an elemental Cerilian box. It's got an entire lake in it." She was obviously excited and almost out of breath just trying to say these few simple words.

Zarx'l instructed Vlagar to bring the cage down to the floor of the forest. Zarx'l followed with two guards at his side. They flew out of the royal den and down several hundred feet before landing. There, they had Jack step out of the cage and show them what he meant.

Jack stepped out of the cage and made his way between a few trees, which were thickly packed and rose higher than he could see. The forest was almost black except for the dim glow of the royal den above. He could see his breath as he walked toward a small break in the trees. He knew it was daytime, but nothing about this place made it seem that way. He stopped in his tracks and turned to face Zarx'l.

"Is this a good place?" Jack knew it did not matter where he opened the box and did not know why he even asked.

"Mmmm" Zarx'l replied back. He was still suspicious of Jack's claim. But he had nothing to lose in letting him try.

Geller shouted out to Jack, "Just think about wanting the water. Set it on the ground and think about wanting the water."

"Here goes nothing" Jack whispered to himself.

He grabbed the Cerilian box and thought about wanting the water to come out. As he did that, he set it on the ground in front of him. He watched as the box opened. Slowly, water began spilling over the sides with more and more power. Remembering how fast it filled, Jack turned and ran toward the cage. A small twister of bright blue water began forming over the top. Then another and another until the scene was all too familiar. It looked just like it did when it filled, but this time the water was spewing out. The water was quickly rising around them.

"We can't stay here!" Cedric shouted to Zarx'l over the rushing water.

By nightfall they were all celebrating in the grand hall. They were no longer caged, and it seemed their mission was no longer a failure. There was a growing lake far beneath them now. Jack watched as leaves slowly began to form on the branches. They were bluish green with blue veins. He smiled. He thought for sure the Frost Birds would be on their side now.

Geller had performed his spell on a large animal carcass from the royal food stores making it plenty of food for a feast. Cedric was playing a large stringed instrument of some kind. The music it made was beautiful, but Cedric's singing was harsh and rough to Jack's ears. Gink and Fink, still bound, were talking to a Frost Bird. It looked like they were unsuccessfully attempting to trade a potion for one of its talons. Gibble was sitting near Cedric, listening to the music quietly. He looked tired and lost in thought. Anna and Selini were dancing together. They looked like they were having fun, having put the dreads of the journey behind them. The music filled the chamber.

Zarx'l looked content with watching his dragons celebrate. It had been a while since there was something to be merry about. There must have been thirty or forty dragons in the great hall. They all chattered amongst themselves, feasting and swaying to the music. Occasionally, a dragon would raise its head and blow frost into the air in excitement. The air was chilled, and a light snowfall had begun in parts of the hall. But even the cold could not get Jack down right now. He was excited that something finally went their way.

Everyone partied late into the night. Cedric had fallen asleep while playing his instrument; ending the music with one last, loud disorganized strum. With that, the party quickly dissipated as each dragon eventually left for their roosts. Gibble still looked lost in his thoughts, but sleep was quickly overcoming him. Without an audience to solicit to, Gink and Fink had come back to the group and were fast asleep. Selini and Anna were also wrapping up their night. They were preparing a place to sleep. Jack had been happy but had not felt like dancing at all that night. He had been perfectly content just watching the frivolities of the others, much like Zarx'l had done. There was much on his mind having let it wander all night. He found it hard to sleep.

Zarx'l looked at Jack and attempted to speak gently in his booming voice, "You should rest. You have done us a great deed and I am in your debt. I also believe you will be pleased to know I have decided that Wyvergia will join the Govilians Council. The fight may seem impossible, but perhaps with the mighty Frost Birds on your side, there may be a chance. I realized just how scavenger-like we'd become; feeding off the remnants of foul creatures." He was becoming angry as he spoke and a small puff of frost blew from his snout, "To think we were forced into these conditions. We remained neutral and still Ghowla attacked us!"

His voice was much less calm now. But, before he spoke, he sighed and held his tongue for a moment. Then he spoke gently again, "Vlagar will stay at your guard tonight. You must sleep now." He then rose out of his throne and walked loudly out of the great hall.

Jack walked over to where the others were laying and watched Zarx'l exit the room. He wondered why they needed guarding in such a great fortress but did not think much of it. He was pleased with himself for having thought about the water in the Cerilian box. Selini had to use her enchanted boat to save them, which led to Jack using the box on the lake. Then he thought about how that would never have happened had someone or something not tried killing him in the cavern. Things could have been much different right now, he contemplated.

"You two get some sleep now, I'll watch over you." Vlagar said as quietly as he could, sounding slightly annoyed. Jack had not noticed that Gibble was still awake, looking lost. He must have really let fear take over him today, Jack thought, as Gibble looked drained.

The next morning started similarly to many of the past mornings. Jack awoke to the smell of Geller's cooking. This time, though, Cedric was playing his instrument again. It sounded like a high-pitched harp, but it was fun listening to. He heard Anna talking with Gink and Fink about a protection potion and Selini talking with Gibble about the storm in the cavern. Vlagar was still near them, having never left his post. He still looked like he was guarding them. Jack wondered if some of the other Frost Birds might try and eat them if they did not have some sort of protection.

Moments later, Zarx'l came into the room. He walked proudly as he made his way to his throne.

"We're all rested, now are we?" Zarx'l asked loudly. "Because today you begin your journey back home with what I can only assume is good news."

Jack's stomach sank. He obviously knew they had to get back home, but it was only just now hitting him that they now had to traverse their whole path all over again.

"Vlagar can get you to the edge of the Joules Storm. From there, you will be on your own. My dragons cannot fly through such a fierce electrical storm."

"Your majesty," Anna spoke before anyone could stop her. "We have a couple potion masters here that might be able to put together a protection spell for Vlagar to get through the storm."

"They might be able to?" He seemed slightly annoyed and shook his head, "I will not ask Vlagar to risk flying through such a storm on the hopes the potion will work."

"Ugh!" Fink made no attempt to silence his disgust at the mere thought that someone did not think he could make a strong enough potion. "I guarantee my work ..."

"What Anna means to say, your majesty," Geller interrupted Fink, "is that with a few more ingredients, we *can* make a strong enough potion to provide Vlagar the protection he needs."

"Hmmm," Zarx'l squinted at Fink and Gink, "I happen to know potions. I'm not very good at them, but I have studied them before. What ingredients are you in need of?"

"AH!" Fink perked up and nudged Gink for the list.

Gink patted his pockets for a moment as if looking for something, then simply bellowed out, "We need a bucket of grave moss and two large eyes of ... er ... um"

"Do you not know?" Selini asked hurriedly and annoyed.

Gink continued after an awkward moment of silence, "Uh-hum, we need one large bucket of grave moss and two large eyes of … dragon."

"I hope you're not suggesting I claw out the eyes of my subjects." Zarx'l said with a hint of a smile on his face looking at Vlagar.

Jack was nervous for Gink and Fink. If they weren't careful, Zarx'l might keep them as his own prisoners.

"Well, you'll be glad to hear!" Zarx'l was almost giddy as he spoke, "I have plenty of large dragon eyes in my stores. As it turns out, fire breathers happen to be our enemies. And we've had plenty of run-ins with them over the last few years."

Gibble gave a nervous laugh.

"Great!" exclaimed Fink. "We can whip up a potion in no time, then."

"Now, before we move on." Zarx'l looked much more serious now, "I must ask you all. Do you happen to know any fire breathers?"

Geller answered almost immediately, "No. We have tried becoming allies with Lumenzian, or 'fire breathers', before, but to no avail."

"So you do not claim to be friends with any fire breathers, then?" Zarx'l looked as if the next answer could have serious consequences.

Selini spoke up this time, "Govilians try to make peace with all of Lunia's inhabitants the best we can. We have tried making an alliance with the Lumenzian numerous times. Every time we have failed. They do not wish to have peace, but we still hold hope that one day that will change."

"Why do I feel like I'm being lied to?" Zarx'l's snout was puffing frost and his voice grew louder.

"If we were friends with the fire breathers, your majesty, we wouldn't have been attacked by them on the way here!" Anna shouted over the puffing sounds of Zerx'l's frost breath.

Zarx'l fell silent immediately. Then he asked, "Why would they attack you?"

Selini chimed back in, "We don't know. We just know they were aiming their attack on Jack. There must have been hundreds of them. They definitely weren't acting as our friends, your majesty."

Zarx'l motioned to the guards who quickly surrounded the group. Jack did not know what was going on. He hated feeling like they had to walk on thin ice around Zarx'l or any of the Frost Birds for that matter. They were all being corralled in the center of the dragons. He felt like they somehow did something wrong, but he could not figure it out.

"You see," Zarx'l said coolly, "we frost breathers have an innate ability to smell a fire breather from far distances. As I told you, fire breathers are our enemies."

A little panicked, Selini shouted out, "We don't know any fire breathers! We are not friends with the Lumenzian!"

"Exactly," snapped Zarx'l, "So you won't mind if we take care of a little mole problem, then!" He motioned to the guards again and they moved.

"STOP!" Gibble stepped forward. "You will never be able to kill us all! We're stronger than your feeble forces, you'll see!"

"Gibble!" Selini tried hushing him. "What are you doing? You're making it worse!"

Zarx'l motioned for the guards to hold their positions. "I was wondering when you would say something." He looked happy but with a look similar to that of Gink's usual grin. Something was going on, but Jack could not figure it out.

"What's he talking about?" Cedric asked the group. "What's going on here?"

"Yeah, what's going on, Gibble? What is he talking about?" Geller was grabbing the hilt of his dagger now. Seeing this, Selini pulled out her wand and faced it towards Gibble.

Anna backed into Jack. He was confused. Did Gibble know something about the Lumenzian dragons that put him in an unfavorable position with Zarx'l? Had Gibble ordered the attack of the dragons somehow?

"Come out, come out, wherever you are," Zarx'l taunted Gibble. "I have too little patience for your petty games." He stood up and the guards all got into defensive positions. "You can face me like a dragon, or you can face me like the coward you really are, it does not matter to me. You're dead either way!" He took a deep breath in.

Jack knew Zarx'l was about to breath frost right at them. He did not know what to do. Was there something about Gibble that he was missing? The whole group backed up as much as they could. That is, the whole group except for Gibble, who remained resolute.

Suddenly, there was a growling sound. Small flames shot from Gibble's nostrils. His back arched unnaturally, and his tail grew rapidly along the floor. His whole body was growing. His wings cracked and fluttered as they expanded outward. The guards backed up to accommodate his growing size but remained defensively positioned.

After a few moments, there stood a large, black dragon with red and yellow eyes right where Gibble had been standing. It looked much like the one he had pierced with the poisoned blade. Jack could not believe what he was seeing. Had they been traveling with a dragon the whole time?

The black dragon took in a large breath. Jack knew they were about to be caught in the middle of a dragon fight. But, before the black dragon could breathe his fire, Zarx'l and the guards in unison breathed their frost at him. Instantly the dragon froze. For a moment, it stood there, solid and covered in ice. Then, it began to tip over. Some of the guards moved out of its way and let the frozen dragon fall to the floor. In one ground shaking bang and crash, the black dragon exploded into thousands of frozen pieces like an icicle smashing to the ground.

Two large, frozen dragon's eyes rolled to Cedric's feet. He backed up; half disgusted half in awe of what just transpired before his eyes.

"Does it help if the eyes are freshly obtained?" Zarx'l asked casually to Fink.

The whole group stood in silence for a moment. Everyone had been taken aback by what just happened. Geller still had his hand on the hilt of his dagger but was slowly releasing it. Selini's wand was beginning to lower as she observed the shattered dragon pieces all over the floor.

"What?" Anna asked confusingly, "What … just … happened?"

"I think you'll notice that your friend here was an impostor." Zarx'l motioned to the guards to stand down. They now returned to their posts in the great hall.

"I've known Gibble for ages," said Geller. "How have I not known?"

"I'm afraid your real friend Gibble is probably long dead. I would imagine this dragon has been acting as an impostor for weeks, maybe longer." Zarx'l explained softly.

"Only a commander acting for the king could have directed those dragons to attack Jack. Somehow, they knew from the beginning that Jack was a threat. But, why? What do you have that threatens them so?" Geller was looking to Jack for answers he knew were not there.

"That explains how we got attacked. First, he tried killing us in the cavern." Selini was explaining aloud, "Then, he tried attacking us in the cavern on the way here. The second time was more powerful. He must have been more desperate to kill you."

"But why not keep trying?" Geller mused.

"He probably figured if he didn't succeed again, it would have been obvious there was someone nefarious amongst you. Indeed, he would have been biding his time; waiting for just the right time to strike. If I was him, I would have waited and watched as the Frost Birds did his dirty work for him." Zarx'l explained. "As I said before, little Mister Jack, you have made friends with us. I could not sit by and do nothing once I realized what was going on."

"Th-thank you," Jack managed to mutter, still in shock.

"We must tell Gubuyis at once!" Cedric straightened up and looked fully alert again. "This treachery could be the downfall of our battle!"

Selini grabbed Geller's arm, "What if Ghowla knows about our plan? He'll have already taken defensive measures to protect Ezjuin!"

"Yes, sister, we need to formulate a new strategy and fast." Geller sounded discouraged and urgent. "How fast until you have that potion ready?" He asked Gink.

"Give us an hour." Gink replied. "We'll whip one up as fast as we can."

"In the meantime, we need to think of another way to defeat Ghowla." Geller sounded worried. "If you have an idea," he announced to the whole group and Zarx'l, "now's the time to mention it."

While Gink and Fink prepared a large batch of a protection potion over the next hour, the rest of the group sat with Zarx'l and attempted to come up with new ideas for defeating Ghowla. Each idea seemed as bad as the last, and none had any promise of working. If they were not able to stop Ghowla, they would not be able to stop his troops.

Jack could not help but replay the image of the dragon smashing into pieces in front of him. The power of the Frost Birds was immense. He wished there was some way to use that effectively against Ghowla himself, but they had warned several times throughout the conversation that Ghowla was too powerful to hit directly. His army was just too strong for them to take on with the numbers they had. Zarx'l warned that the number of dragons he had at his disposal was much smaller than ever, having lost many of his subjects to the extreme drought. He assured them, however, that he could amass several hundred in the time they had.

The image of the dragon smashing replayed again. Jack winced at the thought of it. It reminded him of a winter storm back home that came too early. The bitter cold froze everything. Each individual blade of grass was covered in ice and snapped into a hundred pieces beneath his feet. Tree branches snapped under the weight of the ice and tree trunks shattered like cannons hit them as the water inside them froze. Then it hit him like a ton of bricks.

"I have an idea!" he exclaimed.

Chapter 24: A Newfound Alliance

The flight back was much shorter than the journey to Wyvergia, having only taken a day. The protection spell worked perfectly, guarding Vlagar and everyone sitting on his back from the electrical storm. It lasted the entire trip, so the flight through the mountains was guarded against the bitter winds, too. At nightfall, the group arrived at Gargantulua and landed in front of the large fountain they had set off from. There were not many Valindi in the town center this time of night, but those that were out had quite the scare seeing a Frost Bird. Some had never seen one before. They scattered about trying to take cover.

Geller asked Vlagar to wait while they sorted out the events of the last few weeks. He was especially concerned with the Gibble imposter. There was so much at stake and he knew their next decision would make or break their ability to win this upcoming battle. The group climbed off Vlagar and quickly made their way into the Panthyun's gargoyle lined hallways. Geller ran up to one particular gargoyle that was sitting at a table with a small lantern and asked to see Gubuyis immediately. The gargoyle disappeared into the wall for a brief moment and then came back.

"Follow me" it said in a squeaky voice.

A door large enough to fit even Cedric formed. The other gargoyles around the new doorway looked annoyed that they were being pushed aside and disrupted. Some even muttered their disapproval at the time of night. The group made their way through a long, meandering hallway until they came upon a dead end. Jack thought at first that there must have been some mistake but could not think of any way they could have messed it up. It was only one long hallway, no way to get lost in it. Selini stepped forward and grabbed a small knocker that was perfect for a Valindi's height and banged it loudly against the heavy stone wall. Only a moment passed before Jack could hear clicking and clanking like large gears and machinery doing its work. Then, numerous stones slid into each other until there was a big enough hole to fit everybody through.

They all entered the room. It was dimly lit with the same floating orbs used to light up their tents. The room felt warm and inviting despite its lack of light. There were books lining every side of the circular room as high as Jack could see. In the center was a small wooden table with several orbs of light floating above it; illuminating it fully. A large, aged, but cozy looking, dark green chair sat on one side of the table. And on the table were several books haphazardly strewn about; some closed, some open. There was a large quill in an ink bottle sitting near one corner. And, what amazed Jack the most at the moment, was a large slowly spinning globe. It was made from a distressed brass. The continents glowed with different shades of iridescent colors. There were large bodies of water that looked like oceans. They glowed bright blue and had small waves all throughout.

In the chair sat Gubuyis who had just looked up from a book he was reading. He set it down and looked at a timepiece lying open on the table.

"Well," Gubuyis looked pleased, "either you've turned back early, or someone gave you a ride. And, if you got a ride, then your mission must have been quite productive." He paused for a moment, looking over the group. Then he got out of his chair and walked over to Gink and Fink, "I see you acquired something more along the way." Then he turned to Geller, "What has happened to our dear friend Gibble? Where has he gone?"

Geller began explaining everything that happened. The major parts were filled in by Selini's memory clouds. Gubuyis had many questions, but they were mostly easily answered. When they told him about the treachery of the Gibble impostor, he quickly came to the same conclusion the rest of them had; the plan to poison Ezjuin had to be scrapped. That is when Jack got to explain his strategy to him. Gubuyis seemed to agree that Jack's strategy may work very well in lieu of what they had originally planned on doing. The only problem was that they would need to move quickly.

"Our scouts have reported that Ghowla's army is beginning to empty Ezjuin's roots and fill the ground level. They are amassing for a full-scale assault in the coming days." Gubuyis was sitting at the table again, catching the group up on the current state of things. "If we are to adopt Jack's plan, we must adopt it now." He turned to a pillar in the room that had a single gargoyle on it and commanded, "Assemble the Govilian Council. This is urgent."

"How long do we have until they attack?" Selini asked.

"Based on their haste, we believe they will begin their march within the next three to four days." Gubuyis answered. "We don't even have enough time to assemble all our forces before we expect the attack to begin. It is a blessing that we have the Frost Birds to fight by our side, but we are still too weak to fully fight. We have fortified the walls of the city as best as we can. Our allies are on their way, but, like I said, we won't have everyone ready in time before the attack begins. Jack's plan may work, and if we can do it now, we may win this battle."

Within the hour, they were all sitting at the table centered in the middle of the Council Room. Gubuyis explained to the Govilian Council, which was composed of ambassadors, generals, and politicians from various nations, of the deceit the party faced and the ramifications that brought. There was much talking amongst the members as they all began trying to think of new strategies, knowing now that they had the Frost Birds. Gubuyis did not try to silence the room or explain Jack's idea, but instead let them chatter.

Cedric, sitting to the left of Jack, could see Jack's confusion as to why he was not explaining the new strategy. He leaned over to Jack and explained, "He wants to allow them to try and come up with a solution first. This way they're more likely to listen to one after they haven't been able to come up with anything. Who knows? Maybe there's a better idea out there. We'll see."

Gubuyis let the room murmur for roughly fifteen minutes before asking for their silence and continuing, "As you all know, time is against us like an enemy. Are there any proposed strategies?"

Several times an idea was shouted out only to be shot down by another with a reason for why it would not work. Jack was beginning to feel queasy about his own idea. As he saw the harshness of the others towards their ideas, he began to second guess if his was truly the best one.

After the room calmed back down, Gubuyis motioned to Jack, "Jack here has come up with a strategy that I believe may just win the day."

At that, Cedric gently nudged Jack to stand.

Jack stood and the room went silent. He did not know where to begin, but he knew he needed to start talking before the room disregarded him entirely.

"Many years ago, back home, there was an early winter storm. It was too early. All the leaves were still on the trees and the grass was still green – which is what it's supposed to be like." He had noticed some of the faces of confusion when he mentioned the color of the grass. He had to be careful not to get into where he truly was from, knowing that if he did, he could completely derail the topic. "Not only was it an early winter storm, but it was a bitter cold storm, much like one might expect to see in the dead of winter."

"What is this boy talking about!" a voice shouted out from the crowd. Chattering began to fill the hall again. Nobody was listening to Jack any longer.

Jack stood still. He had no intention on trying to silence the Govilian Council as he did not even feel like he should be there at all. He wondered why Gubuyis could not explain it for him.

Gubuyis tapped his staff against the ground next to his podium. A thunderous booming filled the room and the voices suddenly silenced. He gestured to Jack to continue.

"Um, well, like I said, it was bitterly cold." Jack continued hesitantly. He was not sure how to get his point across before losing the crowd again, but he figured he would go as long as they would let him. "The storm lasted all through the night. By the morning, everything was covered in ice. Each individual blade of grass was an icicle of its own. Bushes were laid flat against the ground from the sheer weight of the ice. Tree branches, entire limbs, crashed down under the weight of the ice. But, perhaps the most important thing here, many trees shattered like a cannon ball had driven through them."

"Jack, get to the point!" Anna, who was sitting to his right, whispered frantically. "You're gonna lose them."

Jack tried talking a little faster, "The point is, the trees shattered the way they did because they were full of water. They hadn't been ready for winter yet, so the water inside their trunks expanded like ice does, and it just destroyed them." There was some murmur, but no sign that his explanation was being followed yet. He continued, "I propose that, er, I think, um, that since Ezjuin is full of water right now, that we do the same thing to her." He rushed his last comment, being too nervous to expand on it. He quickly sat back down.

Before anyone could interject, Gubuyis picked up where Jack left off. "Indeed, Ezjuin has been drinking more than her fair share this last season. Her roots and trees have stored massive amounts of water in them. We are proposing that we freeze her."

The room exploded into multiple conversations and yelling voices. Jack could not tell what anyone was saying, but he felt this response was probably better than he would have received if he had said it.

Then a singular voice came from the crowd, yelling louder than all the others, "How do you propose we get an ice storm all the way to Ezjuin without Ghowla stopping us with a counter curse?"

The room quieted down some. Jack knew they were waiting on an answer, but it felt like the room would not believe whatever explanation they were given. The atmosphere was tense.

"Quite right you are, Sajuaw, quite right indeed." The room fell silent as Gubuyis began talking again, "If we were to enchant the weather to do this job, Ghowla would certainly have the means to stop it before it ever became a threat to him. Plus, it would only instigate him into attacking sooner. Jack's plan is to utilize the Frost Birds in this sense."

Another murmur filled the room, but much quieter this time. Jack could tell Gubuyis had their attention.

He continued, "As you all know, the Frost Birds have immense freezing capabilities. One long breath from a single Frost Bird would be enough to freeze several trees at once. Thanks to Jack, we now have hundreds of Frost Birds willing to fight by our side." He stepped down from his podium and walked in front of the table, "Imagine what several hundred Frost Birds could do to a single Arbolio. Imagine what several hundred Frost Birds can do to Ezjuin – an Arbolio full of water. We can cripple Ghowla's forces to the point they cannot fight. Furthermore, we would destroy his stronghold once and for all." He paused for a moment to let the room take in what was being proposed. Then, he said, "We could possibly rid ourselves of Ghowla once and for all."

Again, the room filled with loud conversations. This time seemed a little more upbeat than before. But Jack was growing tired. It was just this morning that they had learned of the impostor. It all seemed to be moving so fast. After several back and forth questions from the crowd to Gubuyis, there was a general consensus that this strategy was perhaps the best one they had. The Govilian Council quickly voted in favor of it and dismissed.

"We must dispatch Vlagar at once." Cedric stated to Gubuyis, "He will need to inform Zarx'l of when the attack begins."

Gubuyis nodded and wrote on a piece of parchment. He then rolled it up and handed it to Geller. "The attack begins the day after tomorrow."

Cedric and Geller made off for Vlagar while the rest of them remained seated at the table in the nearly empty Council Room. Jack felt relieved. It felt like a large weight had been lifted off his shoulders and he was excited that his strategy was going to be used. His gut was turning over and over, though, as he started wondering about what would happen if his plan failed.

"We need to get some sleep," Anna interrupted his thoughts as she stood up. "Things are about to get crazy."

"Follow me," Selini motioned. "Let's get situated at the cottage. There's a lot to prepare for and we need to rest before we move forward with anything else."

Jack was relieved to hear Selini and Anna were both thinking what he was feeling. Everything over the last several weeks had moved so fast. He thought about home as they all walked back to the cottage. The smell of spirits filled the air as they passed by the tavern and it reminded him of the street near the pub back home. All he could think about was being home. Then it hit him – what if he never made it back home? Even worse, what if his plan failed and all the Valindi were killed?

The group was about to enter the cottage where they had slept before. Jack stopped; eyes open wide, and his chest heavy.

"What is it?" Anna asked.

He held his hand on the doorframe as he tried to brace himself from buckling at his knees, breathing heavily.

"You just need some rest, Jack." Selini reassured him. "It's okay to be scared. Something my father told me once before was that fear in small amounts can be good, but like anything else, too much of a good thing can be a bad thing. If you let it control you, all you'll end up doing is the very thing you fear happening. If you're fearing failure, then you'll probably fail. Focus, Jack. Don't worry about everyone else." Selini spoke very matter-of-factly.

She gave him a quick smile and proceeded into the cottage. She disappeared into the dark as Anna stayed behind with Jack.

"I know you're probably scared," Anna stated, "and I wish I knew what to say."

She paused for a moment. The night air was warm and filled with the smells of the town. They both stood in silence while he calmed down.

"Just …" she began, "just know that you're stronger than you think. Everyone can see that, maybe not you, but we can."

She put her hand on his shoulder as she spoke. She then proceeded into the cottage.

Jack stood by himself for a while. He was not clutching the doorframe any longer as he had collected himself to a small extent. Worry and fear were still very much alive in his head, though.

He leaned against the cottage wall and watched the night. There was a slight breeze blowing through his hair. He had expected it to be quieter, though, especially for the time of night that it was. But, the preparations for battle had taken precedent over everything else, including sleep apparently. There were many more guards than what he remembered from before. There were Valindi bustling about the streets now. The familiar sounds of metals clanking reminded him of the blacksmith back home. He gave a small smile at the thought of his hometown, but quickly dismissed the happiness with fear once again.

"I'd better get some sleep," Jack said to himself.

He also retreated to the warm bed inside the cottage and turned in for the night.

Chapter 25: The Battle at Ezjuin

Morning came quickly. Jack awoke to the sounds of hurried feet and intense conversations from the main room. He did not feel rested but knew there was no time to squander. He quickly got ready for the day and headed out of his room.

"Good sir!" Geller was just outside Jack's door preparing to enter when Jack opened it. "I've prepared you a meal!"

Geller was looking quite content. He handed Jack a small loaf of bread and made off for the main room.

Jack watched in confusion as Geller walked with haste. He could not figure out why Geller would be so content at such a time. He slowly followed Geller back to the main room while he ate the small loaf of bread prepared by Geller.

He was still befuddled by how quickly he became full eating such a small amount of food and it tasted amazing.

"There you are!" Anna was looking displeased with Jack. "Today is a bit bigger of a day than you must think. You can't just waste it away sleeping, now can you?"

Jack stopped in his tracks at the opening to the main room. He felt ambushed by her comment. He felt just as ready as everyone else looked. So, he gave her a scowl to express his displeasure in her remark.

Gubuyis was leaning over the end of the table along with Geller, Selini, and Cedric. At Anna's comment, they had all looked up and greeted Jack with slight head nods and then continued to pour over a large map.

Jack made his way over to the table to see what they were doing. He saw a large animal hide of some kind with a map similar to the globe in Gubuyis's study. There were colored, animated regions. Just the sight of it was wondrous to him, but he knew right now was not a good time to become distracted.

Geller looked at Jack, "Your plan is going to work!"

"We must plan for success and then act on that plan." Gubuyis affirmed without looking up.

Cedric pointed hard at a point on the map, "Right here is where we should begin the assault."

Gubuyis nodded in agreement as he continued to look over the battlefield.

Just then, Gink and Fink came into the cottage. They were arguing about something between themselves like usual. Their arguing filled the room as they entered, and they did not seem to care that it was distracting everyone else. Gubuyis had freed them from their bonds the night before for their part in helping along the group on their journey. With their newfound freedom, the pair was more gleeful and rowdier than usual.

"Would you two just be quiet! Always with you two! The noise and incessant arguing, it's just atrocious." Selini spouted at them when they entered the room.

The pair immediately quieted down at her remarks.

"Well now, what're we up to here?" Gink motioned toward the table.

Jack chimed in, feeling like he could contribute something to the conversation, "It looks like we may have just figured out our plan of attack."

Gink looked awkwardly at Cedric's finger, still pointing at a point on the map.

"I would choose there," he pointed toward the center of the front of Ezjuin.

Cedric stood up, towering above everyone else in the room. He looked annoyed.

"And what, may I ask, would make you choose there?"

"Weeeeelllll…" Gink hesitated, but he looked like he was about to say something intuitive. "Neither of us has been o'er there in some time…"

"You've traded with Ghowla?!" Selini shouted from across the room. "You are a low life!"

"Now, now," Gubuyis waived at Selini to calm down, "I'm sure there's a different story here than you think."

"She's right!" Fink chimed in with a smirk on his face. "But we gave him bad ingredients for a growth potion a while back. Good thing the potion takes weeks to prepare, it was. We got out of there long before he'd ever have known his root o' carldihide was past its expiration, if you know what I mean."

The two brothers laughed as if everybody else knew what they were talking about.

Selini rolled her eyes at the pair and stated, "You two are just a couple of idiots!"

"Why there?" Jack was pointing at the spot on the map that Gink had just mentioned. "Why is that any better than what Gubuyis or Cedric think?"

Jack only asked to keep things moving. He did not feel like hearing another argument between Selini and the two brothers.

Gink looked back at the table, still smirking. "That's where their great forge is." He stood up as tall as he could and smiled at Selini.

She rolled her eyes again and turned away from him so as to ignore the pair.

"I assume that means something significant?" Jack asked, puzzled. "I mean, why does that matter?"

"Hmmm…" Gubuyis sounded while in thought over the suggestion.

Fink leaned in toward Jack, "They'll have fire throwing magi."

"True," Cedric sounded off in agreement, "fire throwing magi, also known as Fironi, need a nearby heat source to draw upon. That's the only way their magic works." He motioned to the fireplace, "with a fire the size of that fireplace, one Fironi can do some damage so long as he is within maybe a hundred feet of it."

"It will likely be guarded by Ghowla himself," Gubuyis said. "and they'll be able to damage our forces pretty significantly once we approach the area."

Jack began to feel worried again despite everyone else's calm composure. "Can we avoid that area until we're almost victorious?"

"Can't." Geller spoke up. "They'll have Fironi planted all throughout Ezjuin. We'll be fighting fire the whole battle."

"I thought you said they have to be near the heat source in order for their power to work," Anna asked worriedly.

Geller spoke up once again, "The Fironi can draw their powers from nearby Fironi. As long as one is close to the heat source, then they'll all have the ability to draw upon it. Rest assured, the Fironi that are closer to the source will be more guarded and protected so as to continue the chain of power between them."

"And once they know we have the Frost Birds on the way," Cedric continued for Geller, "they'll stoke the fires of the great forge and prepare to fight the cold with heat." He looked a little embarrassed for not considering this in his initial suggestion. With a loud sigh, he nodded his head in agreement with Gink's suggestion.

Gubuyis stood up straight and rolled up the map.

"We have no more time to spend." Gubuyis said, "Our troops left late last night. We must now be on our way."

At that comment, Gubuyis walked toward the front door with the map in his hand. Selini and Geller hurriedly gathered their belongings and set off for the front door as well. Fink walked into the kitchen and grabbed some of Geller's bread and gave some to Gink. They both stood there eating while everyone else worked to gather their gear.

"Are you not coming?" Anna asked Fink.

"I don't think we have much to offer in battle," Fink stated matter-of-factly. "I am worn down from our recent journey and neither of us could expect someone to carry us the whole time. We'll simply slow everyone down."

"I'm sure there's something you can contri...," Anna argued back but was interrupted.

"Godspeed as you humans say, good Anna, and may we meet again in good times." Gink spoke lightly.

Anna stood staring at the two of them in a state of disbelief, but she did not know what to say. And, after a moment of quiet, she walked over to the pair of them and gave them a farewell hug.

She met up with the rest of group in the town center. The large fountain was about the only noise left to fill the air. The hustle and bustle of the streets was almost entirely gone. There was no sound of the blacksmith's hammer against iron and steel. The sound of little ones running through the alleyways was missing. The sound of near silence was sobering.

Like a rude awakening, the sound of rushing air through the nostrils of a massive ice breathing dragon filled everyone's ears. Vlagar was there, ready to fly, strapped with his own special armor and several saddles.

"Zarx'l is ready for this?" Jack suddenly felt stupid for asking. He did not feel ready for this and he could tell Vlagar could see that in him.

Vlagar spoke heavily, "He is prepared in his mind, but the forces are scarce as the Frost Birds are scattered across the region. He has assured me that we will see him in battle when the time is right."

It was obvious that Vlagar had his doubts that the army of the Frost Birds could be assembled on such short notice. Jack sighed. This feeling made him even more anxious, but it was a comfort to know that Gubuyis was with them and that they had a strong group.

"Neither Gink nor Fink will be joining us," Anna chimed in sadly. "They are convinced that they will only drag us down."

Cedric responded, not looking too surprised, "There's not much room on a battlefield for a couple of misfits anyway."

Jack wanted to convince him and everyone else otherwise, but not even he could think of something to say that sounded convincing to himself. They were handy to have around on the journey to speak to Zarx'l, but he could not fathom how they could help on the battlefield.

At Gubuyis's motioning and his apparent acceptance of Gink and Fink's absence, the group climbed onto the back of Vlagar. Jack noticed the armor was light, yet metallic. It shined a silverish-blue color in the sunlight. In the shadows, it looked like a thousand rainbows converging upon one another. As he sat in his saddle, he reached out with an open hand and felt the armor.

"It's enchanted to repel heat," Selini said to him. "It has to be light so as not to encumber his flight and wear him down in battle."

Jack nodded. He did not know what to say at this point. He was wide-eyed and nervous. His stomach felt like it wanted to come up through his throat. He had never been in a battle of any kind before. Geller had taught him a few evasive actions and some offensive maneuvers, but that did not make him feel at all prepared. Even with all that they had been through recently, he felt like he should not be there.

After a few large breaths, Vlagar looked back at the group, then to Gubuyis, sitting in the front. Gubuyis nodded and raised his staff into the air. Vlagar's wings unfolded from his side and flapped hard against the air. The water in the fountain next to him began to ripple and as his wings reached full power, the water turned to waves. And, without much hesitation, they were all in the air.

The town quickly grew small and out of sight within minutes. Cedric was sitting behind Gubuyis and the two were obviously intently talking about strategy. Cedric was speaking with much animation of his hands and Gubuyis would occasionally wave his staff around as he spoke, no doubt the two had ideas on how to attack. Behind Cedric was Geller, then Selini, then Anna, then himself. There was an empty saddle behind him for Fink who would have been carrying Gink. Jack felt a little relieved that he would not have to sit next to the pair of them. They were always up to something and Jack did not want to be sucked into their nefarious attempts to prank one another.

The wind rushed past Jack's ears as Vlagar made haste in his flight. In fact, the wind was all that he could hear. He was confused as to how Gubuyis and Cedric were able to hold a conversation so long. They seemed to hear each other just fine.

Anna turned to him and was saying something, but he could not make it out. He gestured that he could not hear her and that she needed to speak up. She reached back and pulled his leather cap down hard. Suddenly, the sound of rushing air fell silent.

"You didn't have that on all the way," she said in a slightly louder than normal voice. "Their head armor is enchanted to hear one another. Quite useful! Just think of who you want to hear and speak to and they will be able to hear and speak to you. Try it!"

Jack thought of Cedric and Gubuyis and suddenly he could hear what they were saying. "… right in the center! If we get them after taking all the Fironi out, we'll for sure have the upper hand!"

Cedric had just finished exclaiming his position on some strategic initiative. Jack looked at Gubuyis who then looked back at him and pointed to his own helmet, smiling. He then turned forward and began looking at a small map.

Jack then looked at Selini who was chatting with Geller.

Selini was explaining something to Geller. "… and without that you have to …" she looked back at Jack and smiled a small smile. "It seems someone is listening in on us, Geller."

Jack looked confused, but Anna quickly noticed and chimed in. "You can hear them, but it's kind of like having someone stand next to you while you're talking to someone else. You just happen to know they are listening. Just like if you entered someone else's conversation in mid conversation and stood there, it may seem a bit rude."

"Oh, I didn't mean to …," Jack started.

"Don't worry about it," Selini interrupted. "It's good for you to find out what we're up against."

"Definitely." Gubuyis interjected as well. Jack looked towards the front where he was sitting and noticed Gubuyis had not even turned around. He was still reviewing his map. "We have too few troops. Our allies have run thin. Ghowla has made strides in picking apart the alliance in many ways. Starvation, curses, murder, blockades, and the lure of power have each worked against us in their own ways. What we're up against is a powerful being full of dark magic looking to expand the boundaries of the Reign as far as he can. He has no weakness for compassion. He has no regard for life. He does not even control his own soul, as he sold it to the Reign in exchange for his great power."

"Ghowla is bent on turning each of us to dust in the end. He will not relent until we're each of us dead!" Cedric stated forcefully.

Jack sighed. "Do we have any good news?"

Selini spoke up excitedly, "We have your plan! It is a good one, Jack. It is almost certainly going to work if we execute it just right."

"We have the Frost Birds on our side, Jack." Anna reached back and patted him on the shoulder.

Jack sat in silence for a bit as he wondered about what they were going into. He was nervous, but he did think the Frost Birds were a big asset. He also knew they had Gubuyis, who was frail looking but extremely powerful. He could not imagine that Ghowla could possibly be any stronger. At the very least, how could Ghowla beat both Gubuyis and the Frost Birds together? After a few minutes, he started to feel relieved and encouraged that things would turn out well for them in the end.

It had only been about an hour or so before they began to descend. In front of them lay a grand forest, tall and thick. There were hundreds of small lights interspersed throughout the foliage of the forest. It was obvious this was the Arbolio known as Ezjuin. All throughout Ezjuin were Ghowla's troops. The sounds of chants and drums could be heard coming from its dark center. Amassing in a great field outside of Ezjuin were the troops of the Govilian Alliance. There were thousands of creatures of many kinds. Most creatures were familiar looking to Jack and Anna, as they had seen their types in the great hall of the Govilian Council.

Gubuyis motioned to a landing spot on a large rock jutting out from the hillside behind the armies. Within a moment, Vlagar had landed and the group dismounted. Drums and chants grew louder from both sides.

Jack looked over the armies. He could see the alliance very well. They looked wide open in the field with nowhere to run if they needed to retreat. He looked as hard as he could into the forest ahead of them. He could hear an ever-growing chanting and what sounded like a thousand blacksmith hammers clanking against iron. But he could not see what they were up against. The forest was too dark, even with hundreds of fires glowing in it.

There were huge beasts like nothing Jack had ever seen before mixed in the alliance's armies. All he could think of was a drawing of an elephant and a hippopotamus mixed together and grown times a hundred. These beasts towered over the armies. On their backs were creatures booming against drums and sounding out battle horns.

"You stay here," Gubuyis motioned to the group. "When it is your time to shine...," with a small nod, he simply left it at that, smiled, and got back on Vlagar with Cedric.

The trio flew to the front of the field where Gubuyis dismounted along with Cedric. Suddenly the field went silent and Gubuyis began speaking.

Even though he was way behind the armies and then some, Jack could hear every word that Gubuyis spoke with clarity.

"My friends! We find ourselves on the doorstep of a dark enemy. This is a powerful foe with plans for each and every one of us. We all know those plans are for our demise. We face a terrible choice today to fight not just an enemy until he yields, but we will be going against some that we used to call our friends. Remember, we have a single mission today. We must focus on that mission. We must fight relentlessly to our last breath. We are fighting for our lives, yes, but most importantly we fight for the future of our children. This is not about gaining land or riches; this battle is about saving what we hold dear – our way of life. That is what is on the line. You must battle as if your children were defenseless behind you on this field today, because that is what will happen. You, each of you, is the last defense between him," he pointed back to Ezjuin, "and your children and their future."

At that moment, a single flaming spear flew out of the dark of Ezjuin right towards the back of Gubuyis. Without hesitation, Cedric pulled his massive sword and swung it in front of the spear. It splintered into a million pieces of wood and sparks while the sword sang the first song of clanking metal.

Without flinching, Gubuyis spoke softly with disappointment in his voice, "And so it begins."

Chapter 26: All Out Assault

J ack's hands instantly got sweaty as he watched what just unfolded in front of him. His heart beat hard and fast as the armies quickly roared into chants, the drums began beating more loudly now than ever, and battle horns sounded the alarm. He watched in awe as the army started moving forward, slowly.

"Where are the Frost Birds? We won't win without them!" Jack's eyes were wide. He felt like he was missing something. He could not figure out why they were starting without the Frost Birds.

"Vlagar has assured us that Zarx'l will show." Geller stated. "We cannot control the time at which we must fight, but maybe we can control the speed at which the fight unravels."

"What do we do?" Anna asked.

"We are tasked with the ultimate mission." Selini said. "We must wait here for the Frost Birds."

The sky above the armies grew dark. They all looked up and saw tens of thousands of arrows flying through the air.

"What'll they do?" Anna asked hurriedly as the arrows began to descend upon the armies of the alliance.

Selini did not look worried, "The Govilian Beasts will play their part."

Just then, the beasts that stood high above the armies called out in a heavy roar. Suddenly, an orange shockwave shot out from each of the drums and flew through the air above the armies. Jack and Anna watched in awe as each and every arrow disintegrated with not one making it through.

Another wave of arrows, some flaming, made its way out of the foliage and toward the battlefield. The Govilian Beasts reacted in the same way and the arrows were disintegrated once again. There was chanting and rejoicing on the field. Then, after a moment or two, a large ball of flames flew straight towards Gubuyis at the front of the armies. It came from the forest, but it was still impossible to make out anything from within the trees. The flame ball moved rapidly across the field. Gubuyis raised his staff and motioned the air from behind him towards the oncoming fire. The air turned from wind to water as it hit against the fire, putting it out in a swirl of smoke. Then, more fire balls shot from the trees. This time hundreds of them made their way toward the battlefield. They flew fast as they melted the ground beneath them. The Govilian Beasts called out a new sound of drums and horns. A shockwave then flew forward and stopped almost all of the fireballs in their paths. One made it through, though, and made its way straight towards one of the beasts. Within seconds, it was engulfed in flames along with anybody immediately around it.

Gubuyis raised his staff as Cedric raised his broadsword. He summoned lightning and channeled it through the sword. Cedric then pointed it towards the tree line as if he was throwing the lightning. The magic turned to a hard and steady stream of fire and lightning as it made its way to its target. Before it hit the trees, it split into a hundred branches. Fires erupted everywhere in front of them for hundreds of feet in both directions.

"Yes!" Jack could hardly contain his excitement.

His elatedness quickly waned as a new threat appeared. Out from the trees could be seen beasts of all sorts. Some looked like large wild hogs wearing armor, others like bears, and yet others unlike anything Jack had ever seen before. They were marching out onto the field with fire and weapons. Jack could see what looked like wizards who held balls of fire in their hands. He could tell those had to be the Fironi. And, as they marched, the Fironi threw massive fireballs towards the alliance. The Govilian Beasts were able to extinguish many of them. Gubuyis was extinguishing fireballs left and right, but he could not keep up with all of them. Neither could the Govilian Beasts. Several fireballs made it through the defenses and incinerated more of the beasts.

The two armies marched toward each other, flinging fire, lightning, water, wind, and rock. Arrows the size of spears flew from both sides. With the distraction of the fight, not all the arrows could be stopped on either side. Losses were being taken from both sides, but the alliance was taking heavier damages as Ghowla's troops were mostly protected by Ezjuin.

In the midst of the ever-growing fight, out came flying creatures from the treetops. There were at least a thousand of them. They flew high and then began to make their way down toward the battlefield ahead of Ghowla's troops. They were the size of small dragons, breathing fire and mounted with two archers each.

"It's the cruzlian!" Geller shouted, pointing at the archer ridden flying creatures.

From the field of the alliance flew out a massive number of winged creatures. They flew high into the sky, towards the cruzlian. The two sides collided in the air. Those on the alliance side did not have riders, but they were smaller and easier to maneuver. After only moments of fighting, bodies of archers began falling from the sky. Those on the alliance side were also falling to the ground in large numbers, as fire and arrows overtook them.

"Look! They're dying up there! We have to help!" Anna was scared and frantic.

"We don't have any way we can help," Jack said sadly.

The Fironi were steadily delivering an onslaught of fire against the troops of the alliance. Vlagar was flying back and forth in the gap between the two armies freezing flame balls and beasts. As the armies got closer to each other it seemed like the fight began to stalemate to some extent. The alliance had regrouped in the front. There were wizards on the alliance side fighting with magic similar to Gubuyis's, but not as powerful. Smoke and fire had billowed up from the trees at this point and was darkening the skies. It looked like late evening, but it was only midday. Ash was raining down on both sides.

Immediately after he extinguished another fireball, Gubuyis lifted his staff and hands. He motioned first from the ground and then towards the tree line. Up from the ground came a large clump of dirt and rock the size of a hill. It rolled at a ferocious speed toward Ghowla's troops, rolling and smashing over them for a hundred feet. It effectively wiped out all the troops in its path. Gubuyis repeated this action toward the other direction in front of the tree line. He then made a similar motion toward the trees and several of them ripped out of the ground. They fell to the ground and shattered like glass as they crushed those beneath them.

Another fireball made its way to Gubuyis. He quickly extinguished it. Then several of the archer ridden, flying creatures nosedived toward him. He gave a slight wave of his hand, shoving them out of the air and into the tree trunks. It was clear there were orders to kill Gubuyis.

Numerous cruzlian were now descending on Jack and the rest of the group. They had been noticed and were now being targeted. Geller cast a small bubble above him as an arrow made its way toward his head. The arrow bounced off and back toward one of the flying creatures. The arrow hit it hard and it fell from the sky. Then, the creatures began nosediving the group, with many archers jumping off and pulling out swords. Jack did not know what to do, but he had to react quickly.

"Get together!" Selini yelled to the group. "They're surrounding us!"

Jack looked around and could see they were being besieged by sword-drawn archers. Their armor was very light, and he figured they would not stand up to several blasts from Selini and Geller.

"Be prepared to fight!" Geller shouted.

In one hand, Geller was holding his wand, and the other was holding his poisoned dagger. Jack pulled out his dagger as well. Anna was holding a small, plain looking short sword. She was wearing armor as well, but it was not enchanted. Jack worried for her, as she likely did not know how to fight much either.

The archers moved in rapidly. There were several dozen of them. Geller shot a red stream of magic from his wand and it blasted some archers. They fell back. Selini did the same. The archers were moving quickly. Several archers shot arrows. Selini managed to make a protective bubble for a short moment, which disintegrated the arrows before they hit them. Then, the archers were close enough and a sword fight ensued. Jack and Anna were able to successfully defend themselves as the blows came, but they were ill-prepared to make any offensive moves.

"I can't hold them off!" Jack exclaimed as he fell backwards, still holding his dagger up against an oncoming blow.

Another bright red light of magic streamed out from Selini and several of the closest archers were blown back. Jack managed to quickly get back to his feet.

Anna shouted, "Jack, watch out!"

An archer had lunged for Jack and knocked him to the ground. It swung its sword straight at him. Jack quickly deflected the swing of the archer's sword. He knew he was in trouble as the others were being attacked by the remaining archers. Before the next blow could come at him, Jack scrambled back to his feet and swung his dagger back at the oncoming archer. The dagger met the archer's sword. This time, however, several small sparks shattered in the air where the two made contact. Then, Jack remembered his dagger was imbued with electrical powers. He instantly thought of the Cerilian box and how it worked by him thinking of what he wanted from it.

Jack prepared himself for another blow from the archer's sword. This time, he thought of the electrical powers of his dagger. As the two clanked together, a small, unfocused bolt of lightning shot out and hit several areas on the ground.

"You have to focus, Jack. Focus!!" Selini called back to him as she fought several archers.

The next blow came with ferocity. Jack was hardly prepared for it, as it knocked him back to the ground. Then, the archer jumped into the air and back down towards Jack; fully prepared to deliver a killing blow. Jack lifted his dagger in defense. This time he tried focusing his thoughts on using the electrical powers against his foe. The two metals clanked together, and a large shockwave of blue lightning shot out in a huge sphere. The archer was blown back. That is when Jack noticed he had blown away all the archers.

Another fireball, and another, and another, made their way toward Gubuyis. He quickly extinguished one and blocked another with a large boulder he summoned from the ground. Right before the other rolled over him, a large black hole appeared behind him and out jumped Fink with Gink on his back. Fink was holding a large potion jar that sucked the fireball in its entirety.

"Pleased to see you, good sir!" Fink shouted at Gubuyis.

Fink tossed the potion jar above him and Gink caught it. Fink turned around quickly, and Gink threw the jar as hard as he could toward the tree line. Gubuyis raised his staff and the bottle flew even faster and farther. It smashed against something in the trees and burst into a violent explosion. The flames lasted for a few moments and then sucked away in a manner similar to Gubuyis's magic. The onslaught of fire and flying creatures diminished against him.

"What is this?" Cedric asked. "A Fironi?"

Fink spoke quietly, "I believe we're about to meet our nemesis."

"I thought you two weren't going to come," Anna said from the hillside behind them. "Did you have a change of heart?"

"Thought we could grab some of that great forge magic!" Fink exclaimed happily.

"You two are something else!" Selini was annoyed.

"We need to focus here." Cedric motioned his sword toward the tree line where the fire had just gone out.

Just then, the trees began bending as if to get out of the way of something big and fast coming from deep in the forest. Within a moment the sounds of a drum and horn along with the massive sounds of something running and stomping the ground came rushing out of the trees. It was a Govilian Beast. Except it looked like a reddish gray color and its eyes were clouded over.

"Necromancy." Gubuyis said unsurprised.

"What? What do you mean?" asked Jack.

Speaking hurriedly, Geller explained, "Ghowla is raising our dead troops against us!"

The dead Govilian Beast ran straight toward Cedric and Gubuyis. Gubuyis raised the ground in front of it into a large boulder, but it busted right through it without slowing down. He then shot lightning and fire bolts from his staff. Cedric raised his sword and ran toward the beast, yelling the whole way. Fink ran after him. Cedric met the beast in battle, making a large cut along the side of it as it ran by him, knocking him out of its way without flinching. It was clear, its mission was Gubuyis.

Just as Fink hopped out of the way of the Govilian Beast, Gink shot a small arrow with an enchanted string. Before Fink was even finished landing, the two of them were being lifted onto the back of the beast. Gink pulled a small potion from his pocket and threw it at the pair of creatures on the back of the beast. It exploded and cleared the way for the two of them to land safely atop it.

Cedric stood back up and threw his broadsword with all his might at the back of the beast as it ran. It landed directly in the back of one of its legs. It slowed down and cried out. Gink poured some kind of potion over the head of the beast and quickly climbed down its side. Gubuyis raised his staff and called the ground once again. The beast was quickly recovering from its wound and picking up its speed again. Gubuyis then pushed the ground toward the beast, but this time it broke into thousands of small rocks. The rocks shot toward it at tremendous speed and filled the beast full of holes. It stopped suddenly and turned to ash as it yelled out.

Before the moment was celebrated, a large fireball flung out from the trees where the beast had been summoned from. It made its way straight towards Cedric. Gubuyis quickly sprang into action and summoned a water ball to extinguish it. Cedric, without his sword, was defenseless. He ran as fast as he could toward his sword and the oncoming water ball. But the flames overtook him before he could make it to safety. The water ball reached him only a second later and extinguished the flames. Cedric, however, had already met his misfortune. He fell to the ground, covered in steam and smoke, reaching out toward Gubuyis.

"NO!!!!" Anna yelled.

Jack gasped. "No! That can't be!"

The battle continued as if nothing happened. The Govilian Beasts were slowly succumbing to the flames of the Fironi, leaving the armies wide open to a barrage of arrows, fire, and rock.

The aerial fight was being lost as only about a hundred of those on the alliance's side remained. Ghowla's flying creatures were beginning to fight air to ground with fire and arrows. The Govilian Beasts that were left were being stretched thin. They were fighting the fires in front of them and the arrows from above. Many of the troops were now dead on both sides. But it could not be seen as to how many troops Ghowla had behind the tree line.

Gubuyis looked around him and saw the carnage of the battle. After a few more fireball attacks, he stated matter-of-factly, "We need to draw him out, lest we lose this battle."

He then raised his hands slowly as if he was lifting something heavy. The ground between the two armies rumbled and shook, then the ground cracked open creating a large chasm between them. Both sides backed up. Ghowla's troops looked frightened as the gap grew the entire length of the tree line.

After demolishing the ground, Gubuyis lifted a large swath of land high above the trees and then dropped it. The boulder was as large as a hill and smashed dozens of trees. As if to fight back, many hundreds of fireballs flew out of the trees and into the alliance's armies. In an instant, many more fireballs flew out, and then another wave.

Gubuyis summoned a wall of water from the chasm that absorbed all the fireballs. The fire was now useless against the alliance's troops.

"We might actually win," Anna said slowly as she gazed at what was transpiring in front of them.

Geller spoke up, "These are powerful defensive measures, but we still need to fight Ghowla, otherwise it is all for naught."

The wall of water glowed red and yellow in the dark of the ash ridden day as fireball after fireball failed to pass through it.

The ground lurched.

Jack nearly fell forward. The alliance army fell to the ground. Gubuyis fluttered, but he kept his stance. The trees began to cry out in a harmonious sound of creaking and weeping. The dark figure of a large creature, a little larger than Cedric, appeared to move toward the front of the trees.

"That's him!" Geller exclaimed. "That's Ghowla!"

The alliance's troops were being bombarded from above. A Govilian Beast was being attacked hard by numerous flying creatures. One such creature was about to make the killing blow when suddenly it froze up and fell out of the air.

"They're here! They're here!" Anna pointed to the sky.

It was the Frost Birds. Leading the army of them was Zarx'l, clad in magnificent armor. As far as Jack could see behind them was a steady stream of Frost Birds. It only took a few minutes for them to purge the skies of the archer ridden creatures. They flew over the water wall and began spewing their freezing breath at Ghowla's armies below. Many froze. The rest retreated back into the cover of the trees. Fireballs flew up from the treetops toward the Frost Birds. With the sudden retreat of Ghowla's troops, Vlagar, with the help of his brethren, froze the water wall. This allowed Gubuyis to concentrate on Ghowla, who was now standing in front of the forest.

"It's your turn," Gubuyis said, speaking to Jack and the others.

Chapter 27: The Great Forge

G howla smiled as he assessed the field in front of him. He walked over to Cedric's body and laughed.

"You couldn't possibly think you were going to win this pathetic excuse for a battle, did you? Look at your losses! I have plenty more troops to fight against your limited and dying number of foolish fighters. You have lost, Gubuyis. You have led your allies to failure. But have no fear, for I will not allow even one of you to walk away this day. You shall all die!"

He laughed maniacally. His voice was shrill and unpleasant to listen to. It was as if his pursuit of power had left his body tired and near dead. He stood tall, but not with ease. It was evident that he was fighting to hold himself up.

He made a parting motion with his hands. All the dead bodies and bits of land and rock between him and Gubuyis suddenly parted. He made another motion and the ice wall shattered and fell to the ground in a glittery dust. He did these things with ease, almost as if he was annoyed he had to do anything in the first place.

He then motioned with his right hand as if he was lifting something. The ground beneath Gubuyis broke away and lifted into the air.

Fink threw a bottle at the ground as it raised itself and a hole formed allowing Gubuyis to fall through.

Irritated, Ghowla flicked the air in the direction of Fink and Gink and they instantly flew backwards across the battlefield.

Vlagar and Zarx'l both descended upon Jack and the others.

"We need to focus on the great forge," Geller commanded Vlagar and Zarx'l. "It will be behind Ghowla."

Several other Frost Birds landed. Jack mounted Vlagar, as the others mounted other Frost Birds. Zarx'l did not allow anyone to mount him.

"This is a two-part mission. First, we have to get to the great forge, and then we have to destroy Ezjuin," Selini spoke as the Frost Birds began ascending.

"How are we going to get past Ghowla? He's not going to allow us to simply pass over his head and we can't flank him. There are too many fireballs." Anna asked.

"That part we'll leave to my father!" Geller exclaimed with confidence.

Ghowla had taken notice of the Frost Birds' presence. "So you believe you can fight my fires with your puny frost breathing dragons?" A smirk filled his face from ear to ear. "Let's see how they hold up, shall we?"

Ghowla motioned his hand forward and the intensity at which the fireballs flew through the air increased. The fireball sizes were larger and their temperatures higher. There were nearly fifteen hundred Frost Birds by the time they were in full force. The battle had now moved from the ground to the sky. The screaming sound of ice soaring through the air, the roaring sound of fire blasting, and the clashing sound of the fire and ice were deafening even on the ground. At first, there was the occasional direct hit and the metallic sound of armor could be heard. But, as the intensity of the fire increased, so did the number of hits. The Frost Birds were only able to defend themselves, as they could not see what to fire back at.

"Ghowla!" Gubuyis shouted. "End this now and we can spare your life. Your path can be changed. You cannot desire to see such loss of life. You mustn't continue."

Ghowla laughed and raised his right hand. A dark red stream of liquid flew from his hand toward Gubuyis. Gubuyis raised his staff and spun it around rapidly like the blades of a fan. The red liquid smashed into his staff and was instantly repelled in every direction. With his other hand, Gubuyis shot out a purple stream of magic.

Ghowla deflected it without effort with a simple wave of his other hand.

"We must go now!" Selini shouted above the sounds of the aerial assault happening all around them. "This is our chance. He is distracted! Go!"

With that command, Geller led the way to the great forge buried in the forest. It was obvious to Jack that the weakest point and most direct route to the forge was to fly over Ghowla. Several dozen Frost Birds joined them, and they all flew toward their target. With Ghowla distracted, Jack felt they had a chance.

As the first few Frost Birds made their way over to Ghowla's position on the field, there was a sudden realization that this move was not going to be easy. Ghowla, still fighting Gubuyis with a strong stream of red magic shooting in many directions but mostly focused on Gubuyis, noticed the movement of Frost Birds above him. He raised his other hand to the sky and shot black lightning high above the trees. It struck several of the Frost Birds, disabling their flight. They fell like rocks to the ground below.

At that sight, Jack commanded to the group, "Turn around! Turn around! We need to regroup and try something else."

Vlagar turned immediately as well as the others. They flew in a circle backwards, dodging fireballs along the way.

"We need to distract him completely!" Anna yelled.

"Everyone focus their efforts on Ghowla, now!" Geller commanded to the troops on the ground.

Within moments, thousands of troops began focusing their efforts toward Gubuyis and Ghowla. Arrows filled the sky as they flew from every direction at Ghowla. Spears and flying swords flew beneath them. And, hundreds of streams of magical lightning and fire of every vibrant color shot from various locations throughout the troops.

"Now! Go now!" Jack felt a surge of adrenaline and courage as he made the command, pointing forward.

The group reconvened and headed back towards Ghowla. Ghowla was holding off every type of assault that came his way. He continued to fire a stream of dark magic at Gubuyis with one hand and the other he held in front of him, creating a powerful shield that disintegrated arrows and absorbed lightning and fire with ease. But, with his shield up, Ghowla was now unable to defend the air above him.

As the Frost Birds made their way above Ghowla on a second attempt, Ghowla took notice. He could not let down his hands, so he stomped the ground with his foot. The ground shook mightily. The trees behind him fell to the ground against their will. Gubuyis fell as did the troops around him. Gubuyis immediately raised his hand and made a shield similar to Ghowla's, but it was a vivid purple and larger. It blocked Ghowla's stream of magic for a large area, allowing the troops to collect themselves. In that moment when Gubuyis had fallen, Ghowla was able to fire another shot of black lightning at the Frost Birds flying overhead. Several more were hit and fell to the ground.

"Push through!" Geller shouted. "Maintain your target!"

Within a moment, Gubuyis had been back to his feet and was fighting Ghowla once again. The Frost Birds broke through. Nearly thirty of them were now past Ghowla and headed for the great forge.

"Follow me," Zarx'l commanded, "I can smell the fire!"

With that, all the Frost Birds in the group rallied behind Zarx'l. The sound of the battle behind them was still audible, but faint. The forest seemed to suck the noise right out of the atmosphere. The air was now less full of smoke and the light of day was shining through. It was a serene view for Jack. The battle had happened so quickly. Now, with the sun shining back down on him, Jack felt a small sense of peace.

"There!" Anna was pointing in front of them at a massively glowing area in front of them. "That's got to be it!"

"Be at your ready," Geller called out. "Here we go!"

The Frost Birds all began descending in unison. In just a moment's time, they were flying through the forest, weaving back and forth around massive tree trunks. The darkness of the forest quickly began to light up. Jack could feel the heat of the forge as they quickly approached it. Then he saw it. It was much like a blacksmith's forge built of dilapidated cobblestone and iron, but on a grander scale. In place of cobblestones were massive boulders stacked in a large circle. The cracks between boulders were aglow with the light of the forge's fire.

Then, there was a smash.

Zarx'l had fired the first shot. The forge shook but stayed steady. Another ice bolt and another and another as each of the Frost Birds fired a shot of their icy breath. All were direct hits. The forge did not budge.

"What if we all fire at once, right down the center?" Jack questioned the others.

"Worth a shot," Vlagar said. "Let's do it!"

Zarx'l led the way once again and the group rounded back to the forge. This time arrows began to fly from the trees. Then, fireballs.

"They know what we're trying to do," Geller said.

"We have to keep trying!" Selini insisted.

The Frost Birds once again descended into the trees and began making their way toward the great forge. Their attempt was riddled with fireballs and arrows. So much so, that it was getting difficult to see their target.

"I got this," Zarx'l said to the others. "You all keep your course."

Without hesitation, Zarx'l turned back into the trees to his side. As the Frost Birds continued their path, Jack could hear the crunching of armor. The fireballs and arrows almost completely stopped, at least they stopped coming in their direction. Now they were being fired into the trees behind and to the side of Jack as Zarx'l took out Ghowla's troops one by one.

Once again, they quickly approached the great forge. This time grouping together and firing all at once. The great forge shook hard and parts of it crumbled. The flames inside dimmed. But, after only a moment, the flames relit to full force. The group circled back around again and repeated their attack. This time the forge cracked, and the flames struggled to stay ablaze.

"It won't be long before more troops than we can handle find their way here," Selini stated. "We have to make this one count."

The trees behind them were bending and rustling violently as if something big was making its way to the forge. The Frost Birds circled back this time and landed, leaving themselves open to attack from air and ground. They each took one large breath and breathed out ice in a long last breath. The forge froze and crumbled, but still stood. Behind the ice was a flickering of light. The fire was still going. Exhausted, the Frost Birds almost looked defeated. Then, from behind them, still flying at full speed, Zarx'l came in with one last shot of ice. He then flew straight into the still standing forge. His massive body shattered the ice-covered forge into a million pieces and a large, final plume of fire and smoke filled the air before finally going out.

"Up! Up! Up!" Vlagar shouted as he took back to flight.

"Yes!" Jack thought to himself.

Just then, an arrow pierced Vlagar's armor. He let out a yelp and plummeted straight back into the trees. Jack watched in horror as the trees grew larger and the day grew dark as they fell below the treetops. Branch after branch rushed past Jack's face and then a hard thud as they hit the ground. He stumbled to get back on his feet. It was obvious they had no time as Ghowla's troops were now so close he could hear their footsteps. The fall had made it hard to think and his sight was going dark. There was a steady stream of loud crashing and explosions all around him. Then, the sudden crash overcame him, and he blacked out.

Chapter 28: Battle Worn

When Jack came to, he could feel rushing wind on his face. He was groggy, but he could make out that he was on the back of a Frost Bird. There were no more fireballs and the air was clear of smoke. He was confused. He wondered who rescued him and where they were headed. It then occurred to him that he was being taken away from battle.

Struggling to fully wake, he mumbled to the Frost Bird carrying him, "Stop. T-turn around." He wiped his eyes trying to wake up, "We have to fight! We can't leave them!"

He was regaining his composure as he spoke. That is when he noticed that he was in flight with hundreds of Frost Birds behind him. He wondered if they had retreated. They had been so close to victory. All Jack could feel was a sense of disappointment. He felt sad. They lost so many, including Cedric and Vlagar. Now they would be forced into hiding.

He wondered about the others, too. He looked all around frantically at the other Frost Birds, but he could not see any of them.

"What happened?" He finally asked aloud to no one in particular. "Where is everybody? Where are we going? What happened to Gubuyis? Where's Ann.."

"Good evening!"

It was Geller's voice and he sounded elated. Jack looked all around but he could not see him.

Once again, Geller spoke, "How are you feeling?"

"F-fine, I guess." Jack was more confused now.

"We did it, Jack! We did it!" Jack could now hear Anna.

He still felt confused. He looked for them again and noticed behind him were several Frost Birds coming up the ranks fast. It was Anna with Fink and Gink, Geller, and Selini. The sight of them made Jack feel immediately better. But he did not see Gubuyis.

Then he heard Gink, "Who knew a mere human would have thought 'o such a plan?!" He sounded both excited and amused.

"What happened? Where's Gubuyis? How long have I been out?" Jack sputtered each question out quickly to whomever would listen.

Anna repeated, "We did it, Jack! We actually won!"

"You've been out for a while now, Jack." Selini said calmly. "We should be back to the fountain any minute now. You just need to relax."

It was hard to believe they could have won the battle after everything he saw. He felt shocked and in disbelief. They had to for sure be retreating. Sure enough, though, after a few minutes he could see the town center of Gargantulua.

Most of the Frost Birds landed outside the gates, but several made their way to the fountain. That is when Jack noticed Zarx'l had indeed made it, as he led the front of the formation. He was carrying what looked like another Frost Bird, dangling under him by ropes. It was Vlagar!

"Vlagar!" Jack shouted in glee.

Roughly a dozen Frost Birds landed in the town. None carried Gubuyis. Jack felt a heavy heart as he feared the worst for his friend.

Before he could fully dismount his ride, Anna had already landed and had run over to him excitedly.

"Jack!" she exclaimed. "We did it! We took out the great forge and then we won."

She was out of breath from her excitement. She looked about as much in disbelief as Jack. Making their way through the Frost Birds were Geller and Selini followed by Fink and Gink.

With a big smile on her face, Selini spoke, "That's right, we took out the great forge. That disabled the Fironi, which let the Frost Birds through the front line."

"In just minutes, they carried out your plan to freeze the trees." Geller also had a smile on his face. "You were right; with Ezjuin so full of water she froze beyond her capacity to absorb the cold."

"The trees froze and exploded into millions of pieces!" Anna was now more out of breath as her excitement and disbelief overcame her.

Looking a little more somber, Geller then remarked, "Ezjuin didn't stand a chance. She died a horrible death."

"We should get the word out to the town," Selini said to Geller.

He nodded and left saying, "I'll leave you with good Anna here to fill you in on the details."

Without any hesitation, Anna began to recount the final minutes of the battle. "Vlagar was shot down, as you know, but that was right after we destroyed the great forge." It was obvious she was still excited, but she was attempting to keep her composure as she continued to speak. "With the great forge extinguished, the Fironi were disabled. Almost immediately, all the fireballs stopped. And then, the Frost Birds moved swiftly to begin freezing Ezjuin."

Jack was feeling great about the fact that they won, but he still felt sad for Gubuyis, who he now assumed did not make it out alive.

"What about Gubuyis?" he asked. "What happened to him?"

"Genius, that one is!" Gink shouted from the back of Fink. "With all of the fighting, he still had the ability to cast a dream spell." Both Gink and Fink laughed.

"You ever wake up from your dreams and realize you ain't yet awake? Like, you thought you woke up but you really didn't?" Fink asked.

Jack thought confusedly for a moment and nodded slightly.

"He made Ghowla think he was fully in battle, but in reality, he was tricked into a dream state for a short bit." Anna continued for them, "Mind you, it didn't last long, but all we needed was a few moments as the Frost Birds made their way into the trees."

"And, once we were in the trees, they were on their knees!" Gink laughed.

"But what about Gubuyis? What happened to him?" Jack repeated his questions.

"He's fine, Jack" Anna stated and smiled at him. "He stuck behind to deal with what remains of Ezjuin and Ghowla."

"What of Ghowla? Did he die?" Jack had so many questions. He found it hard to believe everything that was being said given the state of things when Vlagar went down.

Anna responded, "Ghowla's gone, Jack. After the trees were obliterated, he had nowhere to go; nowhere to hide. He was wide open to attack from every side. But ultimately it was Gubuyis that cast the final blow. The Frost Birds did a decent job of freezing him, but he just kept fighting. Then, Gubuyis opened the ground beneath Ghowla as far down as you can go. Fire and lava filled the hole, and Ghowla fell in. Then, everything stopped. All the magic shots. All the arrows and spears. It all stopped almost at once."

Fink said excitedly, "Ghowla's army just plain gave up at the sight of him being destroyed!"

They had begun making their way back to the cottage where it seemed like forever ago that Jack had departed. As they walked, Anna, Gink, and Fink all chatted. The cobblestone road, interspersed with mosses and grasses, felt welcoming and warming. The sky was growing dark and the streetlamps were already ablaze. The air was warm and clear with the scent of fountain water and flowers.

They returned to the cottage and made their way to the main table where the map had lain just hours ago. There they sat, the four of them, talking and eating until Geller and Selini returned later in the evening.

"My father has returned," Selini said as she walked in the door.

Jack stood up quickly. He looked forward to seeing him.

Geller motioned for Jack to sit back down. "He will be a bit predisposed for a while as you can imagine. He has the Govilian Council to address."

"Well, we should be there, right?" Anna asked.

"He will call upon us if we're needed. But, for now, we should all get some rest." Geller assured both Anna and Jack. "It has been both a great and terrible day for everyone here. Many families will forever be broken. Many heroes will forever be sobered by the fact that they lived while their comrades in battle were not so fortunate."

"We won." Selini spoke softly, "But we lost so much getting there."

It was then that Jack realized the full extent and cost of their win. As this realization set in, he almost felt as if they had lost. He did not know what to say. He was never really good at consoling others, but he knew both Selini and Geller must have lost some of their friends. With so many lives lost, there was a good chance of it.

Jack slowly sat back down and gave a nod to the two of them. He really wanted to see Gubuyis, but he understood this was not a good time to press the matter. The mood was mostly somber for the evening, with the occasional quip from Gink or Fink. It felt good to be back at the cottage, but Jack really missed home now. He had seen more bloodshed than he would ever have imagined possible in his lifetime.

They all sat around the table near the fireplace. After a while, Jack broke the silence.

"I really miss home," he started. "The pumpkin patch and the library made up my home. It would be nice to return there someday."

Anna got up and walked over to Jack and put her hand on his shoulder. "We'll figure it out. There's gotta be a way."

And they sat in silence once again.

The evening quickly turned to night and the night quickly grew late before Geller stood up and excused himself to his room for the night. Soon after, Anna made her way to bed as well. One by one they each made their leave for the night until only Jack was left.

He thought about the day and how long it was. The excitement and anxiety he felt had been quickly forgotten and overshadowed by the intensity of the battle. He could hear the screams of those who died. His mind wandered for at least another hour after the last of his friends had departed the table. His eyes filled with tears as he remembered home and the peace and calm it held. It was not that he was sad that he was stuck away from home. Jack was saddened by all the things he had experienced that nearly cost him his life on different occasions. He did not feel he should be alive and Cedric not. He felt weak compared to everyone else on the battlefield. Eventually, however, his eyes grew heavy and his mind became too foggy to keep his thoughts cohesive. He made his way to bed as well.

Chapter 29: Gubuyis and the Symbol

Morning came much quicker than Jack would have hoped for. The night was tough. His thoughts led him astray of his courageous abilities and left him feeling hopeless. As he stirred awake, the warmth of the sun shining through the window made him briefly feel as if he was back home in his own bed. The delicious smell of something cooking wafted through the cottage and filled his lungs. It only took a moment for reality to set in. He was still in the cottage and it was the morning after the battle. After a short bout of denial, Jack finally stirred out of bed and got dressed in his cleanly pressed clothes, thanks to Gryan. He headed out to the great room and saw, once again, that everyone else was already awake and ready to go for the day.

"There he is," Gink said. "Finally, out of bed he is!"

"Oh, hush up, you!" Selini spouted back, "You've only been up a few minutes yourself! Good morning, Jack. Have something to eat."

"It's nice not having to worry about something bad happening today, isn't it?" Anna questioned Jack quietly as he walked past her.

He nodded in agreement, but he felt like their escape from danger had only just led him down a path of regrets. Everyone else looked cheery with bits of excitement on their faces. So, Jack decided to hide his feelings from the others. He did not want to bring the mood down.

As Selini handed Jack a small dish of food, she told him, "My father will want to see you this morning. Better eat up. It's an exciting time, it is."

Jack ate his food and smiled and nodded as the others recounted their fights and spellcasting. Geller spoke of how Zarx'l demolished the great forge in their last-ditch effort. Selini was excited about how the Govilian Beasts provided a strong defense. Gink and Fink were proud of their potion wielding. And, Anna was amazed by the sheer number of Frost Birds that came to their aid. Stories abounded, but Jack still felt saddened and guilty.

In a moment of excitement, Gink shouted, "We got the powder of a Govilian Beast nail!"

Fink quickly elbowed Gink as if to shut him up. The room went quiet.

Slowly and sternly speaking, Selini asked, "You did what?"

"Well, you see," Fink interjected almost apologetically for Gink, "we, er, we did per se, but hear me out here! We got it from that reincarnated one you see. No harm, no foul! Right? I mean, it wasn't even from a real dead one."

"You two are quite unbelievable," Geller quickly spoke. "Even when your lives are on the line you still have to find a way to steal something for your ridiculous potions and ingredients stock."

Just then there was a knock at the door.

"That's it." Selini stood up from her chair and walked to the door. "It's time to go."

Geller smiled and the conversation stopped. They all stood up and collected their things. Within a minute they all made their way to the door and out to the streets. That's when Jack saw Gubuyis for the first time since before the battle. He nearly cried as he ran to him.

"My good boy," Gubuyis started. "My dear boy. I see in you sadness greater than your heart can handle."

At those words, Jack began to cry. He tried not to, but he could not help it. His words were simple and true and like a sword they pierced through his veil.

Calmly speaking, Gubuyis continued, "We have all lost a great deal. I lost many friends myself." He paused as a single tear welled in one of his eyes. "My dearest friend Cedric meant much to me. I am forever grateful for his sacrifice. He didn't sacrifice just for me, oh no. I knew him well. He sacrificed himself for all of our freedom. He sacrificed himself for the freedom of every race. He will be greatly celebrated for his life back in Monarkia."

"I feel your heart, Jack." Selini said as she grabbed his hand to comfort him. "We have to focus on the future and how to make that a better place for all that survived so as to honor those who have fallen."

Jack nodded his head. He agreed, but he could not help but feel heavy hearted.

"Is there any way to get home?" Jack asked abruptly. He missed home dearly. He missed his dad. He missed the smells of spiced pumpkin bread in the late afternoon. He missed everything about it.

"That is a very good question, my dear boy." Gubuyis said as he pulled a pendant out from under his robes.

It was strung to a golden necklace and was almost half the size of Jack's palm. Jack noticed it immediately as the pendant that Selini had spoken of before. There were symbols all around the edges. And, sure enough, there was a large symbol engraved in the center. Jack recognized it as the same symbol he had seen before in the library back home and on the boulder in the pumpkin patch. His face lit up as he realized Gubuyis might know how to get back.

"I suppose you know this symbol here?" Gubuyis asked as he pointed to the middle symbol.

"That's it!" Anna whispered in excitement.

"Yes, that's the symbol from before. It was on the rock that had a portal of sorts that brought us here. We aren't from this world." Jack was relieved that he could speak openly about it now without worrying about being killed.

Gubuyis looked the symbol over and said, "And I hear you have found a key?"

Jack quickly reached into his satchel and pulled out the trinket with the same symbol. It was warm and glowed purple in his hand. He handed it to Gubuyis and the purple light faded.

After a moment of looking it over, Gubuyis continued, "This will definitely be of use. But I must warn you. I cannot get you home without first learning what this all means. You see, the reason I wear this pendant around my neck is in part because I have not been able to ascertain its meaning."

Jack's face dropped some. All he could hear from Gubuyis was that he could not get them home.

Seeing Jack's growing disappointment, Gubuyis tried reassuring him. "I have many resources at my disposal. And, now with this key, I have something more to go on. I do not believe this key is meant for any portal, though. I believe there is a secret that is yet to be discovered here."

He held the key back out for Jack to hold. Jack grabbed it slowly, not knowing what to do with it. He would rather Gubuyis have it. As it hit his hand it began glowing again.

"You see," Gubuyis stated, "this key seems to react to you specifically. That means something right there. I have to wonder who it was created for before I can ponder what it was created for." He took it back and attached it to his necklace. "I assure you that I will find out what secrets these trinkets hold and will try my best to find you your way back home."

Selini spoke somberly, "I know it's not home, Jack, but know we're forever grateful for your help. Without you and Anna we'd be in a world of trouble right now."

"You're very much welcome to stay here in Gargantulua as long as you need!" Geller chimed in happily. "We would love your company."

Jack looked around. They were next to the large gargoyle statue attached to the side of the large fountain in the center of town. He remembered exiting the gargoyle after the fight with the dragons. He then saw the tavern where they met Bolar. There were many little shops all up and down the streets that ran next to and away from the Panthyun, a massive structure in front of the fountain. The grasses growing between the cobblestone roads made him think of home even more. He looked up and saw the two suns making their way next to each other in the sky. It was not home. But he felt comforted that he had a good place to stay until they figured out how to get back.

Reaching into his satchel, Jack pulled out a small scroll and handed it to Gubuyis. "Can you make sure Zarx'l gets this? I didn't know how it would help the fight any, but it's all I can offer him as thanks for helping."

Gubuyis grabbed the scroll and smiled as if he already knew what it was, "I will make sure of that, yes. He will be delighted, I'm sure."

"I have a question." Jack remarked. "When I was battling the dragons in the cavern before I came here there was a shower of lights that destroyed them. Then, when dragons attacked us in the cavern on our journey, something stopped the dragons again. I know it was Gibble, er, whoever that was, who sent them, but who fought them off?"

Geller and Selini came in closer, their curiosity peaked.

"Well," Gubuyis started, "that is also a mystery. My dear boy, it would seem as if someone was watching over you. Who that was is still unknown. I am hopeful that such acts were of a benevolent nature. But, we need to solve that as soon as possible. Perhaps this individual knows something we do not." He pointed at the spot on his chest where the pendant hung beneath his robes.

A large stone gargoyle the size of Jack came out of the front of the Panthyun and gave a loud, steady shriek. Anna and Jack both covered their ears at the startling sound of it.

"I must wish you ado, Jack, my dearest Captain." Gubuyis said as he prepared to leave the conversation, "As you can imagine, I have much business to do with the Govilian Council. We will have plenty of time to talk later. I encourage you two to read what you can. Maybe you can assist me with discovering the secrets behind your presence here."

Gubuyis then turned and left.

"Well, I don't know about ya, but I feel like a nice spiked Prunklesnider!" Fink said loudly.

With that comment, Fink set off to the tavern with Gink in tow.

"I say we follow," Geller commented. "We could all use a bit of refreshment."

Jack thought for a little while, watching as Fink hobbled through the street and away from them. He looked at Anna who looked like she was indifferent towards whatever decision they made. He thought about how he wanted to get home, but how distant that seemed now. He really thought Gubuyis might have the answer. With a feeling similar to Anna's, he felt like he really did not care what they did right now.

"Sure," Jack shrugged.

The group of them headed to the tavern and sat around a table, joining Fink and Gink. Jack enjoyed regular Prunklesnider while the others enjoyed various drinks. Bolar made conversation with the group. It was no secret how involved they all were with the victory of the day prior. They all sat around chatting about anything other than the battle. This helped take Jack's mind off the tragedy he had seen. It was nice to have something to smile about as they all joked about things Jack and Anna were not informed on. But, it was nice to laugh. Although he was not accepting of it, he was alright with the idea of having to stay here a while longer. He had great friends to get him through.